THE MISTAKES WE DENY

MEG JOLLY

Published in 2021 by
Eldarkin Publishing Limited
United Kingdom
© 2021 Meg Jolly
www.megjolly.com

ISBN 9798548437716

Cover design © Meg Jolly 2021

BOOKS BY MEG JOLLY

The DI Daniel Ward Yorkshire Crime Thriller Series:

The Truth We Can't Hide

The Past We Run From

The Revenge We Seek

The Mistakes We Deny

CHAPTER ONE

SATURDAY EVENING

R obert Craven cut a striking figure, his tuxedo obsidian against the crisp, ice-white of his freshly-pressed shirt. His clean-shaven chiselled jaw swung this way and that as he nodded a wordless acknowledgement to those they passed, many of whom he had already formally greeted before dinner. Those who were worthy of his attention, at least, for plenty fell far below it.

The atmosphere seemed to carve around him—his very presence having a gravitational pull that both tugged at and repelled them. They all wanted him. Envied him. Feared him. Hated him.

Robert smiled, a slight uplift of the corner of his lips in the cocksure, arrogant way that Miranda Craven had once loved, and now loathed. On his arm, she glittered, quite literally, the crystal-specked evening gown draping over her tall, slim figure. It gave her a statuesque quality as she glided alongside Robert, her arm tucked in his, her emerald-gloved fingers matching the gown that turned every head as they passed. With every step, she shone under the chandelier bathing the opulent ballroom in a golden glow.

Miranda smiled coyly, her ruby red lips parting, soaking up that attention as she fluttered her darkened lashes. She was not as young as she once had been, just past fifty like Robert, but she could still capture the attention of the room. And this, after all, was for them. The Cravens. And for him. *The* Craven.

Craven Property Holdings Limited had enjoyed yet another bountiful year, with an unprecedented growth in profits. It was only fitting to celebrate, and in black tie, especially on the eve of signing a major land deal for developing a picturesque Yorkshire Dales village. It would net them seven figures in profits when the project was completed, and a healthy residual income from the leaseholds on the properties that Robert had been shrewd enough to secure.

Harewood House, a stately home just north of the city of Leeds, set in a luscious jewel of an estate that sprawled over the undulating valley, was a fitting tribute to the Cravens' greatness. The Cravens weren't short of their own luxurious living quarters, but the opulence in this place, of the eighteenth-century gentry, drew Miranda Craven like a moth to flame. Or, perhaps more accurately, a magpie to trinkets and treasures.

They had hired out the entire house for the evening— damned be the cost—and now it rang with the clinking glasses, free-flowing champagne, and conversation. The room was so full of bodies the vast space heated itself, the

scent of colognes, perfumes, and champagne filling the air with the bouquet of luxury.

Anybody who was somebody was there: other property magnates, competition of Robert, his associates, his premier suppliers, local minor celebrities, and plenty enough of the local business associations and council networks. Even a Superintendent from the police. Miranda smiled especially graciously as they passed Detective Superintendent Diane McIntyre. The police had been especially helpful with some of the *incidents* they had suffered over the past few years.

Behind the Superintendent, Robert and Miranda's son James Craven chatted idly to an old family friend, a champagne glass held limply in one hand, his other stuffed in his trouser pocket. James did not have the decorum she had trained into his father. Miranda pursed her lips at that. But she was pleased, nonetheless, that he had come, for a change. He needed to step up if he was going to take charge of the family's fortunes.

Robert subtly tugged Miranda to a halt and she turned with practised serenity, her smile widening and her whole body positioning into her best angle for the flash of the camera before them. Of course, she had invited the press. They were not Robert's favourite vultures, but the attention advantaged them. Positive or negative, all press brought business.

'Mr Craven, Eliza Pullman for the Dales Gazette, can you give us an additional comment for the paper?' the young woman behind the camera asked. Her dark eyes

glittered in the shattered chandelier light as she inched forward, her phone outstretched, no doubt recording.

Oh, God. Not her. Miranda's glare sharpened on her. *If only looks could kill.* Miranda had *not* invited her, and the irritating cow had turned up anyway.

Robert's voice was smooth as aged honey as he spoke with practised ease, his voice a soothing low rumble that had lured many a young woman aside from Miranda to bed. 'Craven Property Holdings Limited are proud to be the premier supplier of housing in the Yorkshire Dales for the twenty-first century, bringing jobs and wealth to our local economy.'

'And what of the fact that just today, you have a contract for such an obscene amount of homes on Green Belt lands that will price younger generations of Dales families out of their own villages? *And* they're leasehold, not freehold, so you expect to charge them fees over and above what is reasonable and fair to live in houses on land they'll never own?' The young woman drew closer, her mouth tightening.

'We're very proud to be a *local*, not a national or international home builder,' Robert said, the words each carefully chosen, though he showed no sign of perturbation, unruffled by such a small fly in his web.

Annoyance spiked in Miranda nonetheless, though she kept her face carefully smooth, blank, the hint of a polite smile upon her visage.

'But you're actively—'

'Miss Pullman, if you have an issue with planning, that's one for the council, not I.' Robert stared at the girl

in the intense, overbearing way Miranda used to hate—before he stopped looking at her altogether—until Pullman subsided before his imposing figure.

Wordless—he hadn't bothered to speak to her all night, though she had not broken the steely silence between them either—Robert moved Miranda on, on their turn about the room.

On second thought, Miranda preferred Miss Eliza Pullman's company to what she saw next.

Why the hell is she *here?*

Miranda's gaze hardened as she saw the gaudy red dress of Robert's strumpet ahead. Or 'executive personal assistant' as he termed it. 'Strumpet' was the word Miranda used for Claire Parker. Well. One of them. The politest one.

The womaniser thinks he's a Casanova. But his choice appalled her. Was Claire Parker *really* better than her? Younger, sure. The woman was *ten* years Miranda's junior—time no amount of makeup or Botox could regain.

Miranda's mind suggested other words. *Short. Dumpy. Poor. Vulgar. Look at her box-dye hair job, her cheap makeup.* Her sharp eyes noticed the smudged mascara at the corner of Claire's eye. The fading lipstick. The solid line of root-regrowth underneath the bleach blonde.

Miranda's lip curled in disgust. Miranda quite thought, as a married woman herself, Claire Parker ought to have had more self-respect for herself than sleeping with her married boss—and having the bloody nerve to parade in front of his wife at her own party in a cheap red cocktail dress like a slut.

Men were weak fools, Miranda knew. It was a trait she used to her advantage when she needed to. It was as if they could not say no. As if they *needed* to be wanted, validated constantly, by any woman who'd open their legs. *Let Claire Parker validate his tiny cock and fragile ego*, Miranda thought viciously. Soon, it wouldn't be Miranda's shame, but Robert's.

Now it was Miranda's turn to steer. To show her better class. To show Claire the circles the common slut would never be privy to. Miranda raised her chin, drew herself even taller, gliding past the shorter woman with her cheap, tacky satin dress, to greet one of the Leeds councillors with an audible and exaggerated, 'Oh Timothy, *darling*, so *good* to see you,' and pull Robert into a bubble of conversation with the people grouped there that the strumpet would not dare break into.

Besides Miranda's personal satisfaction of seeing Claire's face redden like her hideous dress at Miranda's bluff, it always paid to keep the wheels greased with such events. After all, it wasn't just *any* firm that could secure a contract for a thousand executive homes in a firmly Green Belt village out in the Dales. It had taken Robert decades to cultivate the precise network of box-tickers, paper-pushers, and red-tape cutters he needed to make sure his building projects were approved one way or another. It was never what one knew, after all, that led to success—more like *who*.

But neither Robert nor Miranda was under any illusion that those who fawned upon them and supped upon their entertaining budget were allies. *Keep your friends close, and your enemies closer* was a saying they were well familiar with. And as they turned to each other and smiled—a picture-perfect smile that was colder than ice as the depths of their gaze met—both of them knew that the enemy they courted closest of all was each other.

The party was merely a shining veneer over the malaise of it all. Miranda would do her duty as his wife and allow herself to be swept around that grand space on his arm, playing the lady as she always did with such elegance and perfection.

Robert would parade her as his prize. A distant daughter of ex-nobility—who had married downwards for money or love or scandal depending on who one spoke to —along with the other subtler signs of his wealth, like the watch flashing on his wrist, or the handmade dress shoes and London tailoring.

And, he would be happy. They all would. Wealthy and happy. That was how it worked, after all, inside that glittering bubble. The reality of wealth and the pretence of happiness.

Perhaps the money was the realest thing of it all.

Miranda knew the pretence would soon be over, at least. Bitterness and relief curled within her.

———

'Don't you dare parade your cheap slut like that again,' Miranda said flatly to Robert, turning to face him as they

stepped into the private quarters of Harewood House—
on their way to separate rooms after the event.

Out of the ballroom, she could smell his cologne in
isolation—a scent that made her sick to her stomach now.
Made her think of all his illicit affairs. Made her wonder
who else he had worn it for, as well as her.

'She's my—'

'Call her whatever you fucking want, she's a whore,
your whore, and I won't have her at our events.' Miranda's lip curled. She curled her arms around herself,
briskly rubbing against the goosebumps the cold air
elicited. 'How you can bear to dip your wick in such slop
is beyond me, Robert. Christ, have you no standards?'

Robert barked a laugh. 'Like you're one to talk.'

'I didn't bring a slut to our corporate event, trussed up
like a cheap call girl.'

'She invited herself. I'll have words,' he growled.

Satisfaction curled within her. She was getting under
his skin. *Good.* 'If you're going to have an affair—sorry,
another affair—at least set some damned boundaries.
Gone are the days when you can hurt me with it,
Robert'—and Lord knows, he had done, not that she'd
give him the satisfaction of knowing it anymore—'but this
is business. No cheap slut is worth what we've worked
hard to build over these past few decades.'

'Stop calling her a slut. She's a good woman,' Robert
growled, advancing on Miranda.

She did not flinch, did not recede, but raised her chin
to him instead, standing proudly. 'Deluded married
woman, shagging her rich married boss, desperate as a

teenager in heat for you, too bloody stupid to see you're just using her for a few months' fun. I don't see it.'

Robert gritted his teeth. 'Don't think I don't know about your little bit on the side.'

'I'm sure you do,' said Miranda airily, drawing closer. In the darkened hallway, her looking up at him, his whole attention focused on her and his body rigid with the tension oozing between them, a distant onlooker might be fooled into thinking they had stumbled upon a lover's frisson. Not the cesspit of resentment that festered in the gulf that separated the two of them.

'But the difference between us, Robert, and it always *has* been, and it always *will* be, is that I have *class*. I was born for this. Raised for this. I don't need to parade my private life for all to see. I know the value of discreteness, and so does Christopher, unlike your strumpet.'

'You had to choose him, didn't you?' Christopher Dawson was an architect she'd met through Robert's business. Robert had been apoplectic when he'd discovered it. Never mind that Robert was on his tenth affair of the decade—that she knew of—and their marriage was irreparably over long before. Robert didn't like sharing. Didn't like other people playing with his toys.

'It's none of your business. At least I didn't shag my own assistant. And the last one. And the one before that. Christ, they might as well have a picture of you in the dictionary next to "midlife crisis". As if you could be any more clichéd.' Miranda smiled viciously, her lip curling in disdain.

At least she'd dated like an adult. She'd let Christopher woo her, made him work for it, before she'd allowed him anywhere near her. As far as she'd heard, Robert had barely had to say 'jump' before Claire had asked 'how high'—or rather, how wide to open her legs over the antique desk Miranda had bought Robert for one of their wedding anniversaries years before.

Robert Craven was not a man anyone said no to, in business or personally, but he seemed to have an extra special way with the ladies. Somehow, his assistants never saw the true him, and what they saw, they mistook for healthy interest, not dominating maleness and an uncompromising will that would toss them aside the moment they lost his interest, or didn't want to play.

Miranda pushed aside the feeling of distaste at it all. If nothing else, Robert had been an embarrassment to her in that regard. At least her father wasn't around anymore to give her a huge *I told you so*.

'You'll be free of me soon, *Merry*,' Robert snarled her old nickname at her, wheeling away, his fists clenched and shaking at his side. He'd never hit her, never come close—for all his faults, Robert Craven didn't hit women —but she saw that he teetered on the edge of that control. He had a fiery temper, and he did not like being made a fool of.

Neither did she.

'And you, I, *Robbie*,' Miranda said, fusing her voice with venomous sweetness. At the very end of the hall, light flooded into the darkened passage. A red dress appeared. Claire Parker, lurking, like a dog awaiting its next meal. Waiting, always waiting, for Robert, and whatever scraps he would throw her.

Stupid bitch.

If Miranda didn't despise stupidity so much, perhaps she'd pity the woman. Miranda turned and strode away, straight-backed, before Robert could retort, or Claire could see her ire.

'Shut up, woman,' Robert's voice rang out at the other end of the hall as he reached Claire.

Miranda didn't need to turn to imagine the simpering fussing of the woman—and how Robert would despise that. She strode into a room—any room to escape, and slammed the antique door behind her so hard it rattled in its frame, the bang echoing in the empty room like a gunshot. Outside on the terrace, the festivities wrapped up, the warm glow of mood lighting falling on empty walkways and lonely shrubbery under the baleful glare of a waning autumn moon above.

Gods, she didn't relish the thought of carving up the business empire they'd built together—it was hers by rights too, all of it. She bloody resented that Claire Parker or any of Robert's strumpets would get the benefit of any of it after the divorce, but maybe it would be worth it to be free of the hatefulness that seemed to govern her life. To be free of Robert Craven.

Or maybe not. Miranda still railed against it all. Miranda didn't like sharing either. Maybe she'd still find a way to take it all. Damned, be Robert. Damned, be the strumpet.

CHAPTER TWO

SUNDAY MORNING

R obert Craven *hated* to admit that Miranda might be right. But as he gazed dispassionately at Claire Parker—or rather, her arse, as she bent suggestively low over the desk before him—he had to admit, the cow had a point.

What *was* he doing? He was a self-made multi-millionaire. He'd bedded and wedded the prized daughter of an old and noble family, decorated with titles, land, and military prowess—and that was no small feat. The thrill of the chase had been legendary to a young Robert.

What on earth was he doing playing around with a past-it married woman, and his PA to boot? It was a cliché, just as Miranda had said. Fine, Claire had great boobs—nice, big bouncy things he loved, that were so far removed from Miranda's almost flat chest—and she was willing to do whatever he liked but honestly, the ease of it *bored* him. Her plainness *bored* him. Her willingness *bored* him. Such a sheep.

He remembered Miranda, and as much as he despised her now, the thrill of that chase. The buzz of that conquest. She had been hard-won and hard-fought for. She'd made him work for it. Gods, she'd had him eating practically out of the palm of her hand. And if he cared to admit it, that was what he missed. That was what he longed for.

Not the hit of a quick shag with Claire, the one that faded quickly into a buzz of annoyance, because really, all she did was lay there and moan, and he was pretty sure she faked it. He was a man. He wasn't an idiot. He wasn't as good as she made out. She simply acted out what she thought he wanted.

Robert sucked the inside of his cheek, staring coolly at her. She straightened and caught him looking, blushed and giggled, then winked and sashayed away.

Yep. He'd have to get rid of that. Things were done with Miranda, and he wouldn't touch the poisonous witch with a ten-foot bargepole, but he was done with shagging the secretary.

'Claire,' he called out. 'Here a minute.'

Immediately, she came running, already a little breathless. Jesus, what the bloody hell had he seen in her at all? She passed under the fluorescent lighting outside his office, and now all he could see were the bags under her eyes so badly concealed, the mascara clumped and flaking around her eyes, the blusher done too bright and red on her cheeks.

He'd thought her naturally pretty. Girl next door. Homely. Warm eyes, kind words, and a comfortable body, he supposed. So different from the hard edges of Miranda's personality. Now she just looked old and desperate. What was worse, he felt it. The thought made him shudder.

When had *he* gotten so old and desperate too?

'Yes?' she said, closing the door with a *snick* so they had privacy. No one came when the boss's door was closed. An unwritten rule. There were few of them in anyway that Sunday morning. Reception was about, and some of the bodies on the phones, for his property business never slept and Sunday was a prime day for house viewings and sales. Plus, he and Claire were there to go through the press releases ahead of Monday's web and paper issues, to make sure they had maximum coverage after the Harewood event. Claire's fingers rose to the wide collar of her white blouse, that she'd already left suggestively open by an extra button.

Robert gritted his teeth. It did elicit some sort of arousal in him, he had to admit, that she came so readily. No doubt she expected him to bend her over the desk again. He stood abruptly before he could think any more on that.

Before she could cross the room towards him, drape herself over him, or the desk, or gods, start undressing him, he shoved his hands in his pockets and spoke. 'Claire, it's not working out between us,' he said, his voice devoid of any emotion. 'I'm ending whatever this is.'

'What?' she said, stopping. And then she advanced, but Robert stepped back, placing the desk between them.

'It's not working out between us,' he repeated. 'We shouldn't have crossed the line. I'm sorry.' He wasn't really, but he was well practised in trying to placate Miranda when she was pissed off. The least he could do was throw a sorry into the mix, insincere as it was.

'You can't…I don't understand…' Horror, confusion, hurt flashed across her face—and then rage. 'Did *she* put you up to this?' She surged forward.

Miranda? Robert snorted with amusement. 'No. Nothing like that.' Not in the sense Claire thought—that he'd be going back to Miranda's waiting arms. If he did, those waiting arms would be clutching a knife waiting to carve him up and bleed him dry, more like.

'Then why? I don't understand. Did I do something wrong?' She looked pitiful for a second, her wide, blue eyes filling with tears she tried to blink away.

'No. I understand if you don't want to stay on here, if it's too awkward. I'll give you a glowing reference.'

'You're firing me?' she whispered.

'No, Claire, no, just if you want to—if you'd rather not work together after having been involved.'

Her face paled, and she drew herself up. He recognised the self-righteous indignation he'd seen a thousand times in Miranda, though Clare Parker's ire diluted into insignificance by comparison.

'You have someone else, don't you? Who are you fucking? It'd better not be someone here. Is it Jennifer? Rebecca? I knew it. I'll—'

'Stop. There's no one else.' Annoyance lashed in him. Gods, why did Claire not accept it? It wasn't as though there were feelings involved. He fucked her. He bought her nice things. It was transactional. End of. This wasn't —had never been, wasn't going to be—a relationship. She'd always known that too. Hadn't she?

'Then let's make this work,' she said, changing tack as quickly as the wind once more, sliding around the desk, her voice husky and low. 'Don't throw away what we have. It's so *special*, you and me, Rob.'

He backed away, but she moved faster, caught him. Pressed herself up against him, her hands groping for his manhood through his trousers. Her fingers were firm, seeking, desperate. His whole body stiffened, and he gritted his teeth at the kaleidoscope of sensations that sparked—his body betraying him at her touch.

Robert placed his hands firmly on her arms and pushed her away—gently, but enough to free himself. 'Enough,' he growled.

She toppled away as though he'd thrown her, stumbling into the desk and crashing to the floor.

For fuck's sake. Fucking melodramatic bimbo. He knew damn well he'd moved her firmly and nothing more. 'You're disgracing yourself. Get up.'

'I'll sue you!' she snarled at him from where she sat, her legs akimbo, her knickers on show.

'Don't make me fire you, Claire. This doesn't have to be difficult. We had fun. Nothing more. It's nothing personal.'

'I gave up my *marriage* for you! He won't take me back now he knows what I've done!'

'That's not my problem—it was your choice, always.'

It wasn't his fault that she'd been so open to forsaking her vows. He wasn't responsible for Claire's choice, much as he wasn't responsible for Miranda's choice to screw the bloody architect.

He was still annoyed about that, if he was honest, and this wasn't helping. Claire had totally been a revenge screw. An, '*if you can screw about, so can I*' defiant blast— but he rather thought Miranda had won this round in her choice.

'You bastard!' she shouted, scrambling to her feet. Shaking, her hands balled into fists, she stood there, thrumming with wrath. For a moment, he thought she'd run at him, strike him. But instead, she turned and ran, hot angry tears streaming down her face as she threw the door open with a bang and stormed out.

'You'll pay!' she screeched, for the whole office to hear.

Robert strolled to the door, hands in his pockets, and watched her go. The few curious faces in the office outside turned to Robert as Claire noisily gathered up her things and stormed out, crashing the door shut.

'Jennifer,' Robert called to the secretary calmly, knowing all eyes would be on him. Knowing the gossip that would be spun from their wild imaginations the moment he shut the door again. 'Mrs Parker's employment with us will be terminating immediately. Please ensure her things are saved in a box ready for her to collect at her convenience, and connect with Jeremy at GrowPro first thing tomorrow to start the recruitment for a suitable replacement.'

As he shut his office door, a hubbub grew amongst the staff.

Let them bloody talk. Claire was all mouth and no trousers. She wouldn't do anything. Robert Craven would make sure of it. No gold-digging slapper was going to ruin his business.

CHAPTER THREE

'Stick to your day job, mate,' DS Scott Metcalfe said. He tutted at the splatter of white paint on the hallway carpet.

DI Daniel Ward stepped back to admire his efforts, paint roller in hand. 'Could say the same for you, Scotty. I daresay I understand why Marie doesn't let you loose with the decorating...'

Scott spluttered in indignation, his jowls illuminating red.

Daniel chuckled. 'Don't worry about the carpet. Getting it replaced tomorrow.' They'd already rolled up the rest, and this was the last to pull up. He glanced around the confines of the living-dining-kitchen space in his first floor rented flat in Thornton, West Yorkshire. That weekend, they'd transformed it from a tired, dated, magnolia dump to a refreshed, bright, white pad deserving of a bachelor. Alright, it wasn't fancy, and it certainly wasn't anything special, but it was *his*.

A home.

Something to put his mark on.

Daniel had vowed to make himself one at last. It had been long enough since he'd felt at home anywhere, he'd had to painfully admit to himself. The divorce was underway, and he had his own space—why not here?

Why not here? he asked himself again. There were still a few homely touches to add—his mother's paintings, for one, once they were framed, and of course, some half-decent furniture—but it was coming along.

'I appreciate your help, mate.' He breathed in the strangely satisfying chemical smell of the fresh paint—so much nicer than the legacy of staleness, body odour, and smoke that had gone before.

'Ah, no bother.' Scott waved a hand dismissively. 'It's good to see you getting back on your feet, Daniel. It's been a hell of a rough time these past couple years. Just glad that you two are finally sorting yourselves out.'

'Aye.' It had taken long enough for Daniel and Katherine Ward to admit that it wasn't working. Longer still, for the anger and bitterness to come to an uneasy truce between them. Ward ran a paint-flecked hand through his unkempt hair.

'I see she finally let you have some furniture.'

'You could say that.' He'd managed to blag a small oak side table for the hallway—to dump his post and keys on—and the spare bedroom furniture. With the new mattress he'd bought, it meant he now had an actual bed to sleep in for the first time in the months since he'd moved there. With the impending new carpets—meaning the removal of the previous ones, along with the stains and stenches of the former occupants—it meant that Ward was dangerously close to having something resembling a *nice* place to live, one that was all his.

'Did you sell the house yet?' Scott dumped his spent roller in the tray and took them both to the kitchen sink. Ward popped the lid back onto the giant tub of paint before he followed—with a paint speckled Oliver the Beagle rising from his bed in the corner, tail wagging, to join them.

'It's on the market and there's been a few viewings, but nothing yet.' Ward bent to stroke Olly with the back of his hand. His fingers were tacky with drying paint. 'Nearly W-A-L-K time, little buddy.'

Ward ached—he wasn't as young as he used to be, much to his annoyance, and painting the ceilings had crippled the pair of them—but he couldn't deprive the dog of a much-needed run out. If Ward was being honest, he longed to escape the pervasive, headache-inducing fumes of paint too.

'Ah, you'll sell it no problem.'

Baildon, where Daniel and Katherine had their home, was a sought-after area. Daniel didn't doubt it either. It was the last thing tying the pair of them together, aside from the divorce itself. 'Hmm', Daniel replied noncommittally. He wouldn't count his chickens.

Scott grimaced as he swigged the cold brew they'd left on the side two hours ago, and tipped the rest down the sink. 'Right. I'd best be off. I promised Marie I'd be back in good time.'

'Have fun.'

Scott pulled a face. 'The things I do for that woman.' Yet, Daniel knew he wouldn't have it any other way. Scott Metcalfe worshipped the ground his wife Marie walked on. He'd booked tickets to see her favourite comedian—a woman he despised—but he'd laugh and smile along for Marie.

Ward grinned as he saw Scott out. 'Have fun. Thanks again, mate.'

Daniel threw on a crumpled hoodie and grabbed Olly's lead, the metal clasp chinking. Before he could call the dog, Olly barrelled out, claws scratching on the bare wood floors. 'Wish I had hearing like that,' he muttered as he bent down and clipped Olly on the lead.

It was late Sunday afternoon by the time he made it outside. The sun had already given way to an early dusk. Seething banks of storm-riddled clouds brewed in the north, carried on blasts of cold wind that funnelled down the valley.

Daniel lifted the hood up as a fat blob of rain splattered down his cheek. 'Just a quick one, Olly, eh?' He wasn't dressed for a deluge, and though the dog liked mud, he wasn't a fan of the rain either.

Olly yapped as he pulled Ward forward. Ward jogged up the Thornton Road towards Keelham, crossed, and turned off into a footpath that led up and over the hills. Still far too exposed, but at least Olly could have a run out round the field for a bit. He hadn't expected the decorating to take all weekend, but it was the way it went. At least it was done. The carpets would come first thing tomorrow before work, so when he returned that evening, it would be like an actual *home*.

The thought still felt strange. Ward unclipped Olly from the lead and let the dog race off into the long grass, standing to watch the dog run loops around himself following this trail and that.

His phone buzzed in his pocket. 'Hello?'

'Hi, is that Daniel Ward? It's Eve Griffiths—from the framers.'

Daniel's heart stuttered at the sound of her lilting voice. He berated himself. 'Ah, yes, hi. Is everything ok?' He pushed thoughts of her aside with ones of his mother's paintings. Were any of them too damaged to frame? That was why he worried, yes. That was why he cared that she'd called. Nope, he wasn't fooling himself. Daniel gritted his teeth, his eyes on the dog, and his shoulders hunched against that biting wind.

'So sorry to bother you on a Sunday.' He could hear the smile in her apologetic voice, and it seemed to dig an ache into his chest.

Get it together, you tit, he snapped at himself silently. 'No problem. What's up?'

'I have the first painting framed, is all. I wanted to check it's to your liking before I frame the rest in the same style. Is there any chance you could pop by? It won't take long.'

Daniel was silent for a second. He hadn't expected that. He'd expected that he'd see her once more, to pick the lot of them up, and then that would be it. Their paths would never cross again. He'd wondered what if, but the dream would be better than any reality he was capable of. Perhaps the universe was throwing him a bone. Or torturing him.

'Daniel?'

Even the way she said his name, light and soft. It ignited in him the desire to connect with her. So very different, whimsically so, to Katherine's cold self-control. *Damn it.* 'Yes, sorry. That's fine. When are you open?'

'Tomorrow morning, from nine, if that works?'

'Sure.' The carpets were arriving at eight, and fitting would take an hour. It was a quick turnaround but he could dash past on his way to work. 'I have work at ten, but I should be able to call in on my way for a few minutes.'

'It won't take long. Thank you. I'll...see you tomorrow, Daniel.'

'Bye, Eve.' Daniel hung up, the mobile hanging in his hand, and his eyes closed for a long moment.

Whatever the fantasy was that he had, he needed to stop it. Immediately. It was never going to happen, never going to go anywhere. He liked her because she seemed kind, because she'd been *nice* to him. That meant nothing, except that she had good manners. He couldn't believe that he'd been so starved of affection by Katherine that he was so desperate for any shred of kindness. Desperate enough to mistake it for the possibility of something more.

Ward tugged his hood down, letting the stinging rain

pelt his face, the sky above him dark and grey with the storm's coming. It was a welcome, freezing distraction. Instead of heading for home, he forged up the hill, Olly looping back and forth, delighted his walk had been extended, despite the rain. Ward strode, but he could not escape his treacherous thoughts of Eve Griffiths.

CHAPTER FOUR

MONDAY MORNING

R achel MacAllister heaved the vacuum cleaner out of her Vauxhall Corsa's dusty boot, followed by the caddy of cleaning products and cloths, hefting both over to the house before her with a well-practised strength that belied her small stature. She tucked a stray strand of hair behind her ear that had slipped out from the ponytail atop her head, taking a moment to glance, as she always did, appreciatively at how the *other half* lived.

Though, it was a short moment that day. A steady drizzle permeated the air, plastering her fringe against her forehead, and it was freezing under the dragon's breath misting the valley. One quick glance at the house.

Well, *house* was probably the wrong word. It wasn't quite a mansion, but it wasn't far off. The former farm-house had been renovated, modernised, and extended across a sprawling floor plan. It spread generously across the vast property that covered half the hillside with neatly manicured lawns and pruned shrubs.

The first time she'd visited, several years ago for her first clean there, she'd been daunted and awed at the size of it. It was hard not to dream that one day, her weekly Euromillions habit would pay off and maybe she could afford a place like that. Live there, instead of clean it.

She didn't mind the cleaning per se. As a clean freak, it was actually a job she rather enjoyed, losing herself in the therapeutic nature of it, whilst her headphones pumped something upbeat to keep her energy up.

That being said, it was the people she cleaned for that she had a problem with, half the time. Top of the list was the Cravens. That was partly why she elected to clean every Monday morning first thing. Mrs Miranda Craven was hardly ever home—though Rachel MacAllister knew *exactly* who she was usually with. She wondered if Mr Craven knew about that. Then again, Mr Craven had his own bit on the side too. Well. Several bits.

Rachel suppressed a shudder. She wouldn't like to get caught in the middle of that.

Monday mornings, for the most part, meant that Rachel never had to endure the haughty, superior snobbery of Mrs Craven. Nor the rude shortness of the master of the house. She'd never met the children—two adults now, a woman and a man—but she reckoned they'd be much the same. And so, she was glad of it.

Her brow furrowed as she took in the sleek, new, black Range Rover Sport on the driveway. Mr Craven was home then. Her stomach flipped and plummeted. She'd do her usual and stay out of his way as much as humanly possible. Though she'd only put one earphone in. Just to be able to hear him coming. The thought of him prowling up behind her...hulking, brooding, impassive, dark-eyed, set her on edge in some primal way she couldn't explain.

Rachel locked the car, picked up her vacuum and caddy, and crept around to the kitchen door. At least she had a key to get in. She'd be as quiet as a mouse, hopefully in and out without having to say more than a 'hello' to the man. She slipped the heavy brass key into the well-oiled lock, which turned silently and slipped inside, the metal handle smooth and freezing to the touch.

It was warmer there, but never *warm*, she always felt. It never had the feeling of a home, well lived in, well worn, and well loved. It always felt slightly cool, distant, unloved and empty, a yawning hole where the heart of it ought to be. But even so, it was dry and away from that chill, and she'd take it.

The vacuum crashed noisily as she set it down upon the stone-flagged floor, the sound echoing through the barren place. Rachel winced. Hoping Mr Craven hadn't heard. The last thing she wanted was to attract any hostility from the man, especially for her best-paying client. She might not have liked these rich snobby folks, but at least she got to earn a fiver an hour over minimum wage. That *wasn't* to be sniffed at. Not when it helped her and Jason make ends meet with three kids to feed.

Rachel put in an earphone and set her playlist going —a mix of classic nineties pop with the Spice Girls, Britney, and some of the good boy bands in there too—before she started with the quieter jobs first. It was still early after all, only eight. Just in case Mr Craven was still abed, unlikely as that was, but perhaps he was ill. Why else would his car still be there? He was normally in the office by the time she arrived.

Rachel swept the stone-flagged floor using the broom from the cubby by the door, and wiped down the marble work surfaces, mouthing along to some Boyzone. It was a welcome reprieve to the chilly silence of the place. She could never quite work out whether it seemed to be sadly quiet, looking for an injection of love and noise to fill it, or dark and brooding, as unpleasantly hostile as its owners.

She cleared the cups away on the table—two cold cups, ringed with the dark deposits of yesterday's coffee, pursing her lips. She didn't mind them occasionally, but she wasn't a bloody dishwasher, thank you very much. Rich people could be so *lazy*, she'd found, but on the whole, the Cravens weren't too bad in that regard—probably because it seemed no one hardly lived here. What a waste of a grand house. The irony of it. The huge place, barely lived in at all, versus her family—five of them stuffed in a three-bed semi down the valley in Embsay.

It left a funny smell in her nose almost as odd as the scent of drains. She sniffed tentatively at the sink, but the smell wasn't coming from there. Nor did it emanate from the sleek, matte black automatic sensor bin at the end of the counter. She glanced up—no leaks coming through the ceiling.

Odd. Must be a drainage leak somewhere. Perhaps the

rich didn't have it all smelling of roses. She chortled at her own joke—privately thinking it served them right, really.

Rachel lugged the vacuum and her caddy across the kitchen to the solid oak door that led into a cavernous living space, dusting feather brush, cloth, and polish at the ready for the matching oak furniture in the living space. Humming along to Destiny's Child, she cleaned over the giant beam fireplace, sweeping out the hearth—which was hardly ever used, to its great shame—and polishing the ornamental fireplace tools that frankly, she didn't think she'd ever seen dirty.

That strange smell seemed stronger here, though the door to the downstairs loo was by the front door, across the vast space, and otherwise there were no drains or pipes in there. Maybe she ought to report it. In case they didn't know. In case they thought she might have done it. Her hands slowed as she warred with that, the unpleasant prospect of speaking with them, or being collared by them later.

Rachel turned, slowly, gritting her teeth. She'd better mention it now. Out of professional courtesy. And to protect her own back. Clients had tried to pin things on her before—things they'd broken and thought it easier to blame her for—and she wasn't bloody having it again. The shame of that getting back to the boss and having to explain, red-faced in his office, how their client was a bare-faced liar. Rachel MacAllister prided herself on the best service, and she'd never broken a damn thing. Much as she'd sometimes wanted to for the rudest of her clients.

Already het up, it took Rachel a moment to register that the huge lump on the stone-flagged floor was, in fact, Mr Craven. But she'd not be able to report anything at all to him. Not with his brains spilling out across the stone.

Rachel screamed.

CHAPTER FIVE

D aniel Ward's heart thumped in his chest, his throat feeling blocked with the tug of each breath, as he pulled up outside *Griffith's Fine Art and Framing* the next morning. He'd left Olly at home with a massive bone to gnaw on, after the carpet fitters had come and gone.

Now, his apartment's soiled and brown-stained hard-wearing carpets were gone, replaced with softer mid-grey ones. It stripped the apartment of any colour of warmth, but he welcomed the blank slate. And the demise of the terrible smell that had plagued the old floor coverings from the apartment's previous occupants.

Self-consciously, Daniel flipped down the sun visor above the steering wheel and checked his reflection in the small mirror there. He was ready for work, his dark cropped beard trimmed, the rest of his face clean-shaven, his chestnut hair combed and waxed. Dressed in his usual professional suit, with his thicker woollen coat to ward off the morning's chill. The storm had abated overnight but a taste of winter came from the north with the turn from September to October.

Irked at himself, Ward snapped the visor shut and climbed out of the car, striding to the shop front before he could change his mind. The bell tinkled as he entered. Inside, the same fragrance of artist paints and the sweet scent of some kind of polish lingered.

Eve popped her head out from the back and broke into a smile at the sight of him. 'Ah, perfect! Thanks so much for coming. I didn't want to just presume before I did the rest. Let me get it.'

Daniel drifted to the counter, staring at the walls hung with artwork around them. Other landscapes of his beloved Yorkshire, and some of the local inhabitants, from sheepdog to cows. One even of the weir by Salts Mill in Saltaire, near where one of his latest cases had briefly taken him on the hunt for a murdered woman.

Rustling and scraping in the back pulled his attention to the ajar door. Eve bustled through after a moment, hefting a frame. Daniel held back his instinct to rush to help her—she had it in hand, her wiry muscles well practised to handling bulky frames.

'Here we are,' she murmured, her full attention on lowering the frame softly onto the surface, facing Ward.

His gaze passed over her—the light brown sheet of hair pinned back behind each ear and falling loose down her back, the navy check shirt and paint-smudged, figure-hugging jeans. He glanced at the painting as she looked up, smiling.

'What do you think?'

A lump formed in his throat. It was the Filey Brig painting. Steely grey seas before a blue sky, the dark bulk of the Brig jutting out into the North Sea, with sandy beaches drawing the viewer in, and those smudges of white, seagulls wheeling overhead.

She must have mistaken his silence for reticence, perhaps disapproval. 'We can change it, if you hate it,' she said quickly.

'No,' he interrupted. 'No, I was just looking. It's been a long time. I've never seen it look so good.' For so many years, those paintings had been unceremoniously rolled up and stored in black plastic bin bags, thanks Katherine.

'These must be incredibly important to you—I don't mean to pry, but I got the feeling your mother...well...that she wasn't around to see them anymore.'

'No,' Daniel replied, his voice soft. 'She's not. They're all I have left of her, to be honest.'

Eve's answer was hushed with silent apology. 'I didn't mean to...'

'It's alright. It was a long time ago now.' Ward forced a smile onto his face, though it didn't quite reach his eyes. 'I decided it was time to remember. This is perfect. Thank you.'

And it was. The painting, slightly faded in places, and with a stain spotting one corner, was carefully held back by a bevelled edged mount under the glass. Somehow, the wooden frame was precisely the same colour as the oak furniture in his bedroom that he'd taken from his and Katherine's guest room. The long, slim painting would hang perfectly over the tall headboard. It was as though that picture had been framed to fit it perfectly. Like it was meant to be. Something seemed to click into place.

'Brilliant. Would you like the rest framed in the same finish and style?'

'Yes please, that would be great.'

'Excellent.' Eve rustled under the counter and pulled out a notebook filled with a looping script, neatly spaced on each line. She flicked through a couple pages. 'I should be able to fit the rest in over the next couple weeks. Would you like to take this one now?'

Ward hesitated, his mouth open, about to say yes. 'Ah —I'd best not. I have to go to work, and I can't guarantee this will be safe in my car all day. I don't want to damage your work.' Perhaps he could slip by to collect it another time...another excuse to see her, even if it was pointless anyway.

'It's no problem. I can keep it here for you.' She looked him up and down casually. 'I'm being totally nosy, but what do you do, out of interest?' She leaned on the counter, propping herself up on both palms, and cocked her head, waiting for his answer.

'Ah, I'm a detective inspector.' Somehow, he felt like a pretentious fool saying it, though he'd worked damn hard for all his experience and his exams to own that title.

She raised an eyebrow. 'Oh, wow. That must be exciting.'

'We get our fair share of cases. It's burglary season

now, to be honest, and I can't say that's too fun.' It wasn't, poking around in the violated shreds of peoples' lives for perps they hardly ever managed to catch due to insignificant evidence. He stopped short of saying he preferred the big cases, murders and the likes. It would sound exactly as horrifying as he imagined, without the context, to a civilian.

She chuckled. 'No, I can imagine not. My dad used to be a copper before he retired. He was an inspector too. Not a detective, though.'

'For West Yorkshire?'

'Aye, though it was back in the day, of course. I don't think you'd know him. William Griffiths.'

'The name doesn't ring a bell.'

'He retired a couple decades ago.'

'Lucky him,' Ward said wryly. Decent pension, decent retirement age—better than Daniel knew he'd receive when the time came.

Eve chuckled. 'I suppose. Not for mum, though. Drives her round the bend having him home all the time, getting underfoot, as she says.'

Ward couldn't imagine it, any of it, without threatening to tear open that terrible void inside him at what had been taken from his own mother and his family. He forced a smile that was more like a grimace onto his face. 'I'll bet.'

His phone rang in his pocket, and he excused himself. His heart sank as he saw DCI Martin Kipling's name flash up on the screen. And the time. He was running late. 'Excuse me.' He took the call. 'Sir.'

'Ward, I know you're probably already on your way in, but I need you in the briefing room when you arrive. There's been a high-profile death and Superintendent McIntyre knew them *personally.*'

Ward could read between the lines. The gaffer would be under pressure to deliver this one quickly. High profile...immediately, he wondered who it was. 'I understand, sir. I'll be there as soon as I can.' He hung up and turned back to Eve. 'I'm really sorry, I have to go. Do you need anything else from me?'

She held her hands up. 'No, sorry to have kept you, that sounded important. I'll let you know when the rest are finished.'

'Thank you. Sorry.' And he truly was as he rushed out of the shop, leaving his mother's painting behind once more, and the woman who seemed to ensnare his attention, he wished he could have stayed a little longer, even though he had no reason or right to.

CHAPTER SIX

MONDAY MID-MORNING

W ard arrived to a steaming mug of tea just the way he liked it in the briefing room, courtesy of his DS Emma Nowak.

She grinned at him and whispered, 'Morning, sir. Thought you might need this.' She handed him the brew. It was in a well-used *Line of Duty* "Mother of God, it's The Gaffer" mug that some joker had brought in a few years back as a secret Santa gift for the DCI. DCI Kipling hadn't seen the funny side. Mind, Ward didn't think he had one.

'Thanks,' Ward mouthed. He hadn't had a chance to sort a drink out with the DCI's rush—Nowak was a star, alright. He owed her a brew on the invisible tally.

He squeezed into the back of the room as the DCI forged a path to the front. They wouldn't all be working the case, of course, momentarily pulled from a tangle of other duties, but clearly, if the fearsome DSU Diane

McIntyre knew the victim, her involvement had Kipling pulling out all the stops.

Metcalfe nodded to him across the room, and Ward raised his brew in salute. Last of all, in filed DS Priya Chakrabarti, heading up the burglary taskforce—and looking gaunt enough to prove it. The long shifts weren't helping any of them.

'Morning all,' DCI Kipling's nasally, measured voice rang out across the room. He surveyed them all, the couple of dozen standing before him from the HMET unit. 'No rest for the wicked, as they say.' It could have been a joke, but he wasn't smiling. Neither was anyone else. Expectant silence awaited him.

'The body of Mr Robert Craven was discovered this morning at his home address in Skipton. Now, I'm sure you'll *all* know who Mr Craven is—a local entrepreneur with good standing in the community and local area, and something of a success story, a local lad who's built an empire from nothing, and a good friend and beneficiary of our force. Just this week-end, Detective Superintendent McIntyre attended an event to celebrate the Cravens' business success this year. As you can imagine, she's personally affected by this terrible news.'

He glared around at them. Ward arranged his face into something neutral. The only feeling he'd ever seen McIntyre express was ire. Oh no, wait, fury too. And wrath. The full spectrum of rage. *Sadness though?* He wasn't sure about that one—but then again, he stayed out of her way too much to know her on any level other than "bloody terrifying".

'Of course, we remain impartial, but it's in our interests to investigate Mr Craven's unexpected death thoroughly. I hope that we'll find nothing more than a terrible accident has befallen him, rather than foul play, but given the high-profile nature of this incident, we must also be sensitive to the volume of press interest I expect shall be received.

'As yet, no one other than ourselves and the attending emergency services are aware of what's happened, and, aside from informing his next of kin, I'd like to keep it that way. Local Uniforms have sealed the scene for now. No leaks. Is that understood?' Once more, DCI Kipling glared sternly at them all.

'Yes, sir,' rumbled through the room.

DCI Kipling's shoulders relaxed slightly. 'Good. DI Ward, you're SIO on this one. Take DS Nowak with you, and attend the scene at once. The pathologist and CSI are en route already. The rest of you are to attend to your usual duties and await any caseload from your DI. Dismissed.'

The team responded with a resounding, 'Sir.'

Ward raised an eyebrow at DS Nowak as they filed out amongst the team. It looked like he'd be putting his coat straight on. He grabbed it from where he'd flung it across the back of his desk chair in the shared office as DS Nowak hurried to her desk to collect her things.

DI Ward chugged the brew, wincing at the burn of it down his throat—but better hot than never—before slipping his coat on and grabbing the car key out of his pocket. No pool car for them today. They'd be making the best of the fast roads up to Skipton in his prized VW Golf R.

'Where to, Emma?' Ward asked as he reversed out of the parking space in the Bradford South Police Station car park.

'Er, the arse end of nowhere actually, sir.' Emma squinted at her phone. 'Just north of Skipton. Head through Skipton as though you're off to Gargrave, and it's just off there.' She reached forward to plug the details into his satnav.

Ward could imagine the property of a local business magnate—some large mansion, set well away from plebs like them. 'Cheers. What do we know about Mr Craven?'

Nowak blew out a long breath. 'Not much, sir.' She scanned her phone. 'He was found dead this morning by his cleaner at the family home, who's still present on-scene, as far as I know.'

Ward logged that one—not impossible for the cleaner to have done it, or be an unlucky witness. Hard to know without meeting her. 'Well then. Better get a move on, hadn't we?'

It would take them a while, time Ward wished they didn't have to spend en route, but it couldn't be helped. He tapped his finger on the steering wheel impatiently as the traffic merged from two lanes to one on Canal Road, a familiar pinch point of congestion—and then they were off, still too painfully slowly. He could open it up as they hit the Bingley bypass—and he did. He had no desire to linger there.

It was still so soon after they had stopped the horrific

killing spree of Henry Denton there. Too close for comfort. Up the Aire Valley, he wove on the fast A-road, out past Keighley and with it, the last of the sprawling suburbia that reached out from Bradford. The rising fog revealed a wide, rich, green valley filled with grassy plains beside the river and the road, hills dotted with villages and hamlets funnelling them on their journey towards Skipton.

Ward took the ring road that swung them around west of the town, listening to Nowak as she directed them from there, pinching and zooming onto her phone and squinting at the screen to check the satnav had them on the right course. The dual carriageway ended at the roundabout, and off they dove into winding country roads towards Gargrave and the famous Three Peaks. The lanes were barely better than a single car's width, with punishing stone walls and towering dark hedges crowding the Golf as it zoomed along.

Skipton was the gateway to the Dales. Out there, there were no more large towns, and certainly no more cities. Villages, hamlets, lone farmsteads and houses dotted through the verdant, weather-worn landscape of grouse-filled moors and craggy, weathered stone.

Ward braked sharply as they came upon an unexpected crossroad buried almost indistinguishably in the tangle of hedgerows and poorly lit with the dark tree branches crouching overhead like grasping fingers.

'Sorry,' he muttered, as Emma squawked in protest beside him.

'A little warning, sir!' she choked out, glaring at him.

Ward sniggered. 'Just checking you're awake, Sarge.'

'One of these days,' she said darkly to him.

Ward couldn't suppress his grin—didn't even try. 'Where to next?'

'Straight across. Onto Bog Lane.'

Ward did a double-take. 'Eh? Come again?' He eased the car across the junction.

'Bog Lane, sir.'

Ward couldn't help it. A little snort came out amidst a rolling chuckle.

'Sir?'

'What? How can you not find that funny? Alright, I admit, a bit juvenile, but still.'

'What's funny about Bog Lane?'

'You're kidding, right? Is this a foreigner thing? You're half-Irish, half-Polish, did you miss the memo on toilet gags?'

'Oh,' understanding dawned. 'No, sir. A jack's as funny here as it is anywhere else, I reckon. A *bog*, you say?' she wrinkled her nose.

'Well, it isn't funny if I have to explain it,' muttered Ward. 'But yes. Bog. Lavatory. Toilet. Loo.'

'Acting your shoe size today, sir?' Emma said smoothly, giving Ward side-eye and raising an eyebrow.

Ward gave the undignified response of sticking out his tongue—something he immediately regretted as Emma smirked and turned to face forward once more. 'You're telling me it isn't funny that some rich guy lives on toilet lane,' he said lamely.

'Absolutely, sir,' Emma said, as mockingly as possible.

'Oh, here we are,' she said before he could respond. 'This track here.'

A dirt track, easy to miss, cut off the winding lane between two high dry-stone walls. It quickly gave way after twenty yards to a gravel driveway and open wrought iron gates. It led to a courtyard, down the hill, and to a sprawling house, well-hidden and private from the road.

'Nice,' Emma said, letting out a low whistle as she took in the full-height stable door that had been converted to a window, and the wooden doors and window frames that nestled in grey stone, under a recently slated roof.

The courtyard, generously proportioned when empty, was stuffed. An ambulance took centre stage, the rear doors open and facing them, the front pointed towards the house. A marked police car squeezed in between it and a shining black Range Rover Sport, whilst on the other side of the ambulance, a red Porsche Boxster blocked in the CSI van and an out of place looking silver Vauxhall Corsa. Nowak jumped out to let Ward squeeze his Golf right up to one of the walls so the driveway wasn't totally blocked.

'Full house, eh?' he said as he climbed out, surveying the chaos. The scent of damp earth, such a change from the city's pollution, carried on the breeze. Still, like the city, it was too busy for his liking—he'd have preferred the cordon to be further back, but this was the only parking they'd find in half a mile, with how narrow the drive and adjoining road were.

They crunched across the gravel past the ambulance. The CSI van was deserted. Ward noted the vinyl sticker on the Corsa, which explained its presence—*Skipton Cleaning Services*.

Outside the solid wooden front door—reclaimed, by the looks of it and otherwise unmodernised except for the CCTV camera over the door—and sheltering out of the drizzle under a solid wooden overhanging porch was a PC, holding the scene. The doorway behind him was taped over with cordon tape. The PC looked thoroughly miserable—but not because of the crappy job he had, or the rain. No, that was thanks to the woman berating him.

Tall and slender, approaching her fifties, Ward would have said, she was immaculately put together. Her sleek dark hair was somehow impervious to the rain, and the navy tailored pantsuit flowing across her elegant form stuck out as out of place in the middle of rural Yorkshire.

'It's my damn house, so let me in!' she snapped at him, clutching her maroon leather handbag closer. A yap sounded from inside, as if to agree, and the head and shoulders of the most ridiculous dog Ward had ever seen popped its head out.

Small enough to be a hairy rat, the poor sodding thing had its fur tied in a red bow between its ears.

The PC's eyes flicked to it, and then back to the woman as she leaned towards him, raising a clawed hand and shaking it at him with ire. He bloomed red, stuttering as he shrank away.

Ward marched across. 'Ma'am, may I help you?

Detective Inspector Daniel Ward. Senior Investigating Officer.'

The PC wilted, relief evident on his sagging face as he clocked Ward and Nowak striding purposefully towards the pair of them.

'Well, I hope you can!' exclaimed the woman, wheeling on them, the full force of her presence falling upon him. 'This is *my* house, and I need to go inside at once!'

'Mrs Craven?' Ward hazarded a guess.

'Yes, Miranda. Charmed.' For a moment, she was all smiles as she extended a limp hand. It was more like a claw with talon-like false nails. He grabbed it—smooth and cold—gave it a weak shake, and let it go. Then, it seemed, she was all business again.

'It's freezing cold and throwing it down.' The drizzle was fine, but he wasn't about to correct her. 'Can *someone* please tell me why I cannot enter my own home?' Her icy tone told him she wasn't looking for an explanation, but someone to blame.

'Mrs Craven, are you aware why we're here?' Ward asked, as Nowak flicked him a glance.

'Well aware, thank you. My husband's dead, so I hear.'

Ward blinked. Not the response he was expecting. 'Aye. We're very sorry for your loss, Mrs Craven. Do you have anywhere you can stay? At the moment, we're looking to recover your husband's body and make sure no suspicious circumstances are surrounding his death. We'll make sure a liaison officer is made available to support you at this difficult time.'

Mrs Craven snorted. 'How ridiculous. Do you not have better things to be doing? Fine, fine,' she said, raising a hand to dismiss Ward before he could speak. 'Can I at least go and get my things? My darling little Trixiebelle' – the dog yapped at its name and Ward resisted cringing with every fibre of his being— 'needs her special food and I have to collect some clothes.'

'I'm afraid not, Mrs Craven—not now at least. Perhaps later today, when our forensics team is further along, we may be able to recover some items for you that aren't material to any investigation we may open.'

Mrs Craven huffed with sheer disgust and turned back to the PC.

'Sorry, Ma'am, what he said,' squeaked out the PC, wilting before her withering stare.

'Fine,' she spat, glaring again at Ward and Nowak. 'I shall have to *manage*.' She spat the word out as though it were the worst thing she'd ever had to do.

'Mrs Craven, we could do with speaking to you first, please,' said Ward.

'I have a meeting,' she said irritably. 'I'll give you my number. Call me to book into my diary.' She rattled off a number which Nowak had the good sense and speed to write in her already-open pocket book.

Mrs Craven turned and strode straight-backed to the Porsche before Ward could insist that she needed to stay. It was a difficult feat in the gravel given her stilettos, but she did not falter once. The engine rumbled into life and a hail of gravel peppered the CSI van as she accelerated away.

'Christ,' muttered Ward. 'What the hell was that?'

'I have absolutely no idea, sir. I can't say I've seen a grieving widow like that before.'

'Aye. The trouble is, I didn't see that she was grieving at all.' Grief didn't always hit people immediately, but the shock of it usually did. Mrs Craven seemed as unfazed and unbothered by it, as though she'd passed comment on the mild inconvenience of the weather, not the death of her husband and father of her children.

Why, also, did she need to collect things for the dog and herself? Why was she arriving home on a Monday morning? Something didn't add up, and that sixth sense of his was tingling with the premonition of *something* there. Ward's eyes followed the red car until it passed out of sight at the end of the drive. He heard the engine roar as she raced it down the lane.

'Thank you, sir,' said the PC, giving him *a look* that he translated as mixed exasperation and fear of the woman.

Ward chuckled dryly. 'You looked like you needed help before she ate you. Is the victim through here?'

'Aye, sir. First thing you see as you walk through the door. Rather spoils the view.'

'I'll bet.' Dead bodies weren't his favourite ambience in a luxury converted farmhouse. 'Let's go speak to the cleaner first,' Ward said, changing tack now the wife was gone, and striding over to two figures he had missed before. Another PC and a woman huddled at the side of the ambulance for what shelter they could get from the wind there, with the PC holding a brolly over the woman's head.

Ward made their introductions.

'Mrs MacAllister,' he said. 'I understand you found Mr Craven.'

'Yes.' Rachel seemed folded in on herself, her arms wrapped around her torso and her head bowed as if she were trying to comfort herself. Her mouth twisted and she covered it with a hand, as though she could suppress the sob that escaped by clutching her lips shut.

'I need you to tell me what happened—how you came upon him, if you can.' Just from her body language, Ward could see the woman was upset—more upset than the uptight wife, at least.

With a shuddering breath, Rachel nodded. 'I clean every Monday morning. The pair of them, Mr and Mrs Craven, they're usually not here. Robert's car—the black one there' —she pointed a shaking finger at the Range Rover— 'was here, and I thought that was unusual, but maybe he was ill or...I don't know.' She shook her head.

'I went in just like normal, about eight. I found him there and I called 999. I could see...his head...his...' She shuddered and paused, turning away, as though she were about to vomit. Slowly, she stood once more. 'Sorry,' she murmured, still grey-faced. 'He was all burst open l-like an egg.'

'Not at all. It's a hard sight to see. So, it was clear he was deceased?'

Rachel nodded and brushed her eyes with the back of a hand.

'And you made the call at...' Ward checked his pocket book. 'A quarter to nine, right?'

'If you say so. I didn't check.'

'But you entered the property around eight?'

'Yes?' Watery eyes looked up at him.

'So, can you account for the forty-five minutes it took you to make that call, Mrs MacAllister? Our PC there says you can't miss him the moment you walk in.' Ward kept his tone even, unthreatening. A routine follow-up question, that was all, nothing more. Yet.

'I didn't go through that door. I don't use that door—it's for family and guests only. We use the side door that goes into the kitchen. I start cleaning there every week.' She faltered as some realisation passed through her. 'God, he was there the whole time I was cleaning the kitchen.'

Revulsion warred with fear on her face. 'I cleaned the kitchen, then I went through to the living area...if I had just turned...' she shuddered. 'I cleaned the fireplace... then I turned around and I saw...I saw him. Just lying there, all split open, like he'd fallen from the sky.' She balled a fist and pressed it against her pale lips.

'And did you ring then?'

'Aye...when I'd stopped screaming.'

That made sense. It would have taken her time to clean, after entering the property, before discovering the grisly find. CSI would determine the time of death. Unless it was immediately preceding the 999 call, he could discount the cleaner. Boy, had she been in the wrong place at the wrong time.

'Are you certain it was Mr Craven? It couldn't have been anyone else?'

'No. It was definitely him,' she said past her fist. 'It was him. I can't stop seeing him.' She looked at Ward, her face slack with horror, her eyes wide.

'It's hard, I know, but it will pass, Mrs MacAllister.'

'He was so pale, and looked so cold and grey...he wouldn't move, and I didn't dare...I didn't dare go...' She burst into tears and covered her face with her hands. 'His head was such a mess!' she wailed.

The PC next to her awkwardly patted her on the shoulder.

'Mrs MacAllister, if you could remain on the scene a little longer.' He nodded to Nowak. 'My colleague Detective Sergeant Nowak here will need to take a full statement from you, and your contact details, before we can let you go. I suggest you take the rest of the day off and call someone to help keep you occupied today.' He smiled sympathetically as Rachel nodded, already staring at the house behind Ward's shoulder again as though Robert Craven's reanimated corpse were about to stumble outside.

Ward trudged over to the house, hating the crunch of gravel under his feet, and slipped shoe covers and gloves on before the PC lifted the cordon and let him through.

The aged door opened on silent, well-oiled hinges into a warm but cavernous space. The warmth, along with a blast of the cloying, heavy, pungent scent of death greeted him. Ward steeled himself and strode in. He was in a vast room that stretched through to the other side of the house—he could see the hills on the other side through the windows there. It stretched up to the rafters too, a mezzanine level opening up to a gallery landing upstairs. Exposed oak rafters upheld a whitewashed ceiling, and Velux windows pooled light into the otherwise murky depths below, illuminating the scene like a theatre spotlight. Below that mezzanine...

Victoria Foster and her CSI team were busy at work, photographing the body and surroundings, and gathering samples. As two paper-suited figures shifted, he caught sight of the contents of Robert Craven's head dashed across the floor like some creative paint throwing artistic expression. DI Ward suppressed a shudder, steeled his stomach, and crossed to the portly figure standing back, observing the scene.

'Well met, Baker.'

'Now then!' The pathologist, Mark Baker, turned to him, a smile lighting up his ruddy face. 'It's been a while, m'dear boy. How are you, Daniel?'

'Good thanks, and you?'

'Oh, quite fine, quite fine. You're keeping me on my toes, I can't complain.'

Daniel chuckled. Only Mark Baker could make such a morbid crime scene feel so warm. 'Keeping you out of trouble, you mean.'

Mark offered a conspiratorial wink.

'What do we have here, then?'

'It looks like he's taken a nasty fall, from my first

impression. Landed at the wrong angle. Feet first, and he'd be alive and kicking—or maybe not *kicking*, given he might have broken his legs. I think he tumbled right off that mezzanine up there. Headfirst. He didn't stand a chance against this.' Mark Baker gestured towards the original flagstones they stood on.

'The railing's not damaged and hasn't given way or anything, so he didn't fall through it,' Daniel mused aloud, folding his arms as he and Baker looked up. 'How would he have fallen over? The railing's standard height. Not something he'd trip over.'

'Precisely, my dear boy, and so I took a closer look. Now, it's very hard to make out given the substantial damage he's sustained, as you might imagine, but he's suffered additional head trauma by the looks of it.'

Ward raised an eyebrow. 'Caused by?'

'Someone else, I do believe,' the pathologist replied solemnly. 'I shall need to take a closer look to determine which came first, but there's every possibility that he suffered some trauma, and then the fall. I can't be sure which killed him yet.'

Unease curled in Ward's belly. Murder. They were looking at a murder.

Mark continued, 'I've done a few calculations and based on those and my observations, I think he's been dead since yesterday afternoon, probably sometime between about lunchtime and suppertime. I'll be checking his blood-alcohol levels, and of course, for other substances, in case that was a factor. Seems unlikely given the timing, but I need to rule it out for you because it closes another significant line of enquiry for accidental death.'

'Do you think he could have been pushed?' That was the other logical conclusion. Pushed or thrown—though, for a big fellow, the latter was unlikely.

'Quite possibly. He may have fallen after the trauma, or been forced, but of course, if that's the case, no one hung about long enough to tell us.' Mark sighed and shook his head. 'Terrible this, though, isn't it? Terrible. He's in this morning's papers, too.'

'What?' Ward turned sharply to Baker. How had the papers gotten hold of this? It was a sealed crime scene, and—

'Oh, not *this*.' Mark waggled his finger. 'Some shindig he had at the weekend up at Harewood. Glamorous, it looked. However, the piece was less about that, and more about the backhanders he's suspected of delivering to the council to get permission granted to build on greenbelt land up in the Dales.' Baker pursed his lips and shook his head. 'I don't speak ill of the dead, but my word, it was scathing.'

'Can you forward that to me?'

'Of course.' Baker patted his pockets until he found his phone and messaged the article's link to Daniel's phone.

It buzzed in Ward's pocket. 'Thanks, Baker. I'll check it out. Better take a look around first, and speak to Victoria.'

Ward departed to prowl around the house, through the clean and empty kitchen, the large, open-plan living space, and upstairs through the mostly deserted bedrooms and bathrooms. It seemed as though no one *lived* there. Not in the sense Ward recognised.

There were so few personal items scattered about, just a photograph here and there, mostly of Robert with his wife and two children as babies, children, teenagers, and adults, but all formal. No fun photos. No personal effects in some of the bedrooms—though Ward surmised, that with the children all grown up, they no longer resided there.

Two bedrooms seemed to be in use. One, decidedly barer and more masculine, with a fresh business suit hung on the wardrobe door. The other with a dressing table lined with perfume bottles and makeup, and a wardrobe filled with evening dresses. The chest of drawers in there was empty.

It seemed Mr and Mrs Craven didn't share a bed anymore, then. It seemed like Mrs Craven perhaps didn't even live there anymore. Ward decided he *definitely* had plenty of questions for Mrs Craven.

He examined the mezzanine rail in detail, putting his weight on it to test for any weaknesses or fissures, but could find none. The thing was solid. Robert definitely hadn't gone through any point of it...which meant, if he'd fallen, he'd gone over it. Ward was a tall man, but even so, the mezzanine came high enough that it would be a struggle to accidentally fall. He'd have to lean out perilously far.

Ward peered over the railing. Craven lay spreadeagled below. Hard to tell precisely how he'd toppled over. Ward chewed a lip.

He stood back and surveyed the creamy carpet at his feet. Dark specks leapt into focus. He bent down. *Blood. Shite.* Blood spattered the carpet, and as he cast around, the walls too, small specks dashed, as though flung at high velocity.

Ornamental stands lined the landing. Each plinth upholding ornaments that looked incredibly old—Roman antiques, perhaps, he wondered. Several were small statuettes as long as his forearm. But the one closest to him was empty. He peered over the mezzanine again. Nothing immediately stood out that could have been an item on the plinth laying abandoned below.

A paper-suited figure looked up. Victoria Foster, going by the glasses—today, bright yellow plastic rims, covered in purple blobs. 'Are you going to stand up there all day or come and do some work, DI Ward?'

'Morning, Victoria,' Ward said with a cheery wave he knew would annoy her. Sure enough, she scowled at him —her masked face hidden but for her thunderously furrowed brows.

He thumped down the open stairs at the end of the space and joined her. 'What have we got?'

'Well, you can see for yourself, I think. A pretty nasty mess. Fallen from a height—Mark here confirms that it looks like we're looking for any weapon causing blunt force trauma too. Well, in addition to the floor.'

'Solid stone will do that to a head, yes.'

'Quite. We've confirmed his ID from the wallet in his

pocket and what's left of his face. Also seized his phone for further examination in case you need that. We're going up to check the mezzanine above next. Just finishing up down here. We'll need to match those against family and anyone else who was here for elimination or identification purposes.'

'There's blood up on the landing too, by the way. And an empty plinth that could have contained the object he was hit with, going by what's on the others.'

'Excellent.' Victoria beckoned one of her team over and set them on analysing that immediately.

'Make sure you get the cleaner. She's outside now. She would have been handling things this morning, so she'll be all over the kitchen, perhaps in here too.'

'Thanks.'

'Any sign of a break-in?' He hadn't seen any—no unsecured windows or busted locks.

'No.'

They both stared at the body for a moment. 'You don't think it's accidental?'

Victoria pursed her lips. 'Not a chance. When we move the body, we'll know more. We need to investigate this one further.'

'The boss would agree. Apparently, the Super knew him. Personally. She'd attended some event with him on Saturday night.'

Victoria let out a low whistle. 'Christ. All our arses on the line, then.'

'Death by Di.' A famous threat back at the station. Anyone who crossed DSU Diane McIntyre usually wished they'd died, because it would have been easier than facing the dour Scotswoman's eviscerating ire.

Victoria groaned. 'Well, I'll send you whatever we have, and God help us, our fate rests in your hands.'

Ward had the good grace to not meet her unimpressed stare.

CHAPTER SEVEN

MONDAY LUNCHTIME

'What do you make of the cleaner, then?' Ward broke the silence as they drove back to the station to start with the mammoth task of figuring out where on earth to begin and set the team to work. Robert's body was already on its way to Bradford Royal Infirmary's morgue for a post mortem and Mark Baker's ministrations. Victoria's CSI team would shortly be finishing at the scene, ready for it to be released back to Mrs Miranda Craven.

Nowak had taken the cleaner's statement. 'Understandably shaken. But she did say something that struck me as odd. Whilst cleaning the kitchen, she washed up two used mugs that had been left on the table overnight, she said. When I asked her how she knew, she said because the coffee inside had dried out and she'd had to give them a good scrub.'

Ward pulled out onto the fast single road that wound

through the top of the Aire Valley from Skipton to Keighley. 'Hmm?'

'Well, Mrs Craven clearly hadn't slept there last night. And seeing that she didn't seem to care about her husband's death, and that you reckon they're sleeping in separate bedrooms, I doubt they were sharing a cosy cuppa together.'

Ward couldn't wait to hear Mrs Craven's alibi—and figure out what on earth was going on between her and Robert to give some context to the situation. 'So, you think someone visited Craven yesterday around the time of his death?'

'I do, sir. I don't know if they're connected to his death, or responsible for it, but it could help us narrow the window of time in which he died, and discover what happened to him, if we can figure out who that mug belonged to and why they were there.'

'Aye. Good thinking, Nowak. I don't suppose...'

'Nope, afraid not, sir. There's no forensic details Victoria can pull from the mug now it's been cleaned, I already checked with her.'

Damn. The cleaner had unwittingly gotten rid of some prime forensic evidence there. 'If whoever drank from that cup was the one who killed him, however, Robert Craven knew his murderer.' *And they shared a drink before the despicable deed was committed.*

'Yes, sir.'

'They have a CCTV system, so perhaps that will hold details of who dropped by.' With no signs of forced entry, had Robert let them in? Or had they entered themselves?

'I'll get on that when we're at the office.'

'Can you arrange for liaison too? I want eyes on the wife. I think we need to keep a close eye on her, and we need to arrange a chat ASAP.'

'I've already got Geoff on it, sir.'

'Brilliant.' Geoffrey Mason was one of their top Family Liaison Officers, or FLOs. The elderly man was a pro at putting families at ease and had a knack for being able to draw out sensitive information to help investigations. Though, Ward rather suspected that Mrs Craven wouldn't be too impressed to have an old man trailing after her. He reckoned Geoff's home-knitted Aran sweaters didn't fit with her glamorous lifestyle.

———

Back at the office, Ward briefed the team with the handful of findings they had, and the starting point, namely Mrs Craven. Plus, there would be their children to inform. The DCI had already collared Ward and told him that the DSU was visiting them personally to inform them. That had given Ward pause for thought—the DSU must have been close to them indeed if she was this personally invested in the case, accidental or not.

'Right. DC Patterson, I'd like you researching family and friends, known connections and the like. Pass them through to DS Metcalfe.'

'Yes, sir.' Young Jake Patterson sat up straighter in his

chair as they all looked at him across the Incident Room. Behind Ward, on a bare Big Board, was pinned one single image, a photo of Robert Craven. He stared out at them all with dark eyes, imposing in death as he was in life.

'DC Shahzad, I need you to investigate the Craven's CCTV security system—what devices they may have, alerts, footage, that type of thing. We need to find out who visited Robert just before he died, and eliminate them from our enquiry, or see if they're someone we should be looking into more closely.'

Kasim nodded, jotting down some notes in his pocket book.

'I also want you to do a thorough check on Robert's phone. Work with Patterson to identify any contacts of interest we need to speak to. If there's anything suspicious on there, I want to be the first one to know.'

'DS Metcalfe and DS Nowak, see to Patterson's and Shahzad's findings—chase up any likely leads. DS Chakrabarti, DC Norris, you two are still on with your caseload, right?'

A weary Priya and David nodded. Priya Chakrabarti took point on the deluge of burglary caseload they had at present now the winter sprees had started again, with a team of DCs reporting to her, whilst David Norris worked on the Varga case, partially overseen by Metcalfe and Ward.

'Busy busy busy,' Ward muttered. 'I know we're stretched, team, but what's new, eh? Let's get to the bottom of this so we don't have the Super on our tails. Alright?'

'Aye, sir,' rang through the room.

'What're you doing now, sir?' DS Nowak asked as they filed out together.

Ward scowled, but not at her curiosity. 'I'm going to interview the delightful Mrs Craven.'

'Rather you than me.'

'Cheers. I just need to read this article that Baker sent me before I track her down.' Geoff's mention of the article, of council backhanders and bribes, of controversial buildings...if Mr Craven's death wasn't accidental, it would be a good place to start.

Ward perched on his desk and clicked into the article, written by one, E. Pullman. As he read, his eyebrow rose. It did not paint a generous picture. Ward wasn't sure what he'd expected, but it wasn't that. From the glamorous photo at the top of Mr and Mrs Craven in black tie at a glittering event at Harewood Hall, he'd expected it to be a celebration, perhaps, of all they had achieved. A local lad who'd grafted to become one of the most successful businessmen in the county.

What he actually read was an article so scathing it threatened to make his eyes water. The editor had been smart—nothing that could be legally challenged as libel, per se, but the vitriol was clear. There was no love lost for Craven Property Holdings Limited, its ventures, or Mr Robert Craven.

The article featured front and centre a new petition from the residents of a luxury estate built by the company on the outskirts of Skipton. They were petitioning for their roads to be tarmacked, their community to have the streetlights it was promised, and for the snagging issues on their properties—amounting to thousands between a handful of residents—to be addressed.

Ward wrinkled his nose as he read on.

"Five devastated residents endured three weeks of raw sewage flooding into their homes, and as a last resort, had to privately finance Yorkshire Water to assess and amend the issue—an issue which should have been Mr Craven's highest priority given the promised life he had sold them on the estate. It seems Mr Craven's life of riches and glamour is financed by less than savoury business practices. Will the greenbelt estates he plans to build in our beautiful Dales be subject to the same problems—and will the local community be left to pay the price and pick up the pieces again?"

He forwarded the article to his team via email with a note to read it, and to gather any press coverage on the company and Mr Craven too. By the sounds of it, Craven was not a well-liked figure, and this would be helpful background information they might not receive from any witnesses or interested parties.

Ward scranned his unpleasantly warm cheese and pickle sarnie, and rang Mrs Craven to arrange a chat, feeling slightly apprehensive about meeting the woman after the way she'd treated the PC earlier that morning. He was interested too, to see how she'd behave—perhaps now, would the shock of it all have set in? In what state would he find her?

The number redirected to a PA who booked him into Mrs Craven's diary that afternoon. To his surprise, she was in Harrogate, far away from Skipton and the events unfolding there. What on earth was she doing there? He'd find out one way or another.

Ward set off from the station in his Golf, with the pleasure of knowing he'd get a good drive out. When the route was clear, the journey to Harrogate was half decent, as his work travel went. At the very least, it got him out of the city and out of the suburbs and into the countryside.

CHAPTER EIGHT

MONDAY AFTERNOON

Miranda Craven awaited him at Rudding Park, a luxurious stately home that now served as a hotel, conference centre, wedding venue, spa, and golf course. The type of place that DI Daniel Ward rarely got to visit in his job—and never, personally. Even smartly dressed for work, he felt under-presented in a place like that.

He parked in the generous car park and marched up to reception where an impeccably dressed and haughty receptionist told him to wait if he didn't have a room or reservation for any of their services. He leaned against the arm of an armchair—earning him a disapproving glare from the receptionist, which he returned with bland indifference—and rang Miranda's number again. No answer. He sighed. The place set him on edge, so far beyond his class was it. He didn't want to stay longer than he had to, nice as it was.

'Detective,' a smooth, husky voice greeted him.

He looked up from his phone to see her. Gone was the navy pantsuit. Now, she wore a cream silk blouse, the top button open, and flaring chiffon black pants that parted like tulip petals at the ankle to reveal delicate, strappy stilettos. Her hair—chocolate brown with a hint of red—was styled like a movie star, all luscious waves and sleek curves. Ruby red painted lips parted in a coy smile as she extended her hand to him.

Ward shook it, not sure whether she expected him to bow and kiss it, given where they were, because she presented herself like royalty. He didn't subscribe to such bullshit pretentiousness either way, that was for sure.

'Detective Inspector Daniel Ward. Thank you for meeting with me, Mrs Craven. Is there somewhere private we can talk?'

'Of course.' She turned and led him through grand wooden double doors, as though she owned the place. 'There's seating through here, and we can order a coffee—or something stronger, if you like.'

He didn't miss the suggestive edge on the woman's voice.

'Diane said she'd be making sure we were taken care of, but I didn't know she'd be sending anyone to see me.'

Diane. It made Ward shudder inside to hear someone speak of the eviscerator that was DSU Diane McIntyre so informally. However, it was an important reminder for him to toe the line. He didn't know what he was getting into, how much history the Super had with Robert, Miranda, and their family. The last thing he wanted was to step out of line and risk Death by Di.

Unaware of his cringe, Miranda continued, 'I'm afraid I won't be much help to you.'

We'll see about that. Ward followed her into a dark, sumptuous room decorated in shades of chocolate, with tall, white wood sash windows looking out onto a verdant garden. The space hummed with the quiet chatter of the half-dozen people in there seated at tables of their own—and who entirely ignored their entrance. He could practically taste the scent of cake and coffee hanging in the air. His stomach rumbled unhelpfully.

Miranda paused at a corner table with two dark leather armchairs set beside it. A newspaper, phone, and handbag sat on the table—but the rat-dog was nowhere to be seen, to Ward's relief. A dog fan he was, but he didn't like the tiny yappy things one bit. Give him his joyous, bean-filled Beagle rollicking through the muddy fields over a dog that needed to be carried on a walk any day.

What is *her deal?* She didn't seem to be a woman in mourning at all—rather that she was having an entirely ordinary day. And that, for DI Daniel Ward, rang alarm bells that deafened him.

Miranda perched on the chair, crossing one leg over the other so her long, slim ankle infringed on the space before the other chair. Ward sunk into it awkwardly. The corner felt away from prying eyes—good—but altogether too intimate considering the close proximity between them.

Miranda watched him, her expression neutral, her head cocked slightly, as though waiting for him to make the first move. She seemed guarded, as though everything she put on was a carefully chosen behaviour. Ward didn't know how much to read into that, but there it was, that serpent of a sixth sense uncoiling in his belly, warning him of trouble afoot.

A waiter hurried over and she ordered a coffee, before looking expectantly at him.

'Tea please.' He was thirsty, now he thought about it, but definitely nothing stronger whilst he was on duty. Especially with a woman he suspected would be as feisty as Mrs Craven.

'Do you need to see a menu? We have fourteen different varieties, sir.'

Of course, you bloody do. Ward suppressed a groan. 'Black tea will be fine, thanks. Yorkshire Tea if you have it.'

'It's Twining's, sir.'

'That'll do,' Ward said with a grimace. *Christ, even the brews are pretentious here.*

He waited for the man to vanish out of hearing. 'I'm sure Detective Superintendent McIntyre has already extended our deepest condolences to you, and expressed that we will do everything we can to understand what happened to your husband.'

Nothing. She gazed at him with nothing in her—no flicker of sadness.

Ward cleared his throat, and softened his face into something he hoped resembled open friendliness. She didn't grimace. That was promising. He couldn't help his face after all...Katherine had so sweetly referred to its taciturn resting state as "resting knobhead face". Perhaps if he could draw Miranda out of that immaculately prepared shell, he might be able to fish for something. 'If you don't mind me asking, you're a long way from Skipton. What brings you to Harrogate, Mrs Craven?'

She waggled a hand and looked at him through lowered eyelashes. 'Oh, call me Miranda. I hate "Mrs Craven". Makes me feel ancient!' She shifted in the chair, sitting taller, leaning forward just a tad. 'I have business here. I'm starting up a fashion boutique and our first branch is over on Princes Street. We launch in three weeks and I'm here to oversee the refit.' That did explain why she would have been collecting clothes from the house that morning, and why she didn't seem to be staying there.

'I see. Whereabouts were you yesterday afternoon, between midday and say, eight yesterday evening?'

'I was here, why?'

'As in, here at Rudding Park?' That seemed odd—why wouldn't she go home on a weekend, people's traditional downtime? Why wouldn't she pick up fresh clothes on a weekend, rather than a Monday morning?

'Yes,' she said slowly, frowning at him as though he'd said something utterly imbecilic.

The waiter arrived, announcing himself with a small clear of his throat. 'Madam. Sir.' He doled out the drinks onto the table—to Ward's annoyance, he hadn't gotten a *cup* of tea, he'd gotten the entire damn tea set.

What's the point of going out for a cup of tea if you have to make the bloody thing yourself?

'Thanks,' Ward said instead, turning back to Miranda

as the waiter left. 'I see—it's a lovely place,' he lied through his teeth as he glanced around, resting his hand on the cold, smooth, leather arm of his chair. 'Were you here all day, or did you venture out?'

'I don't see why you need to know that, officer.'

'Detective,' Ward corrected. 'Routine, I'm afraid. We have to try and build a picture of your husband's last known movements. Knowing where you were, as one of the critical people in his life, helps us establish that.' He kept his tone light and easy. She wasn't under suspicion, after all.

Officially.

Yet.

Miranda stirred, drawing herself away from him now in the chair as she leaned back and lifted her chin. 'I met a friend yesterday afternoon.'

'What time, and whereabouts?'

'I visited his home, around two-ish, for a couple of hours. I had a vicious migraine after all the excitement on Saturday night, and I was completely exhausted. I actually fell asleep there, but he was so good about it and let me sleep it off in one of the spare bedrooms.'

'And if I may have your friend's details? Just for the records, of course.' Ward gave an apologetic shrug, glancing down at his pocket book to give the impression he would be entirely dismissing this as box-checking.

'Mr Christopher Dawson.' She rattled off an address in the older quarters of Harrogate, a well-to-do area by Harrogate Ladies College.

'Thanks. So, if you were here in Harrogate—at

Rudding Park, or visiting your friend, Christopher—I wonder, do you know what your husband's plans were yesterday in that same time window?'

Miranda pursed her lips, and her hands clasped on her knees. 'I don't have the foggiest idea, I'm afraid.'

'None? Surely, you're his wife, you must have some inkling.'

She laughed, a reflexive huff that spoke volumes of derision. *Not a close marriage, then.*

'Alright, when did you last see him?'

'Saturday night, at Harewood House. We had an event there for the business.'

'Yes, I saw that in the paper.'

'So did I,' she said, shooting the newspaper on the table a glare as though she were not best pleased about its contents. As Craven's wife, Ward supposed she wouldn't be.

'Alright, so you saw him Saturday night. Did you stay over that night at Harewood?' Presumably, they would have been too drunk to drive, and it was a good way from either Harrogate and even further still from Skipton.

'Yes.'

'So presumably, wouldn't you have seen him on Sunday morning?'

Miranda froze for the tiniest moment, but Ward saw it, and then that coy, easy smile was back, and she raised an eyebrow at him. 'No. If you must know, we didn't share a room.'

'Why not?' He was pushing it now, dangerously so.

Miranda laughed darkly. 'We don't have that kind of

marriage.' Whatever that meant. 'Robert had other people to warm his bed.'

Oh, shite.

'An affair?' The sole of Ward's shoe squeaked on the parquet wood floor as he shifted with discomfort. Gods, he hated this side of things. It made him cringe to pry.

Miranda nodded, pursing her lips. 'One of many. He was a real Lothario—in his eyes.'

'I see. I'm sorry. So, the two of you weren't close?'

Miranda huffed. 'Not anymore.'

But they still shared a house, a business, a marriage... A prickle of that sixth sense. What wasn't he understanding here? 'Estranged?'

'Yes.'

That sense uncoiled further. 'Separated?'

Miranda clenched her jaw and chewed on her lip.

Ward waited.

'Not yet,' she admitted.

There it was. Something for that instinct to bite down into. 'But you were in the process of divorcing?'

Miranda's reply, when it came, seemed strangely grudging. 'Yes.'

Ward nodded and offered her a sympathetic smile. Inside, that sixth sense was roaring for his attention, but he casually sat back, jotted down a few notes, and let the pen rest once more. 'I'm sorry. I appreciate this is very personal. What led to the breakdown of your relationship, if you don't mind me asking?'

'I do mind,' Miranda replied, her tone prickly. 'How is this relevant?'

Ward shifted in his seat. 'It helps us to build a picture of Robert and his life—to understand the circumstances which may have led to, caused, or be connected to his death in some way.'

Miranda reached for her cappuccino and took a small sip.

Suppressing a curse, Ward dropped the pen in his lap and reached for the teapot on the table. He'd be able to stand a spoon in it, the tea was brewed so strongly. He poured the almost black liquid into the teacup with a sigh. He was sure to have had worse. At least this was Twining's. It would be a posh cup of shite.

Miranda watched him, and crossed her arms, rear-ranging herself fussily in the chair to face her body away from Ward, as though to distance herself from it all. When she looked up, she didn't meet Ward's eyes, but her gaze was hard.

He sipped at his bitter tea and said nothing.

'We met as teenagers. He got a job with my father's business. One thing led to another—I suppose I found him quite charming. So different to the men and boys I grew up with, moving in the circles Daddy did. This is my world.' She gestured around them, to the splendour of Rudding Park. 'Whereas Robert...he's a mechanic's son from Keighley. Young love, I suppose.'

She paused for a moment, lost in that memory. 'We married young. My father gave us some money to start up with—an investment, repaid long ago, you understand. A matter of pride, I'm sure you'll agree. Neither of us wanted a handout. We worked night and day on the business. I suppose I brought the start-up money, and Robert brought the grit.

'We built it up, and we had everything. We thought we could take on the world.' She smiled, but it was tight, bitter. 'And then I found out that he'd not been quite so hardworking as I'd thought. All those late nights at the office, the business trips...they weren't as they seemed.'

Ward waited, but something within him crumpled at that. *What a mess.* He was glad that for all his and Katherine's struggles...at least, to his knowledge, they had both stayed true to their vows. It had been an unhappy union at the end, but neither one had strayed.

Miranda sighed. 'It was the first of many affairs. I found out there were some that came before. There've been several since, and his latest tart is ghastly. It's hard to love a man who treats you like that. He wasn't repentant, wasn't sorry. He was beyond forgiveness.'

She shrugged, and he could see the way she tightened, closing up before him once more, that cool exterior walling away any hint of feelings within. Her eyes, when they met Ward's, were bare of emotion. Calculating. 'I stayed because it was practical for the children, and my own self-interests. But they're grown up, and I won't be made a fool of anymore. I'm taking what's rightfully mine, and I'm going to finally start living the life I deserve without his daily humiliation.'

'So you stand to gain a lot in the divorce?'

Miranda raised an eyebrow, as if the answer was obvious. 'We built that together from the ground up—Robert doesn't dispute that, at least. There's plenty to split.' On some level, Ward knew only too well how messy that was...though his and Katherine's 'estate' was tiny by comparison. Perhaps that was a blessing, really.

'It depends on which side you sit, I suppose. Perhaps, I have a lot to gain. I walk away with half of everything. Perhaps I have a lot to lose—I helped to make it *all*, and only receive half.'

Ward paused for just a moment before he asked the most delicate question. 'And who would be the main beneficiary if he passes away before the divorce finalises?'

Miranda furrowed her brow for a moment—and then to Ward's surprise, she laughed, and a wry smile spread across her face. 'I see what you're doing there. Me, of course. If either dies before it's finalised and our new wills are ready...it almost all goes to the other. I suppose, I stand to gain a lot more from his death than anyone else. There you have it.'

She spread her hands wide, as if inviting him to arrest her there on the spot for such speculation. She knew what he assumed—that she'd bumped him off to take it all, so as not to lose out in the divorce to Robert, or his mistress.

Ward regarded her gravely. 'You do indeed have a lot to gain, but you know as well as I that it doesn't mean anything without further evidence.'

She met his gaze levelly, that smile cooling off.

'So, you two weren't close at all. Did you spend much time together at the business or at home?'

'I hardly saw him. We stay out of each other's way these days.'

"Stay", not "stayed". A common tell. In her mind, Robert was still very much alive. Perhaps she would crumble when it hit her eventually. *Or is she truly made of stone?*

Miranda continued, unaware. 'I leave him to his bits on the side to put up with, and since the last few have been in the business, I leave him to that too. Why do you think I'm here?' She gestured to their opulent surroundings. 'I'm done following him around, waiting for whatever scraps he might throw. I'm done finding other women in my home.'

'So, you still have a stake in the business, you just don't help run it?'

'Precisely. Robert, James, and I have a third stake each. He's not getting rid of me that way. But I won't get in his way. He can run it however he likes now. I don't care. I've started up my own business here, and I'm in no need of him anymore.'

'Your daughter doesn't have a stake?'

'Oh goodness, no. She has no interest in the business. Sarah's always wanted to be a vet. She's just qualified over in York, in fact, specialises in equine health for the racing over there. A *very* prestigious racing team just took her on.' An edge of maternal pride coloured her voice and lit up her face with a momentary joy that flickered and was gone.

It was replaced by annoyance. 'I didn't appreciate Diane interfering there, actually. I should have been the one to tell the two of them their father's dead, not her. You can tell her that yourself.'

I most certainly won't, Ward thought, but he kept that to himself. 'I can only apologise,' he said instead. 'Are they both coping?'

Miranda snorted, drawing a couple of stares from those sitting at nearby tables. But when she spoke, her hiss was calculatingly quiet, given the public nature of their surroundings. 'Of course, they won't be! They found out their father was murdered this morning! He might have been a complete and utter arse—Sarah wasn't too fond of his less than discreet conduct, and him and James were forever blowing up with each other—but he was their father, for all his faults.'

'I am very sorry for your loss. We do have support in place for you at this difficult time as you come to terms with it, and whilst our enquiries are ongoing.'

'That old man?' Miranda asked, her voice rising with incredulity. 'Oh goodness, don't bother. I gave him the slip in Skipton. I can't be doing with someone trailing me.'

Annoyance spiked in Ward at her disrespectful tone. Geoff was a kind and very capable FLO. 'Be that as it may, Mr Mason, Geoffrey, is here to help you and act as our point of contact. He's not just here to ensure you can access any support you need in such a traumatic time, but also to make sure you're appraised of what we're doing.'

Miranda returned her cup to the table, deliberately slowly, placing it upon the saucer with a small *chink*. As she sat back, sheer silk rippled over her supple form in a way Ward supposed would be alluring if she was trying to win him over. She reclined regally in the chair, crossing her legs once more. Watching him. For whatever his next mood would be. Not willing to respond to that, it seemed.

'So, you say Sarah wasn't close to her father?'

A shake of the head.

'They didn't see much of each other?'

Another shake.

'But James and Robert worked together, is that correct?'

'Yes.'

'And he'll step up to run the business now, I presume?'

'Without a doubt. He'll get the board onside and Robert's shares will probably be split between myself and him, so we'll each be joint shareholders of equal stake. Unless he wants to buy me out.'

'Was that always the plan?'

Miranda placed her hands delicately atop her knees. The picture of calm. Still entirely unaffected by her husband's suspicious death that morning. 'Of course. It's a family business, after all. Robert had no intention to let it go after all our hard work, and James has always been groomed to step up.'

Unlike his sister, James Craven had a lot to gain from his father's death. 'So they must have got on well then? For James to be Robert's protege?' She'd mentioned they argued fiercely. *How did that work?*

Miranda laughed. 'Hardly. At times, it nearly came to blows. James has my intelligence and grit, but his father's arrogance and temper. Those can be a winning combination, or a recipe for disaster. But, he's good at what he does. He's young, but with help, he can step up and be successful, I'm sure of it.'

'Will you be there to help him?'

Neatly manicured fingernails tapped in a flutter on Miranda's knee before they stilled. 'Well, with Robert gone, who else is there? He needs a guiding hand for now at least. I may not like Robert anymore, but I don't want to see our business fail.'

'Is there anyone else at the business who can help?'

'Oh, of course. The management team there are all excellent at their jobs. Well, except for the strumpet, of course, but I imagine she's there for her body, not her brain, and even that is poor.' Miranda's laugh was bitter.

'One of Robert's affairs?'

Miranda's lips pursed. 'The latest. The tart dared to invite herself to our event on Saturday night. Shameless!'

Ward frowned. 'You know her?'

'No, thankfully.' Miranda's nose wrinkled in distaste, and her curled lip exposed the tip of a whitened tooth.

'I know it's not comfortable, but if you have her details, I'd be interested to speak to her too.'

Miranda oozed bitterness as she replied, 'I understand. After all, she's more likely to know where he was that day than I—they were probably together. She's Robert's 'Executive Personal Assistant' as he likes to call her, so she's aware of all his movements. The title makes her sound fancy. Glorified filing clerk and shag, in other words. If you contact the business, they'll have her personal details on file. Claire Parker.'

'Thank you. Sorry. I appreciate that's an uncomfortable subject to discuss, especially in the midst of Robert's death.'

'Oh, don't be,' she said tartly. 'Robert made his bed. He can lie in it.'

'Do you have any reason to believe anyone would have wished Robert harm?'

Miranda's snort of genuine amusement shocked him. 'Who didn't? Goodness, the line would be as long as Skipton.'

'What makes you say that?' he asked, though the newspaper article gave him some clue.

Miranda looked him up and down for a second with a raised eyebrow, as though to decide whether he was being serious or not. 'You only have to know a little about the business—what it is, who he is now, to understand that. We started out as a local building business. Robert got too big for his boots. Now, he's building all over the Dales, and he owns half of Skipton's commercial premises, not to mention plenty of residential assets.'

'You benefit from all of that too?'

Her mouth twisted. 'Well yes, I suppose so, But I don't control any of it. I stepped back from being active a long time ago.'

'From holding him to account, you mean?'

Miranda shot him a coy smile. 'You don't say no to Robert Craven, Detective Ward. But if you try to, well, he makes life very unpleasant indeed. I learned to pick my battles. Self-preservation, call it.'

Ward glanced up from his notes. 'He was abusive?'

'Oh no. Robert is a gentleman through and through. He'd never raise a hand to a lady. But he was raised in a different time, with different values to our children. He was The Man of the house, and what he said, at home or in business, went. To him...I think he liked my father's money as much as me, to start with. After that, when things started taking off, I was nothing more than the mother of his children or the glamour on his arm to be paraded when he needed it.'

From the resentment in her tone, Ward could discern what she thought of that. 'I can see you disagreed.'

'Yes, but as I've grown, I realised that I don't hate him for it. It was as much my fault as it was his. I won't let a man treat me like that now.' Her eyes had glazed over, her gaze cast aside, as though for a second, she was in another time and place.

But to Ward, her answer was altogether too neat when he considered what she had to lose and gain, and the raft of seething bitterness he caught glimpses of beneath the surface. It wasn't that tied up and finished, he reckoned. 'You said that he had plenty of people who don't think of him kindly though. Are there any who bear him specific grudges?'

'Enough to want to kill him, you mean?' Miranda arched a dark brow. 'I can't imagine it. Oh, he was hated alright, but who would take it so far?'

'People can act in unexpected ways when put under pressure, believe me. If you have any specific individuals in mind, it would be very helpful.'

Miranda rolled her eyes. 'Where to start? There's the

Resident's Association of Skipton, run by a ghastly woman, Florence, Frances...*Something*, I don't know.' She held up a finger as if checking off a list. 'Banging on about Robert's estates—the homebuilding arm of the business, I mean. They're forever campaigning, and that did get nasty last year with a protest outside the company offices. She burnt an effigy of Robert, you know. There's a video on Youtube somewhere.'

Ward raised an eyebrow and jotted that down. That definitely sounded worthy of investigating.

Miranda waited until the sound of his pen scratching on the page stopped before she spoke again. 'There's a young lady who writes all sort of nasty things in the press and causes a nuisance. Eliza Pullman. The foolish woman chained herself to the gates so the plant machinery couldn't get in or out. Robert tried to get a restraining order against her, but that didn't go anywhere.'

Ward scrawled notes, trying to keep up.

Up went another finger. 'Then there's half the shops in Skipton. The Skipton Retail Group, they call themselves, but all it is, is a way to try and pressure Robert into lowering their rent, or footing the bill for their refits, and whatever else. The council put paid to any case they had with a good dose of common sense. You know what people are like—entitled.' She waited for Ward to offer her his agreement.

He murmured something that sounded vaguely placating, before she continued.

Another finger rose. 'Then there was the incident with the farmer last year. That was a messy one.'

'Farmer?'

'Yes. Robert bought some land, or perhaps he didn't— I can't remember. Either way, this farmer was up in arms —quite literally, with a shotgun and all—about whatever Robert had done. He made threats against Robert. The police had to be involved.'

Ward blinked. 'A shotgun? Do you have a name for this man?'

'No, sorry. You'll have to...' She laughed, a lighter tinkle rippling through her. 'I nearly said you'll have to ask Robert then, how silly of me. I believe Robert didn't press charges on the old fool, but it was in the papers.'

'Right. Anyone else?'

Miranda was still chuckling. 'Isn't half of Skipton quite enough?'

Ward smiled wryly. 'Well, if you do have any other information that might help us, it would be appreciated.'

'Of course.' Miranda waved a hand, the picture of refined elegance, as she attracted a waitress' attention to get another drink. 'Can I tempt you?'

'No, thank you.'

'Pity,' she said, and the way her eyes lingered on him wasn't lost. Ward felt as though a predator's gaze ensnared him. *What* is *her deal?* He wondered if she was as blameless as she tried to appear.

'Just a few more things if that's alright, and then I'll leave you to your busy schedule, and to grieve.' Not that he had seen any sign of her grieving yet. 'May I ask about the security system at your house? The cameras?'

Miranda furrowed her brow. 'What about it?'

'Did you both have access to that?'

'Of course, I could use it if I wished to. I don't have it on my phone, though. I'm rarely there these days, so I deleted the app. The security company keeps the footage in the cloud, and Robert handled it all. I don't use it these days.

'With the divorce, and finding a woman in my bed, I made it a point to move out and I don't like to see who's stopping by. I just go back to check everything is intact, to store my evening wear, and I have Amazon deliver all the Subscribe and Save things there for Trixiebelle, so I pick that up. Oh, and I like to check that he hasn't moved some tart fully into my house.' She smiled thinly but her glare was sharp enough to cut.

'Can you access the system to see comings and goings, on Sunday?' He didn't hold out much hope if she'd deleted the app.

'You'd need Robert for that, sorry. He set up the account. I don't recall the company's details.'

'Do you have any other security cameras around the property?' It was a long shot. There'd been no sign of forced entry, but it was worth an ask.

'Yes, the camera at the door, one watching the cars, and two around the back.' Miranda had plucked an iPhone out of her trouser pocket, and was tapping away on the screen, her attention having firmly wavered.

Ward held in a pang of annoyance. She was something alright. He had no idea what, but she was something. 'You said you moved out. Where do you live now?'

'I'm staying here, and with a dear friend when I need more amenities. Ah, speak of the devil.' Somehow, she transformed. No longer disinterested, and to the point of slouching. She straightened, a smile rising unbidden to her lips, a light charging into her eyes, as she raised an arm and waved.

Ward turned.

A silver-haired man strode toward them, a warm smile illuminating his grey eyes, well-built and well-kept, radiating strength. Older than Ward, Ward placed him in his late forties or early fifties, similar to Miranda.

Miranda stood. The man kissed her on the cheek and pulled her into an intimate embrace that lingered a lot more than Ward would have embraced a friend.

'I'm *so* sorry, Miranda darling.' Those brows were furrowed with unbridled concern, his body angled towards her. Miranda retreated, but his hand still rested intimately on the small of her back. He glanced over to Ward with mild curiosity and raised an eyebrow.

'Christopher, this is Detective Inspector Ward. He's investigating what's happened to Robert. I didn't tell you everything.' For the first time, Ward heard a flutter of distress in her voice. Perhaps she wasn't hiding anything —only her own emotions, tightly clamped.

Ward's ears perked. *Christopher?*

'Why? What's happened?' His cautious smile turned to a frown as he held out a hand for Ward to shake.

Ward squeezed his hand back in a silent battle of

wills before they both dropped away. 'I can't comment on an ongoing investigation. Christopher...?'

'Dawson.'

Ward waited.

'I'm an architect. My firm, Dawson and Alistair, does a lot of work for the Cravens. Is everything alright, Miranda?'

Ward examined him with refreshed interest. Christopher was the 'friend' Miranda had alleged to be with at the time of Robert's death. Who she now alleged to be partially staying with. And yet, he described himself primarily as a business contact of the Cravens.

Miranda shook her head. For the first time, Ward thought he could see a flicker of unsettled agitation run through her. 'It's bad, Chris,' she said quietly. 'He was murdered, Diane says.'

'What?' Christopher breathed, aghast.

'Did you know Mr Craven well, Christopher?' Ward asked.

Christopher wrenched his attention away from Miranda. His face smoothed, with visible effort. 'Only in a professional capacity. We haven't worked together in a year or so now.' Christopher's eyes slid to Miranda once more, betraying himself.

Ward glanced between them. Miranda seemed at ease with Christopher. Perched on the edge of the chair arm, her attention casually focused on him. *Lovers?* he wondered. It was certainly plausible given the limited information he had. Maybe his relationship with Miranda was more personal than professional. Why else would Robert's former architect be meeting with Miranda?

'So you didn't happen to see him yesterday?'

'No, absolutely not. I was at home all day.' That lined up with Miranda's explanation too.

'Give us a moment, Christopher, please. We're almost done, right?' Miranda looked to Ward, an eyebrow raised.

Ward nodded.

Christopher inclined his head and retreated to the bar. 'I'll get a coffee.'

Miranda's attention followed him for a few seconds before returning to meet Ward's. 'Christopher is over-seeing the remodelling at my new venture.'

Sure, he is. And the rest of you, Ward thought. He wasn't convinced. 'There's just one more thing I'd like to ask at this time. On the mezzanine gallery, there are several stands, with various ornaments on them. I don't suppose, if one of those items seemed to be missing, that you'd know what it was?'

'Of course. Are you saying we've been robbed? Those are very valuable.' Miranda paled. Perhaps the shock of it all was beginning to sink in.

'We're not assuming that right now, as there are no signs of forced entry. But if you could give me a list of what's on those plinths, we can cross-check what's there, and see if anything is missing.'

Miranda swallowed. 'They're antiques. Robert always had a fascination with the Romans. The patriar-chal nature of their culture, I imagine. There was an amphora from Pompeii, a wax tablet and stylus from...oh goodness, I'm sorry, I can't remember. I think that was Etruscan, actually. And then four statuettes. Roman deities—Mercury, Mars, Venus and Minerva, I believe. They all espoused traits that Robert admired.'

Her mouth twisted in a smile tainted by bitterness and grief. 'War, wealth, victory, sex. Some such poppy-cock like that. I don't know much more about their history, I'm afraid, only that they're incredibly valuable.'

Ward would have to look into that. Perhaps one would be missing, and perhaps it would fit with the blunt force trauma Robert seemed to have suffered at or around the time of his death. 'You wouldn't happen to have a picture, would you?'

'Of course. They're heavily insured. The appraisers documented them in detail. I'll get my PA to send you the details.'

Ward stood, flipping his pocket book shut, and sliding a card from his pocket. 'I appreciate your time, Mrs Cra—'

She scoffed. 'Miranda, please.'

'Miranda,' he acquiesced. 'I'm sorry to have to question you at a time like this,' He still wasn't all that convinced she was a grieving widow. 'I'll be in touch if we need anything else. Here's my details. Call me any time night or day if you think of anything that might help us, or to let us know if there's anything you need.'

Ward left, not giving his regards to Christopher, who stood facing away at the bar, unaware of Ward's presence as he collected two coffees. Ward stepped out and paused, feeling an absence where his wallet ought to have been as his hand grazed over the pocket in habit. A moment of swooping horror, worrying if he'd dropped it somewhere, passed over him and he looked back.

Just as his fingers caressed the supple leather of his wallet in another pocket.

And just as he saw Christopher Dawson draw Miranda Craven up into his arms and give her a lasting kiss on the lips whilst his arms encircled her waist. She rested her head on his shoulder, face turned into his neck, and they stood there unmoving, as he held her.

Gotcha.

If the post mortem and CSI report came back with anything suspicious surrounding Robert's death, which was as close to guaranteed as he could bet, DI Daniel Ward had the first place to look. At the almost ex-wife and her lover who had each other as their alibi, and everything to gain from Robert Craven's death.

CHAPTER NINE

MONDAY LATE AFTERNOON

'Hi,' Ward said, his voice gruff as he took the call. He was thankful that his marriage and divorce didn't seem half as messy as the Craven's. Mind. That still didn't mean he welcomed it.

'Hi,' replied Katherine, his estranged wife, on the other end. 'Um, I just wanted to let you know, that we've had an offer on the house. Five grand under asking.'

'What do you think?'

'I think we should push to get asking price.'

Ward wanted shot of the place—and the memories. But that extra five thousand pounds would cover some of their legal fees. 'Alright. Push if you want. I'm happy to accept as is if you can't get any more.'

'OK. That's it. Thanks—bye.'

'Bye.'

At least they were civil, Ward thought as his hand dropped to the flat bottom of his steering wheel once more after disconnecting the call. For a moment, the rolling Yorkshire hills around him fell away as he sped back towards Bradford.

That was an advance on how acrimonious and unpleasant things had been between them, even just so recently. Now, they could hold an entirely hostility free conversation. It was a relief of sorts. Maybe it would always be hard, but it didn't need to feel impossible.

———

Bradford South Police Station hummed with activity as usual. Ward grabbed himself a much-needed brew—he'd be working overtime again, it seemed. Unpaid, as per usual. He always sent the DCs and DSs home, because they simply didn't have any more paid overtime in the budget, but he didn't keep a check on his own hours.

What did it matter? Aside from Olly the dog, it wasn't like he had anything else waiting for him.

That had still been a huge adjustment since Katherine had finally relinquished the Beagle to him. In the few weeks since the dog had permanently arrived in his life once more, Ward had had to be much more mindful of not working all hours of the day so he could be home to walk and toilet Olly enough, not to mention, socialise him. The last thing he wanted was to leave the pup alone all day in the small flat.

Don't finish too late, he reminded himself. There was just enough time to check in with the rest of the team before they called it a day, at least. Maybe he'd be out vaguely on time after all.

'Briefing on the Craven case, please,' he called out over the shared office. Those staff working on the case immediately moved, stretching back in their desk chairs with a groan for the most part, before standing and gathering any pertinent material.

Ward didn't wait for them, but went to the Incident Room to fill in a Big Board for the case. He noticed that Nowak had already started one—her neat capital print listing the victim and the few details they had. As he waited for his team to assemble, Ward scrawled on more details from what he'd recorded in his pocket book.

Nowak audibly moaned as she entered and saw what he'd done to her neat, clean board.

'Sorry, Sarge,' Ward said with a grin.

She simply gave him an exasperated stare.

'Call it a test on your OCD, eh? You'll have to resist re-writing it. We don't have time.'

The exasperated stare turned into a dark glare.

'Oof, if looks could kill.' He turned to the team and clapped his hands together. Assembled before him were DS Nowak, DS Metcalfe, DC Shahzad, and DC Patterson. 'Right. Where are we? I have some interesting findings, which I've started adding on the board here, and I want a check-in from each of you for the day, and where we're kicking off tomorrow, please. I'll start.'

Ward took a deep breath. 'I've spoken to the *very* interesting Mrs Miranda Craven. Turns out, the Cravens were in the middle of a divorce after a long, unhappy marriage, and couldn't wait to be rid of each other. They no longer live together. Robert's had numerous affairs but his current mistress is Claire Parker, his PA. Miranda is in a romantic relationship with a former business associate of the Craven empire, Christopher Dawson.'

Ward had already looked for Dawson on the PNC. No priors, and not a hair out of line. No cause for concern, in any case, and most probably a helpful dead end given the wealth of suspects they were unearthing. He'd need to clone the team at this rate to chase them all down.

Ward continued, 'Most notably, Miranda is practically the sole beneficiary of Robert's will, and has significant financial gain in the event of his death.'

DC Shahzad let out a low whistle through his teeth.

'My thoughts exactly, Kasim. Miranda is perfectly placed with motive, means, and opportunity. To be honest, on a personal level, she really didn't seem too bothered at all that her husband's been murdered in their family home. There was barely a flicker of emotion. Can you really be so far estranged from someone that you feel absolutely nothing if they were to die—and in such a way?'

He opened his palms, looking around. His team shared glances but no one spoke up. He knew that he would never be able to do the same if Katherine met such an end. For all their differences, he had loved her, and he didn't want to see her hurt. Wasn't that a basic human level of decency?

'She claims to have been in Harrogate around the time of Robert's death with Dawson, who backs up her alibi, but they could well be in league together. So, I'd like to dig more into the pair of them to make sure that alibi holds. We'll need to pull her phone records if possible—I want to see if the location data backs up what she's saying. We also have potentially identified the murder weapon.'

As promised, Miranda's PA had emailed across details of the artefacts, and Ward's team had identified the missing item. 'One statuette, about forty centimetres tall, of the Roman god, Mercury.' God of financial gain and guide of souls to the underworld—both of which seemed fitting for the wealth-minded and prematurely departed Mr Craven, though Ward did not say it. 'This is our potential murder weapon, and it hasn't been located yet.'

Ward gestured to the Big Board, where a printed photo of that statuette was now pinned up, amongst other things. 'Miranda also identified some other possible sources of conflict with Robert that need digging into. Their daughter lives a distance away. According to Miranda, she has no involvement with the business and is somewhat estranged from her father.

'The son, James, however, is an equal shareholder with Robert and Miranda, takes an active part in the business, and has been groomed for succession. According to Miranda, he also has a fierce temper and James and Robert are reputed to have had explosive arguments. Who knows the truth of that, but we'll need to look into the business—speak to people who work there, and of course, to James himself.

'Other than that—well, as if that isn't quite enough,

seems the chap was hated universally by all of Skipton. The Residents' Associations on his domestic estates, and the Skipton Retail Group made up of their commercial tenants hate his business practices, and there was an alleged incident with a farmer and a shotgun, over which no charges were brought but there was some media coverage. Plus, a potential issue with a local journalist against whom Robert failed to obtain a restraining order. Right. That's me. What have we got?' Ward folded his arms and looked at his team, waiting for someone to start.

DC Patterson cleared his throat and stepped forward. 'I've been looking into friends and family, sir. You've already covered the main relatives. Other family are cousins, a few aunts and uncles, and I'm looking into any that they might have been close with through social media. Nothing yet. Robert doesn't seem to have been active on any networks.'

Ward nodded. 'Good. Take point on gathering information on Miranda and James particularly, please, and if you can scope out Christopher Dawson too, that would be helpful.'

'Yes, sir.'

'We need to understand the business structure for shareholdings—look on Companies House for that—and from a management standpoint to see how much sway James holds in the company. Miranda too, to be fair. She downplayed her role, but you never know. We could do with seeing the will too, to understand who benefits in the event of Robert's death. I'll bet James is on that list. Kasim?'

DC Shahzad cleared his throat. 'I've downloaded the contents of Robert Craven's phone that CSI brought in, and I'm analysing his messages, contacts, and so on. The calendar suggests he was in the office that morning, even though it was a Sunday, but the afternoon was blank. The mistress, Claire Parker, is definitely a person of interest—I think they had a fight the day Robert died, as there are a lot of text messages from her of varying content from pleading to threatening, and no replies from Robert. These messages cease on Sunday night.'

'Add her to the list, Patterson,' Ward interjected before Kasim continued.

'There's not much from Miranda, suggesting they didn't have much contact, or at least use that method to speak to each other. I can't access some of the apps like business emails, for example, where I imagine he communicates with James on company matters, but there are some texts with James. They don't reveal much.'

'Did you manage to get into the CCTV account?'

'No, sir. The app needs a password and doesn't automatically login.'

'Damn.'

'Yeah. I'm putting together a warrant to get that information directly from the CCTV company, but it will most likely take days, sir.'

'It's not like Craven's in a rush, is he?' Patterson piped up with a bemused grin. 'Being dead and all.'

Ward raised his eyes skyward. 'God help me deal with you, son. Anything else, Kasim?'

'That's it, sir. From the phone's contents, Claire Parker looks like a very interesting prospect.'

'We'll speak to her too then. And I need to see those messages to know what we're dealing with.'

'Yes, sir. I'll email them across.'

'Nowak, what have you got?'

Nowak flipped open her notebook. 'Robert Craven is a local property magnate at Craven Property Holdings Limited. He's fifty-three. He's a multimillionaire—apparently worth in the region of about twenty-five million quid—who's made his wealth by acquiring land, building mainly executive residential homes on it, and selling for huge profits. The lands are typically leasehold, so there's residual income from all the charges associated with that.

'I've looked up the Resident's Association, and the video you told me about. It makes for interesting viewing. Frances Hodgson, the RA's head, is *definitely* someone we need to speak to.

'Basically, Robert Craven has his cake and eats it. These developments are in sought-after areas—Burley in Wharfedale, Grassington, Kettlewell, that sort of place. Beautiful Green Belts that shouldn't be developed on, in small Dales villages...and yet somehow, it happens. There seems to be an overwhelmingly negative view of him.

'Locals are up in arms wherever he develops, because youngsters are priced out of their own villages, and the homes are often going to wealthy out-of-towners as holiday or second homes. It means younger generations are forced out, but not being lived in full-time, the houses go to waste, and the villages are dying. He's seen locally not as a star businessman anymore, but as someone exploiting the Dales for his own greed.

'The landowners he buys from typically don't receive favourable deals, and it's reported that they often suffer adverse consequences from his developments in terms of noise, pollution, hazardous waste, runoff problems with the surrounding agricultural or moorlands, poor access... the list goes on.

'In addition, he also holds a large number of commercial properties in Skipton, again, whose tenants aren't too happy with his high rental and management fees. As far as I can tell, their petitions, pleas to the council, and protests against Robert—or rather, the company—have amounted to nothing. Almost all of this information is filtered through the press, so of course, they have their own spin on it, but by all accounts, it makes out that he was a greedy bully, who forcefully pressured people into complying.'

'I see.' Ward mused for a second. Miranda Craven had told Ward that one didn't say no to Robert Craven. Perhaps she'd alluded to that too. 'It seems there's plenty of motive, then.'

'Not half, sir.'

'Did you find any mention of an incident with a farmer and a shotgun?'

'Oh, Bill Turner, yes. That was...' Nowak flicked through her notes. 'Last summer. The Dales Gazette reported that there'd been an altercation at his farm. He claims he was coerced into selling land to Robert Craven, who then overdeveloped it to the point that his farming land was compromised by pollution and water runoff from the site. He allegedly fired warning shots to stop Robert trespassing on his remaining land.'

'No charges were brought, though?' That would tally with what Miranda had said.

'No, I've checked. Insufficient evidence.'

'Right. Anything else at this stage? Sarge?' Ward turned to Metcalfe.

'That'd be it. We'll be waiting until tomorrow for CSI and pathology at the earliest.'

Those would be the most illuminating, perhaps. Ward examined the board. 'So far, then, we have more digging to do on the almost ex-wife, her fella, the son, the mistress, and the farmer. We'll need to speak to each of them. And feel out the Residents' Association and the Skipton Retail Group. See if there's any ill will there. I'd like to nose at the press too, if we have a chance. I can't imagine Robert would be too chuffed to have his name dragged through the mud all the time. Who's writing all these articles?' He looked up with one raised eyebrow.

'I'll check,' offered Nowak.

'Good. Could be motive there, or at least, they can join the queue behind everyone else who seemed to despise the man.' He let out a wry chuckle. 'Right. That's the priority for tomorrow then. Lines of enquiry with those individuals and groups—interviews, phone records, location data, general information. Whatever we can pull without needing a warrant. Kasim, keep chasing on the CCTV warrant, that could be our best line. And here's hoping Victoria and Mark can shed some light with their reports on Mr Craven's death.'

It was the CCTV he was hoping for. That it would give them the precise time and identity of the person who'd arrived and murdered Robert Craven. Otherwise, they'd never be able to narrow down the list from every man and his dog.

That was a point he'd not considered.

Maybe the ghastly rat-dog had done it.

Case closed.

Ward wished it would be that bloody easy.

CHAPTER TEN

'DC Norris, where are we with Varga?' Ward's last port of call before he sent the remainder of the team home at six was to catch up with the largest case of them all. Bogdan Varga, the Slovakian crime lord using West Yorkshire as his own personal playground and revenue stream for his illegal affairs.

David yawned, covering his mouth, and tore his eyes away from his computer screen. 'Hello, sir.' Ever polite, DC Norris was the best mannered and least foul-mouthed of them all. 'Brown's verdict is tomorrow.'

Ward knew. He'd been trying not to think about it all day—the Craven murder, Eve, and Katherine had at least accomplished that. It had been completely pushed from his mind.

'What do you reckon?'

'It's in the court's hands, sir. They start at ten.'

None of them would be attending—like they had the time. The DCI had given evidence on their behalf at the trial. It had been nearly a year since they had discovered, that fateful November morning, the horrific contents of that innocuous lorry in a Liverpool dock. Victims of Varga's trafficking ring. They'd not managed to connect it to Varga with strong enough evidence to charge him, but they'd nicked the driver, Brown. He faced trial for dozens of counts of manslaughter, and a ream of other charges.

Ward's stomach turned. He wasn't sure what he wanted the verdict to be. After all, he didn't know how complicit Brown was in any of it—he hadn't been at the trial, hadn't heard the evidence for and against. Did it really matter, in the end? He thought back to the most recent lorry they had intercepted, driven by a desperate Slovakian, Miroslav Ferenc, who had been coerced by Varga's thugs to work for the crime lord.

Was this driver any different? Did any of it really matter when they could not cut the head off the snake itself?

'Sir?' David said.

'Aye, sorry, David. Just thinking.'

David, a man of few words anyway, nodded under-standingly.

'What are our current lines of enquiry?'

David clicked to a different window on his computer. 'Here's what I'm following at the moment. We have last November's lorry, and we'll see what the court says as to his guilt. The brothel raid this summer and the unfortu-nate gang murder of the young lady we interviewed from there remain unsolved and I think we'll have to shelve those for now—no new evidence, you see.'

Damn. The young woman's green-blue eyes, her wide, petrified stare as Ward had uncovered her hiding, cowering, in the brothel, had still not left him. They'd tried to rescue her from that life, rehabilitate her in a woman's shelter, and ensure she was safe...but Varga had gotten to her anyway. Made an example of her. He owned those women in life and death, to do with as he pleased. Their protection wasn't enough to save her.

David continued, 'The investigation of possible collusion by port staff with regards to allowing Varga's imports into the country is to be handed over to Anti-Corruption.'

'What?' spluttered Ward. 'That was supposed to be our bust!'

David grimaced. 'Would have been nice. But the Super doesn't see that we have the manpower, and anyway, it would fall under Liverpool's Major Crime, since it'd be investigating staff over there. We're to assist and data-share where possible and necessary, but as far as we're concerned, it's not our problem anymore.'

'Not our problem?' Ward growled. 'I'll give them "not our problem". This whole damned case is our problem! And never mind about the manpower. Christ, if they have some secret pot that's not been affected by these bloody budget deficits and cuts, I'd love to know about it.'

'Sorry, sir.'

'Not your fault, David. I'll take it up with Kipling, so don't offload that yet.' And he would take it up. Vociferously. For all the good it would probably do. But Ward would be damned if he'd let any part of this case go. He'd worked it for years now, and it had cost his life, his marriage, his sanity.

'Yes, sir. There's one other thing...'

'Oh?' Ward's mental tirade faltered.

'Our investigation is really moving beyond our jurisdiction now.'

Ward sighed. 'Slovakia.' Miroslav Ferenc's interviews had hinted at widespread criminal activity in Slovakia that supported Varga's trafficking and smuggling organisation. They had known as much, really. There was no way they'd be able to investigate that from the United Kingdom.

'Yes. So, we have limited resources and legal legs to investigate Bratislava Logistics Solutions, as they're based in Slovakia. However, I was able to do some digging from what we can use. Something very interesting turned up, in fact.' David paused a moment, glancing at Ward for suspense. At a glare, he hurriedly continued, 'The owner of BLS is related by marriage to Bogdan Varga. Bogdan Varga's sister is married, and it's her brother-in-law that owns and runs the firm.'

Ward's eyebrows rose. 'Bloody hell. It's a family affair.'

'Yes, sir. Coercion or complicity...I can't say. But they're involved.'

Ward chewed his lip. 'Christ.' Post-Brexit, intelligence sharing had become much harder. Revoking membership of the European Union had had far-reaching consequences for national security and the usual channels were closed. 'Do we have any options?'

'You'll be pleased to know I think so, sir.'

Ward clapped Norris on the shoulder. 'Good man. Go on.'

'I've reached out directly to the Slovak Police Force, SPF, specifically to their Organised Crime Bureau. It's taken a few weeks, and the red tape has been enormously frustrating, but I've finally managed to get somewhere, I think. If we can work jointly with the OCB, we might be able to close the net around Varga.'

A wicked grin stole across Ward's face. *This* was a much-needed breakthrough. 'You think that if we pool our intelligence, we can nab him?'

'I do, sir. It seems they have plenty of active lines of enquiry for Varga, and they'd very much welcome the opportunity to close a few of those off successfully in our mutual interests.'

'And if we could get him...*actually* get him...' Ward trailed off. It was a dizzying hope. Certainly unachievable at present.

'Indeed, sir. It would be a huge weight off our caseload and a monster taken off our streets and Bratislava's.'

'Excellent work, David.' And he meant it. 'Set up a meeting as soon as you can with the OCB. Let's do this.' Between Anti-Corruption, his team, and the OCB... maybe they, at last, had a chance. More than a chance. A *fighting* one.

Ward thought back to the various instances he'd met Varga. A slimy, unpleasant, cruel man with no regard for the law or anyone but himself. In his wake, lay only victims and devastation. He did as he pleased, and silenced anyone who crossed him—Ward had been on the receiving end of his warnings several times already.

It had felt, to Ward, as though Varga drew closer to him, dogging his steps with shadowy threats. The photographs that Varga had taken and sent to Ward, tracking him, showing him just how close the crime lord could get to him personally. The T-shirt left at his door, a stark reminder that Varga was always watching Ward's steps—and, God forbid, his team's—after the seizure of the lorry full of counterfeit clothing. The young woman from the brothel that Ward and his team, Nowak especially, had tried to save—and Varga had made sure to execute her anyway. Just because he could.

No more, Ward thought, as a spike of resilience lanced through him. He clenched his jaw. *Now I'm coming for you, Varga.*

CHAPTER ELEVEN

MONDAY EVENING

DI Ward left not long after the team—tomorrow would be a long day with such a queue of possible leads to follow up for the Craven case, following up on the forensics and pathology reports, and collaring the DCI to find out what the bloody hell was going on with shifting part of the caseload to Anti-Corruption.

He followed Thornton Road out of town, calling in at the Morrisons at Four Lane Ends, as it was locally known —the giant crossroads just up from the Seabrook Crisp's factory—so he could grab a bite for tea. Ward schlepped around the store with a basket, grabbing milk and making a mental note to get bread too, since he was fairly sure he had neither. He picked up a stir fry kit on a whim as he walked past. After a second, he stopped, and put it back.

Balls.

He didn't even have a wok. *Can you make a stir fry in a frying pan?* He deliberated for a second. *Ah, bugger it. Live a little, Dan.* He shoved it in his basket once more. *If it turns out that bloody bad, bread and butter for supper it is*. Though he might not have any butter, either, now that he thought on it.

He lugged the basket to the bakery—just why did they put the best carbs the furthest away? Retail psychology, or some such thing, he'd once heard it called. He preferred "a giant pain in the arse", frankly.

Daniel chose a fresh tin loaf as a treat, with a momentary pause as he picked it up and inhaled the familiar scent. It reminded him of his grandad, who used to bake tin loaves at his old sheltered home. Ward still remembered eating them, warm and fresh out of the oven, slathered in melting golden butter...Those had been better times, before his grandparents had passed, and before his father had ruined all their lives.

Ward swallowed and dumped the loaf in the basket. A small tray of scones caught his eye. He'd already planned to drop by the hospital on his way in tomorrow—the Bradford Royal Infirmary, BRI, was practically on his route anyway with only a small detour. He'd been hoping to speak to the pathologist about his findings. Mark Baker, ironically true to his name, adored baking, but Ward was pretty sure it was more than his turn to bring a treat for the jovial pathologist.

Mind, Ward's wouldn't be home-baked—at least, not by him. Ward didn't know how to bake. Frankly, he liked Mark, and he didn't want to poison him by trying. Morrison's *"The Best"* branded scones would do nicely instead to keep Mark onside.

———

Ward pulled up in the half-full car park outside the apartment blocks. It was already long dark and freezing, early October heralding a long Yorkshire winter ahead, but at least it was dry for a change. Ward hurried inside, fobbing through the front door and collected his post before climbing to the first floor.

He stopped, frowning as the apartment door *clicked* shut behind him. *Grey.* For a moment, he forgot. As though he'd walked into the wrong place. Then, it flooded back. Of course. The new carpets had been fitted just that morning. It already seemed an age ago. With his and Metcalfe's matte white paint job brightening the walls, it did look like a different apartment.

And then, he couldn't think at all as a brown-and-white blur barrelled into him, barking fiercely. Olly the Beagle jumped up, peppering him with licks, his tail wagging so fast Ward could hardly see it. Ward dropped to a knee, relinquishing the shopping bag so he could fuss the dog.

'Now then, bud, alright, alright, I missed you too.' He gave the dog a thorough loving before getting the lead, which sent Olly into another frenzy of excitement. 'Just a quick loo trip alright? I'll take you out for a proper walk after dinner.'

After the warmth of the apartment, it seemed extra cold as he stepped out once more for a brisk walk to the common so Olly could do his business. Ward's stomach growled. The cheese and Branston pickle sandwich seemed an aeon ago. He hoped the stir fry would stand up to merit. After a few minutes, Olly finished up and Ward jogged back with him, eager to eat.

Ward kicked his shoes off by the door and took off his jacket, noting again that he really did need some hanging pegs on the wall. For now, same as always, he dumped it on the floor, scooping up that day's post and the shopping. Olly trotted ahead, tail wagging.

Ward chucked together the stir fry—noodles, greens, chicken, and some sweet and sour sauce—stirring the pan with a wooden spoon, before checking out the mail. Bills, as per usual, and a letter from the solicitors. He opened it.

Decree Nisi.

The divorce.

Something in him stuttered. He scanned the letter. The *Decree Nisi* had been granted. Now, it would be a formality to get the *Decree Absolute* and end his marriage. It was a strange feeling. *Divorced.* He rolled the word around in his mind. Still not knowing quite what to make of it. He'd be free, he supposed. And yet, *divorced.* The word alone carried so much weight. So much baggage.

Ward swore as smoke reached his nose. He nearly tripped over Olly as he galvanised. A quick stir later, and his tea was only *partly* charred. He turned the heat down and glared at the hob—as though it hadn't been his own fault entirely.

This was it, though. One huge step closer to everything being done. To the tangle that felt like his personal life finally, perhaps, yielding. What would life look like after Katherine, once it was formalised?

Ward would be the first one to admit, he'd been muddling through since they'd separated. He'd been treading water, doing his best to juggle finding a home, getting the dog back, managing work...so much so, he'd not even really had a chance to dwell on what it all meant for him and his future. It would be months, perhaps weeks, and he'd officially be *divorced*.

He hated to admit it, but for the first time since he'd started the process, he felt apprehensive. Katherine had been almost his entire adult life. He'd dared to daydream, almost childishly, for a moment, about Eve Griffiths, knowing full well it was nothing, but there would be a life after Katherine, right? Did he have to spend the rest of it alone?

Ward stirred the pan. Took it off the heat. And just stood and stared at it.

What does the future hold? he asked himself.

I don't know, came the answer.

That's not helpful, he warred with himself.

Anything you want. And that was the scariest part of all. He had no idea what he wanted anymore. What he even was without their relationship defining him outside work.

Ward picked up the pan, scooping out the contents into a large bowl. He couldn't think on it. Something to figure out another time. He had enough on his figurative plate already, damn it.

As if heaven-sent, his phone pinged with a message.

He checked it, wondering if it was one of the team, or perhaps, it was a blue moon and his long-estranged brother had replied to one of his texts. No such luck. But, sod's law: it was Katherine.

House has sold for asking, she wrote. *There's a chain, so might be a wait—I'll let you know.*

So, she had been right to hold out. Ward appreciated that, he supposed. The extra five grand would cover some of the legal fees. Unlike the Craven's empire, his and Katherine's assets were simple. They'd divvied up a small pot of savings, and they'd split the house. End of. Job done. Life together over.

Katherine's message continued—*Decree Nisi came today. I think you're getting a copy too.* That, he already knew—just. It was strange to talk about such life-changing matters over text. Not that he'd have preferred to do it over the phone, or even in person, for the unwelcome turmoil it would bring. But...what an end to a life together. *In with a bang, out with a fizzle.* He read the rest.

Also found Olly's paperwork. I've updated his registered owner to you. Will post across/keep here and you can pick up. Let me know? K.

Ward hovered over the reply button. He swallowed. There was no point putting it off. He typed a reply.

Thanks. I'll pick up whenever I next pass, no rush. Happy days on the house. Let me know if you need anything from me.

He hit send. The phone weighed down his slack hand. Ward sighed, and dumped it on the small foldaway dining table. He snagged his half-charred sweet and sour and downed a glass of water, realising yet again he'd forgotten to buy in drinks of any sort. He'd run out of tea and coffee after the weekend's decorating spree.

He looked at Olly, about to call him out for a walk. He needed it too, he realised. The cathartic rhythm of step after step after step pounding away his cares. Olly snored gently on his bed beside the television cabinet.

'Heh.' Maybe not, then. Ward left his dirty dishes on the table, eased out of his chair, and took himself to bed. Thoughts of Eve Griffiths tempted him once more as he laid there in the blackness of his darkened room, a hazy orange outside the only illumination from the car park lights. He'd soon be a free man. Free enough to ask her out, if he dared. The problem was, he didn't.

You don't have the guts, man. You don't deserve it anyway.

Ward scowled at that inner voice, but he didn't bother turning away from it. It wasn't one he could escape. He'd learned that long ago. Maybe he'd spent so many years caught up in it all that this, the not knowing, would be a good thing. Maybe it would lead to finding or making what he did want. Maybe Eve was nothing more than a wistful fantasy. Maybe what he really needed was to be alone for a while. Not alone and throwing himself into work—his old trick—chasing Varga and the rest of them.

Maybe for a change, he needed to be alone to have the space to figure out what the hell he wanted with *any* of his life anymore.

CHAPTER TWELVE

D aniel prised himself from a snug bed—complete with Olly throwing out the heat of a radiator on full blast weighing down his legs—far earlier than he wanted. But, such was his life now, as a dog-dad. He took Olly for a good long walk before he slung some breakfast down his neck and headed into the office, ready—maybe —to begin a heavy day of advancing the Craven case.

He'd almost forgotten to pick up the packet of scones, jam, and clotted cream for Mark Baker the pathologist from the kitchen counter, and had to dash back in. Out of breath and flustered after racing up the stairs, he legged it back to the car and set off. The hospital was close, at least, but in rush hour Bradford traffic, it would be a bloody nightmare—and that was without considering parking.

Pathology was at the south side of the hospital off Duckworth Lane, and the car park there notoriously bad for being able to get a space. Ward took a chance and left it in the first space outside on the main road that he could find. It was the best of both worlds, really— extra steps, and not being extorted for hospital parking, which, as a Yorkshire man and thus as tight as a duck's arse, went against every fibre of DI Daniel Ward's being.

As he swung through the doors into the pathology department, he was greeted by the familiar scent of bleach. He remembered the first time he'd had to visit— more years ago now than he cared to remember as a DC —and how nervous he'd been. After seeing his first body, he'd expected the stench of death to pollute and dominate the place, but Mark Baker and his team kept a tight ship. The place was spotlessly clean, and to a young DC Daniel Ward's relief, stench-of-death free.

'Mark?' Ward called, loitering at the end of the hall. One didn't go into Mark's domain without a good invitation. The jovial pathologist had a dark streak when it came to protecting the sanctity of his operation and the dignity of the deceased he worked with. Daniel had heard the story of his apoplectic rage when a post-mortem had been burst in upon unannounced by a team of junior doctors, mid-procedure. He'd never heard the man raise his voice, but he wasn't about to test Mark and see if it was true.

'Who is it?' called the deep voice of the man himself. Mark Baker bustled out of a side room with an armful of paperwork, his open white lab coat flapping. 'Ah, Daniel, m'boy! How good to see you, good to see you indeed. How do?'

Ward smiled. It was impossible not to be put at ease by Mark's warm charm. 'I'm alright, thanks, you?'

'Oh, never better, you know me. I presume you've come for the Craven report?'

'Aye, and I brought something to get in your good books. Home-baked.' Ward held up the armful of food—realising at that instant, that of course, wrapped in Morrison's packaging, he wouldn't get away with claiming to have baked the scones. *Oops.*

'Oh, you scoundrel,' chortled Mark, but he beckoned Ward in. 'Come on. You can put them on my desk. I shall sample them later with the team and check they're up to scratch.' He winked.

'I'm doing you a favour, really, Mark. Anything I made would be inedible.'

'You do yourself a disservice!' Mark held a door open with his foot for Ward to follow.

'Not at all,' Ward chuckled. 'Stick to the day job, as they say. That's me, when it comes to baking.'

'Hmm. Pop them there.' Baker nodded to his desk as he dumped the papers on it and eased heavily into his well-worn, creaking desk chair. 'Do you want to see Mr Craven?'

Good lord, no. 'Just your report will do.'

Mark nodded. 'As you wish.' He turned to his computer and spent a long minute pulling up the files. 'Haven't quite finished it yet—you'll have the full report by the end of today, but I can tell you everything now. Mr Craven died from blunt force trauma to the head, in a nutshell. He was forcefully struck across the left side of his face and head. That's what killed him—the fall just made spectacularly sure of it, and broke or fractured plenty of his bones.'

'Left side?' Ward interjected.

'Yes, exactly. So one would presume his attacker was right-hand dominant.'

Ward suppressed a groan. 'Great. That only leaves ninety percent of the population as a suspect, then.'

'Quite, though with Mrs Foster's observations, I'm sure you'll be able to further narrow that down.'

Ward certainly hoped so. He was hoping to get the crime scene report from the CSI team that day too and really start tearing chunks out of the case. As it was, they had a line of suspects as long as the River Aire and no way to know who on earth had killed Robert Craven.

'There's some foreign residue in the headwound— dust, mainly—but nothing from the foreign object itself, so I can only surmise from details like that, and the effects on his skull and facial bones that the object was heavy and very dense. Perhaps metal, or stone, something of that nature, to have made *such* a devastating wound and killed him.'

Ward frowned, folding his arms. A heavy object. He thought back to the empty plinth. 'What about say, a small marble statuette? Small enough to be carried by one man, large enough to be used as a weapon?'

Mark blinked and paused before he answered. 'Well, yes, I suppose so, actually. That would be perfect.'

That was what they needed to find then, the statuette of Mercury. 'Was there anything else you noticed?'

'I'm afraid not. He wasn't in a good way when he came to us, to be entirely honest, Daniel. It took a while to establish that there had been two incidents—some kind of assault with an object *and* the fall—and determine *which* had killed him. After that, our observations were very standard. There were no foreign substances in his blood like alcohol or drugs, so he was *compus mentus* as far as we can tell. There were traces of medication for high blood pressure and some related degradation and damage to his body from the condition, but nothing to be concerned about with regards to your investigation.'

Baker hadn't told Ward anything surprising, per se, but he had confirmed what Ward thought, without saying it. *I reckon the missing statuette is the murder weapon. Craven's assailant clobbered him, and he went over the mezzanine—either on purpose, or by accident. Did they mean to attack him?* So far, the attacker was in the house, with no signs of forced entry, or a concealed hiding place...Ward chewed on his lip.

'Penny for your thoughts, Detective?'

Ward chuckled. 'Just mulling it over, Mark. You've confirmed the MO for me, and that's very helpful. Trouble is, I have no idea where to start searching for the murder weapon, and the list of possible culprits is taller than me.'

Baker squinted up at Ward. 'My, that is saying something. Well, I have every faith in you. You always manage it.'

Ward smiled grimly. He didn't. Thoughts of Varga played on his mind, the spectre of the crime lord never too far from his waking thoughts. It was nice that Mark had the confidence in him, at least. He wasn't sure he had it in himself.

'Thanks, Mark. I appreciate it. Right, I'll leave you to it. Back to the circus I go.'

'Oho, I'll tell Scott you said that,' chuckled Mark.

'Be my guest. I can run faster than him.'

Mark's laughter followed him out of the pathology department. Ward sped back to his car. He had a missing statuette to find. Pronto.

CHAPTER THIRTEEN

W ard arrived to a hive of activity that morning, though his sarge was nowhere in sight. 'Where's Emma?' he asked DS Scott Metcalfe as he passed to his own desk.

'Ah, you know these young things. She's using that whatchamacallit, *initiative*. Off out to interview Frances Hodgson and Eliza Pullman.'

'Who?' Ward's head was still in the pathology report.

'Hodgson is the lady that so kindly filmed herself burning an effigy of Robert Craven. And, turns out there's one name that keeps coming up behind the press articles slating Craven's company and who even reported on that incident—Eliza Pullman. Nowak's gone to have a chat, see if there's anything worth sniffing at there.'

'Oh, aye. Good.' Ward frowned. It was good, he supposed. Emma being so self-starting, he had to have expected it sooner or later. *Future DSU there, after all*, he was certain.

'Mmm. Well, she didn't want to risk you landing her with the shotgun chap, I reckon. I'm taking a look at Miranda's phone data now. Can't do much without a warrant, but I have basic triangulation data.'

'Christ, didn't know you could use big words like that, Scotty.' Ward slung his jacket over the back of his chair.

'Cheeky bugger. You want to know, or what?'

'Sorry, your Lordship. Go on.' Ward shot Scott a wicked grin, but his interest was entirely piqued. The more he thought about it, the more he knew it had to be Miranda. Motive, means, and opportunity—she had all three in spades and more.

Scott tsked and shook his head. 'The bloody cheek of you nippers. It looks like she was in Harrogate all day. Just like she said.'

Ward's shoulders fell. 'Damn. Wait—her *phone* was in Harrogate. It doesn't mean she was.'

'My thought exactly,' said Scott, leaning back in his chair and taking a big swig from a steaming mug of tea— or witch's piss, as Ward said, since the Lancastrian had it so damn weak it might as well have been water and milk shown a teabag.

'Right. Check ANPR for the car. Both of their cars, actually. I want to know if Miranda left Harrogate, or perhaps Robert made a trip, picked someone up.'

'Already put in the requests.'

'Good. Keep on them. Do we have anything back from Victoria?'

'Not yet. End of day. I already asked.'

'Damn.' It would have helped inform his questioning that day. Always better to hold too many cards than too few, after all.

Ward looked up as DCs Shahzad and Patterson strolled in, leisurely as you like, brew and biscuits in hand. 'Lads, what is this, a bloody picnic? Get to it!'

They snapped to attention. 'Aye, sir. Still waiting on the warrant for the CCTV company to access the cloud-hosted video backups,' Shahzad offered.

'And you?' Ward glared at Patterson. He'd softened on the new DC over the last few months—the young lad worked hard, when he wanted to. The trouble was the *rest* of the time.

'Er, um...'

Ward grinned so menacingly, Jake shrank back. 'Well, if you're at a loose end, I have the perfect task for you. You can go chat to Bill Turner for me.'

'W-what?' yelped Jake. 'Isn't he the nutjob with the shotgun?'

'Yep,' said Ward.

'B-but...you...you can't just send me in there,' stammered DC Patterson, eyes wide.

'You're more than ready for it, Constable,' growled Ward, enjoying every tremor in the young DC.

'Did you not hear the part where he's *mental* and has a flipping shotgun!?'

Ward guffawed.

'What if he shoots me!?'

'Then we won't have to put up with you. Winner winner, chicken dinner, lad!'

Patterson just gaped at him. Then Scott. Then Shahzad. All were too busy trying—unsuccessfully—not to laugh, to offer him any backup.

'Off you trot then, son, that's settled. Go on.'

Patterson looked fit to cry or piss himself at the prospect, but he wasn't stupid enough to disobey a direct order from his senior. 'Yes, sir,' he croaked.

'Don't worry, lad,' Scott called after him as he sloped out, head firmly ducked. 'We'll scrape all the bits of you together for your mam.'

The door shut behind Patterson with a guffaw of laughter from the office.

'Are you sure you don't want me to go with him, sir?' DC Shahzad asked.

Ward did feel slightly sorry for him. Maybe. Perhaps. Or maybe it was just a bubble of gas passing through his constitution. 'He's as ready as he'll ever be.' He shrugged. 'I need you here chasing the tech. That CCTV is *the* bit of evidence we need to prove who visited the property when Robert Craven died.'

'Well, we've all been pushed out of the frying pan and into the fire on this job,' said Scott, still chuckling. 'About time we stopped coddling the lad.'

'Aye. Patterson can deal with a nutjob and a shotgun.' Maybe.

———

DCI Martin Kipling prowled the halls of Bradford South Police Station—a sight to fear, for his office was upstairs and out of the way compared to the main office. 'DI Ward. A word.'

Scott pulled a funny face at Ward and mouthed, *you're in trouble*, with a cheeky wink.

Ward gave Metcalfe a sly middle finger as he stood, even though it had to be bad if Kipling had replied to his email by coming to find him in person. 'Yes, sir.'

'I wasn't about to barter emails with you all day, Daniel,' Kipling said with a stern glare as he walked with Ward down the hallway and into the canteen. It was empty save for some bods from downstairs, who promptly cleared out as Kipling stared them down.

'We just can't give this up, sir,' Ward began, but Kipling cut him off.

'We can, we must, and we already *have*, Detective Inspector,' Kipling said, a stark warning of their differing ranks, and a reminder that he would not tolerate insurrection. 'If we have possible corruption, collusion even, in British authorities with Varga's operation, we have to tread carefully, and we have to be thorough. Remember, we all want the same thing.' He stared at Ward, holding his gaze, until Ward nodded.

'I know you understand, Daniel. I know you feel personally responsible for this, and goodness knows, I don't expect that will change.' Kipling had tried to get him to back off, to care less. He was finally understanding Ward couldn't do that.

Good.

Kipling sighed. 'We're ruffling a lot of feathers here, Ward.' He pursed his lips for a moment before he continued. 'There's to be a full audit of port staff by Anti-Corruption, for starters. Maybe that net will widen. Maybe not. Either way, a chain of events has been set in motion now, and we have to understand and respect that. This is a one-way street—our information flows to them, and not the other way around.'

Ward shuffled his feet and crossed his arms. That was what he didn't like about it. Loss of any and all control. 'How can we be sure they're doing it properly?'

Kipling huffed in exasperation. 'You can't be serious. They're Anti-Corruption, for goodness sake! Don't make me regret giving you this case back, Ward.'

Ward gritted his teeth and bit back a reply that he knew he'd regret. He only wanted justice. His team did. For Varga and his victims. It was hard to let that go, to trust someone else with so much. Didn't Kipling understand that?

'I'll find out what I can, but I can't promise anything. Now it's in the hands of AC, I'll be fishing for any scraps from the Super too. I can't say I like it either, Ward,' said Kipling, 'but it's the right thing to do. I need you doing what you do best.'

It sounded like Kipling was trying to butter him up. Ward wanted to squirm. He was used to clashing with the DCI—especially when it came to Varga—not whatever this was.

'We need to focus on Varga, and only Varga. AC will handle the rest. Do you understand?'

'Yes, sir.'

'Good. Did you hear the verdict?'

'No.' Ward felt a momentary rush of shame. He'd been so caught up in...everything else, that he'd not even checked.

'Guilty. Full counts of manslaughter for every single victim.'

Ward couldn't breathe for a second. The court had convicted the lorry driver after all. It had been the HMETs team's worst fear that the evidence they'd gathered to support the prosecution would have gone to waste, would have been for nothing. The driver wasn't Varga, sure, but their evidence had suggested he might not be entirely innocent in the matter. A jury had seen fit to take it as far as the letter of the law allowed.

'That's...wow,' Ward forced out. He leaned heavily on a table, almost physically reeling as he tried to absorb the unexpected news.

'Good work. It's our team that secured this conviction. Every single hour we put in. It was worth it. I'm personally thanking everyone now. Assemble everyone in the Incident Room.'

Kipling left him there.

Ward watched him go, mind churning. They'd collared the driver, sure, and he'd be sentenced accordingly...but he wasn't Varga. The ringleader. Handing off part of their investigation to Anti-Corruption would make HMET's work harder. Ward wanted the case for HMET—*every* aspect of it—to hunt Varga down. Damned be the red tape that held him back.

CHAPTER FOURTEEN

DC Jake Patterson pulled up outside the dilapidated farm in his wheezing Fiat Punto with no small amount of trepidation. He killed the engine quickly—it seemed too noisy to him, even though it was only a one-litre engine. His hearing strained overtime, as did his sight, scanning the dismal, fog-wreathed moor around him—peppered with sheep but deserted of people —for any sign of a completely deranged farmer with a shotgun about to blow his brains out.

Nothing.

Sheep quietly grazed the moor above Grassington, a sleepy village in Upper Wharfedale that he'd never been to. To him, it looked much like the others he'd passed through on the way. Quaint stone-built houses, shops, pubs. Cobbled streets. That Dales vibe that one couldn't seem to put into words, of slower-paced days and folk as solid as the earth, of fresh air and good, hearty food and drink.

Then, there was the estate.

Looming over the village, the newbuild houses were an eyesore, even to Jake, entirely out of keeping, as though they'd been uprooted just like Dorothy from Kansas and plonked somewhere entirely ill-fitting. The huge estate sprawled, hugging the top of the village, obscuring the view of the moors beyond in part. A modern aberration in that beautiful old place.

The farm before him, with its stone and ramshackle outbuildings half reclaimed by nature, looked far more in keeping with the landscape there. Jake wanted to head back into the village. Maybe he should have called to one of the pubs there for a dose of courage before he'd come— much as the gaffer would have clobbered him for it.

Patterson eased out a shaky breath. 'Pull yourself together, son,' he said in a deep voice, impersonating DS Metcalfe. 'It's only a shotgun.' He gave a nervous laugh to himself.

He heaved out of the car and buttoned his jacket, turning the collar up against the bitter wind that drove down from the hills. The jacket felt paper-thin. No bloody protection against a shotgun, that was for sure. But Ward would never have let him take a bulletproof vest—HMET didn't deal in that kind of uniform.

Jake folded in his wing mirror manually, conscious of the narrow country lane. Never mind that he had a Fix-It-Again-Tomorrow Punto, he didn't fancy a smashed wing mirror, thank you very much.

He'd half parked the car in the drainage ditch at the side of the road, causing it to be an upward struggle to get out—at least he'd find it easier to get back in, he reasoned. Possibly advantageous. He tried not to think about being chased back to his car by a maniac with a gun, but, oh, wait, nope, there was the thought again.

Miserably, Jake locked his car and slouched up the long, rutted, dirt track that led to the farm buildings. He wasn't ready for this. And he definitely wasn't paid enough.

A haphazard array of buildings—stables, sheds, barn —greeted him in a courtyard filled with all manner of machinery that looked like it had rusted solid to the earth for more years than he'd been alive. At the far side of the courtyard, which was little better than a pot-hole filled mess of broken cobbles, dirt, gravel, and ruts, a farmhouse nestled.

Framed by weeds half as tall as Patterson, and covered in a tangle of ivy that seemed to be giant hands choking the life out of the poor, decrepit building, Jake could instantly tell it had seen far better days. The single-paned, wood-framed windows were clouded and dirty, the white paint long peeled from the wood, with panes cracked in several windows.

Jake's heartbeat notched up another level as he padded through the courtyard, peering into the yawning maw of a broken stable door and the cavernous darkness beyond with trepidation, as if some beast would come barrelling out at him. It seemed too quiet. The space was sheltered on three sides from the wind coming down from the hill, and it was too far from the hubbub of the village.

Why did he feel as though he was in a horror movie all of the sudden?

A nervous laugh bubbled up before he could contain it. 'Hello? Police?' he called out before his nerves could desert him entirely.

At the front door—wooden, old, and peeling like the windows—he rapped sharply, even though every instinct wanted him to turn tail and leg it. He couldn't. DI Ward would bollock him, no doubt in front of the rest of the team, for dereliction of duty and cowardice.

Was that worth it? *I mean, the alternative is this mad old bastard blows your head off with a shotgun, Jake.* Now that he thought about it, nope, it wasn't worth it, and frankly—

The door opened.

An old, grizzled face peered out. Wiry grey-white hair in a shaggy bush on a face and head that hadn't been trimmed in a decade. Deep-set wrinkles. A glint in eyes so deeply veiled he wouldn't have been able to tell what colour they were if he glanced closer—but he didn't.

Jake sprang backwards, landing on his arse with a painful jarring as the man bellowed, 'GET OUTTA HERE!'

Jake yelped and scrambled to his feet. 'Hello, sir, I'm—'

'GET THE FUCK OFF MY PROPERTY BEFORE I GET MY GUN.' The man turned and lurched back inside.

Fuck's sake! wailed Jake internally. How far did he have to go in the line of duty? How far was good enough before everyone agreed he'd been very brave, thank you very much, in the face of such astounding danger.

'Police! I just need to chat, sir!' His voice came out as a high-pitched squeak, and he wanted to fold himself into the ground, let it swallow him up.

Thank God no one was there to see him. 'Specially not the girl he'd been talking to. First chance out on his own, and he was screwing it up.

They'd joked they'd be there to pick up the scraps of him left on the ground. Maybe they hadn't been joking. Had they? DI Ward wouldn't have sent him into danger alone. Would he? *Would he?* Doubts lurked.

The man was back. 'I warned yer!' he roared, waving a massive double-barrelled shotgun in Jake's face.

Fucking fucking fuck! Jake clenched his arse together —just to make sure he didn't lose the contents, before he gathered what little scraps of his courage remained. 'PUT DOWN THE GUN! I'M THE POLICE. STAND DOWN NOW, SIR,' he bellowed in his best imitation of DI Ward.

The man blinked at him. 'EH?' he hollered, squinting at Jake, and the warrant card DC Patterson held up. 'P'lice? Yer shouldha said, lad. Thought tha were nobbut trouble, tha's ony a nipper, eh? What's tha want?' He scowled at Jake. But he didn't put down the gun. Distrust oozed from him.

'I just need to ask a few questions about an incident, if that's alright, sir,' Jake said, trying to draw himself up tall even though the back of his coat was crumpled and caked in mud. 'Mr Turner?'

'Aye, well I 'ant got all day, so chivvy it along, eh?'

'Would you be able to tell me where you were this Sunday afternoon just gone, between about twelve and eight PM, please, Mr Turner?'

'Eh? Why's tha want to know that?'

'I just have to ask, sir.'

Mr Turner grumbled unintelligibly to himself for a moment. 'Well, Sunday I were up on't hills, sorting t'gimmers and t'ewes fer market next Sunday.'

Sorting what and who-now?

Mr Turner barked a sharp laugh that made Jake jump as he saw the blank look in the lad's eyes. 'Sheep, lad. Sorting out me sheep fer market. Tekkin' em down Leyburn to sell some off so I can feed t'rest and missen through winter.'

In Jake's mind, he had to run the equivalent of an auto-translate to understand the man's broad Yorkshire. *He's selling off some sheep to raise money to feed himself and his livestock through winter. Got it. Maybe. Maybe not.*

'Do you have anyone who can back that up?'

'Eh? Why would I need to?' That scowl deepened. 'If I sez I did it, then I did it, lad. Why's tha so fussed what I'm doin' wi' mi own livestock?'

'Because we're looking into the murder of Robert Craven on Sunday, sir'—Patterson didn't think Turner's face could become anymore thunderous. He was wrong— 'and seeing as you had a significant disagreement with him that involved a firearm'—probably the one the old man wielded now, which Jake glanced nervously at again

— 'then, er, sir, we have to make enquiries. Sir.' He swallowed.

'Craven's dead?'

'Yes, sir.'

'Well good riddance to the bastard,' roared Turner. 'Get his comeuppance, eh?' He barked another laugh, and then hacked an explosive cough after it, pausing for a long moment to catch his breath. 'Yer can see he's fair ruined Grassington, eh? Criminal, bloody criminal it is, what he did.'

'You had a disagreement about the houses with him, didn't you?'

'Disagreement?' Turner rounded on Jake, blazing. 'He ruined the place! Three of my sheep were poisoned with whatever crap were running off that land. He didn't offer no compensation, and I had to put 'em down missen to end their sufferin'!' He looked red with rage, and Jake could understand why—if he was a farmer, and his animals had suffered...of course he would care.

'I took mysen round to his site and I said, I said "I won't bloody stand for it!" and thannoz what he did, eh? Didn' stand wi' me, man to man. Talk, 'pologise, figh', whatever. Coward that he were, he called you poor wee sods up and got me hauled off teh t'nick.' Turner spat on the ground between them and cursed under his breath.

'So you bore him quite a grudge then, sir?'

'Aye, an' who wouldn't? He's ruined my village wi' these bloody monstrous houses, ruined mi' farm, and he di'nt give a shite! Good riddance to the bastard, wish

134

they'd rip that damned estate down too whilst they're at it,' he finished thunderously.

Patterson wasn't sure who "they" were, but he nodded carefully. 'Do you have anyone who can prove what you were doing on Sunday?'

'Eh?' Turner gazed up at him incredulously. 'Does tha have wool in tha's ears? I were separatin' t'gimmers and t'ewes for market. Wa'nt tha listenin'?'

'I was, sir, but is there anyone who can verify you were here? Would you be able to come to the station and let us take your fingerprints to discount you from our investigation?'

Turner turned a deeper shade of beetroot, and he hefted the gun back up from the floor where the barrel rested into his grip. 'Now, see here, lad. I gave yer time o' day with tha sayin' that was from th' police, but I aren't about to suffer no fools. Get off me land, *now*, before I lose me rag with yer. I aren't going 'round in circles. I have a sheep to sort wi' t'vet and I aren't bein' tardy on your account. I've answered yer questions and it's more'n what yer deserved. Now, get the bloody hell off my land!' the man finished on a roar, bristling as he stepped forward, brandishing that shotgun.

Jake turned and fled. Launching himself over potholes and ruts. Darting between the ruined, skeletal remnants of the old machinery. Expecting at every moment to be peppered with the burning punch of shotgun cartridges blowing him into oblivion.

Only when he was back in his car, doors locked, and driving, just driving, in any damned direction, as fast as the aged Punto would let him, his wing mirror still tucked in, did Jake Patterson relax enough to let out a squeak of fear, and a stress-trump from the other end's sphincter.

Jake pulled over, in the middle of God knows where, still on some narrow country lane up in the hills above Grassington. Handbrake on. Indicator on. And rested his forehead on the steering wheel, taking great shuddering breaths as he thanked every god he could think of for letting him walk out of there alive. Like a traumatic memory, he was already reliving it, dodging out of that farmyard, expecting obliteration, as though he couldn't quite believe he was alive.

Am I alive!? Jake felt his arms, his legs, ran a hand through his hair, cupped his face in his hands. It felt real enough. There'd been no pain. He looked in the rear-view mirror at himself. Sweaty. Dishevelled hair. And as he glanced down, dirtied pants from the tumble onto his arse he'd taken.

'Come on, Patterson,' he groaned. 'Pull yourself together.' He'd be the laughing stock of the office if they found out the whole truth, and that he'd pretty much wet himself running away. Never mind that he'd literally risked his bloody life for the case. He wasn't sure if he still felt too weak at the knees to stand, or whether it ought to make him the cocky little shit DI Ward seemed to think he was half the time.

He'd hardly gotten anything out of the man, and it wouldn't be good enough for DI Ward. But Jake Patterson would *not* be going back to Bill Turner's farm. No way. Not a cat in hell's chance. Certainly not without backup. Jake needed enough to go on to make sure that didn't happen, anyway. What did he have?

His heart slowly starting to calm, the adrenaline making him buzz finally fading away...DC Patterson turned over the car, eased it into first gear, and did a three-point turn to head back down into Grassington and to the office. Soon, he was out the other side of the village —having not been shot at on his way past the once more apparently deserted farm. That eased the last of his fraught nerves. A relieved laugh escaped, and he eased into the sweeping roads leading down the valley, back to relative civilisation as he knew it.

With every twist and turn of the undulating road, he tried to figure out what he could take away from that bloody awful meeting. For one, Jake wasn't diminutive, but he wasn't a giant. Mr Turner, gnarled and hunched with age, was no doubt strong for his shorter stature and advanced years if he was still out farming by himself, by the looks of it, hardy as the hills and sheep he tended... but Jake didn't think he would have been able to over-power Robert Craven, not even by surprise. From what he had seen of the victim's specifications Robert Craven had been a tall, well-built figure, full of strength and vitality—more than enough to match Mr Turner.

Besides which, there'd not been a forensic track of sheep-shit and mud through Mr Craven's luxurious home that he'd heard about. And, as Jake had gazed down at Mr Turner's ragged clothing, all greying with age and dark with crusted dirt, the man's boots caked in dirt and sheep shit, he'd thought, terrifying shotgun or not, that he'd never seen a more unlikely candidate for Robert Craven's murder.

Least of all because the grizzled old man would have probably just blasted Craven's head off, and there wouldn't be enough of the man's face left to identify him. Jake shuddered at the thought—but he was sure he was onto something there. The MO didn't fit Mr Turner.

Either way, DC Jake Patterson was mightily glad to be away from the bloke. Now, he just had to come up with a better story than 'a mad old hatter with a shotgun terrified me into almost pissing my pants, and I didn't get any concrete evidence to prove he didn't do it.'

That would be a bit trickier to convince the gaffer.

CHAPTER FIFTEEN

Varga haunted Ward's steps all the way back to his car and to Skipton to visit Mr Craven's company headquarters to speak to the staff there, who by now would be wondering where their boss was, for the death had still not been formally announced, unless James Craven had informed them.

Would he have? Ward wondered. He couldn't imagine that it would be particularly high on a grieving son's list, yet, if James Craven possessed the same work ethic as his father, perhaps he would be far more pragmatic.

He pulled up outside the offices, built in the signature pale yellow stone of newbuilds these days, and noted the high-powered Jaguar F type parked closest to the doors, with the personalized plate reading 'J14'. Ward couldn't help but be envious at that—the plate alone would have cost an eye-watering amount, and then the car itself...He slowed as he walked past it for a quick nosy. Gunmetal grey, with yellow accents. Special edition.

Nice. James Craven wasn't short of a bob or two either, then. *How the other half lives.*

Maybe if Ward saved his entire salary for a decade, he could afford one. Probably not. Ward strode inside, trying not to dwell on that sad fact.

'Can I help you?' a woman's voice sounded as he stepped inside and stared around the plain, modern office interior—like the bland, nondescript reception space of probably a thousand other offices. He turned to the woman behind the desk. She hovered, poised, with a face that said "this had better be more important than my sudoku game/Facebook stalking/gossip column, thank you very much".

Ward held up his warrant card. 'I need to speak with James Craven, please.'

The woman's face crumpled and paled a little. 'Yes, of course,' she said quickly. 'I imagine this is about Robert?' A trembling hand covered her mouth. 'We're all in such shock, we just don't understand.'

So James made it to work to tell them all then.

That didn't sound like a grieving son to Ward. Mind, if the apple didn't fall far from the tree, perhaps James had inherited his mother's cold and calculating streak.

'If James is available, it's a matter of urgency,' Ward said impassively. He had planned to make contact with James next...two birds, one stone.

The woman trailed off. He thought she was about to shoot him a glare—how dare he be so disrespectful—but she quickly swallowed, and nodded. 'Of course. Please take a seat.'

Ward didn't, remaining standing.

She made a quick call, and then stood. 'I'll take you through now.'

Jennifer, Ward noted as he saw the name badge as she passed him, fobbing herself through a set of double doors into an open-plan office with mostly full desks, and the chatter of a dozen mouths on headsets, and the conversations of a dozen more between each other. Ward supposed there was quite a lot to talk about that Tuesday morning, if their boss had been found dead. He wondered how much they knew.

'Here, Detective. Robert's office.' Once more, the receptionist looked like she was going to cry. She knocked twice, a sharp rap, opened the door for Ward, and scurried away. A stifled sob reached his ears as she retreated.

Ward stepped inside a sumptuous private office, his feet instantly muffled from the hard floor outside on softer carpets. Wide windows on double aspects flooded the space with light, the vertical blinds open and pulled back offering uninterrupted views of the Aire Valley from the large antique wooden desk and matching leather chair.

A man in his early thirties awaited beside that desk. The spit of his father, though decades younger, James Craven had the same dark hair and eyes and the same confident stance that Ward could see mirrored in the professionally framed photographs of Craven around the room—at award ceremonies and company events, suited and booted.

James Craven seemed entirely out of place, awkward, like a child caught in the pantry. Like he didn't fit in his father's office.

It must be difficult, sympathised Ward silently.

James shook Ward's outstretched hand before returning both hands to his pockets.

'I'm sorry for your loss, Mr Craven,' Ward offered, though as usual, it felt insincere and underwhelming. 'We're doing all we can to seek justice for your father.' James had been briefed by DSU McIntyre—he would know the circumstances, or at least, what was pertinent for the public domain.

'Thank you,' said James. He looked drawn and tired, darker shadows hanging under his eyes than Ward would expect from a man of his relatively young age. Perhaps he did bear some grief—or more, at least, than his mother. Perhaps he didn't know how else to deal with it, save to get up and try to carry on.

'I have to ask you some questions, if that's alright?' Ward said, firm but not harsh. He hadn't prepared for this entirely—he'd expected to gather some basic information at the company, details of Claire Parker, for one, and arrange a meeting with James. That he was there right at that moment...

Wing it, Daniel told himself. He had enough years on the force to be able to do that, at least.

James nodded. He moved around to the chair—glancing at where his father had probably sat thousands of times—before halting. Thinking better of it. Crossing to the window to lean against the sill instead.

'You're not under caution, and this isn't a formal interview, so you don't need any legal counsel, but you're more than welcome to if you so wish.' Ward paused, and raised his eyebrow.

James waved a hand dismissively. 'Go ahead.'

'Thanks.' That made things easier and quicker at least. 'I'd like to get some background on you, your father, and the company, if I can. You're a pretty big part of the business here, right?'

'Yes. In three years, I'm due to take over as managing director so my father can retire.' James' face twisted in a smirk that quickly soured into grief, and Ward could see as he visibly tamped it down. 'I suppose he won't get to swan around ordering me about from whichever luxurious destination he was going to retire to.'

Ward smiled sympathetically and waited.

'I've worked at the company for ten years now. I own a third of it—though that wasn't always the case. Dad said I had to prove myself first. I'm the operations director now—for five years. I live and breathe this place, like he doe-*did*,' James corrected with an awkward wince.

'As much as anyone can, anyway, anyone who's not him. There was no one more invested in all of this than my dad.' For a moment, a lost look flitted across his face. The hint of a child who had just lost a parent, wondering how they could pick it all up and carry on.

'You must have enjoyed working so closely with him for so many years.'

James laughed. 'Yes and no. I think we were arguing more than we weren't, to be honest. Dad likes things done his way—my way or the high way, you know? Me...I wanted to be a bit more modern, inject some fresh blood into the place.'

'So you disagreed on that?'

'Oh yeah, but nothing serious. Occasionally, he'd let me run with one of my ideas. Sometimes they work, sometimes they don't. But at the end of the day, he's the boss, and he's built this from the ground up. I know why he's always tried to protect the business, even if it means he could never really let go.'

James stared at the photograph on Robert's desk as he spoke, a slight upturn in one corner of his mouth—he spoke of his dad with affection, to Ward's perception.

'And now, there's just me,' he said slowly, dragging a hand through his sleek hair, rumpling the carefully coiffed look.

'You argued last week, or so your mother tells me. Can you tell me about that?'

James looked sharply at Ward, before blinking a few times and folding his arms. 'Sure.' He swallowed. 'I mean, just another blowout, really. I wanted to run a PR campaign to get the Dales folk onside for the new village building projects...Dad wouldn't hear of it.'

'Go on?' Ward jotted down notes in his pocket book, his attention casual.

'That's it, really. He thinks that since he has the backing of the council, the planning permission committee, and all that, that it's a licence to do whatever he likes.

However, I know that the goodwill we need to build will be vital in selling those houses for what they're worth—for maximum value. You catch more flies with honey, not vinegar, right?' James waited for Ward to nod.

'Exactly. I think he's getting stubborn in his old age, to be honest.' James picked up an ornament from the windowsill—a small trophy, Ward realised, shaped like a rugby ball. 'He wouldn't hear it. I admit, it got a bit heated, but apparently, we both feel strongly on it, and if you talk to my mother, you'll never hear the end of her saying I've got the same stubborn streak as Dad.'

Ward noted that he kept referring to his father in the present tense, as though he were still alive. That would take a while to sink in.

James put the trophy down. 'I regret it now. I haven't seen him since. I didn't...I never thought...if I knew that the last things I said to him would be so awful, I never would have...' he trailed off, his voice thick. Ward watched him force down his feelings.

'I'm here now, because I'm not quite sure what else to do with myself,' James admitted quietly. 'Without Dad...there's no one running the place. So, I figured, if I had nothing better to do, well, I'm sure it's what he would want. For me to come here, take charge, make sure everything's still running smoothly.' He glanced at the desk. At the newspapers upon it.

Ward could spy some familiar and not entirely complimentary headlines, no doubt some written by Eliza Pullman.

Perhaps not as smoothly as he'd hoped.

'These were entirely the kind of thing I'd wanted to nip in the bud with my PR initiative,' James muttered, crossing to the desk and shuffling through the papers. He pushed them aside with a huff.

'Where were you on Sunday afternoon between twelve and eight, James? For our records, you understand.'

James stilled for a moment, his eyes flicking to Ward's and wondering as he understood what Ward was asking of him. 'I was out with my wife and children at Bolton Abbey. We went walking in the Strid wood—they have a Halloween trail for October. Then out for Sunday dinner at a local pub. Then home, and putting the kids to bed.'

'I see. Do you—'

'I have photos,' James cut him off, his tone growing more hostile. 'With time stamps.'

'Of course. Thank you. I know it seems petty, but we have to check. It's very common for the victim to know the perpetrator.'

James froze, his attention whipping to Ward, the phone in his hand entirely forgotten. 'You...think someone we know killed Dad?'

'It's a possibility.' Ward couldn't comment, but that was his suspicion—after all, the house bore no signs of forced entry, which meant Robert had let them in. In all likelihood, that meant he knew them.

'We'll update you as soon as we can,' Ward offered. He hoped that the Super was done meddling. He couldn't work a case if the high aboves were leaking information to key witnesses and possible suspects. Though he was chiefly thinking of one suspect so far, to be honest. Miranda.

James nodded, but he looked far away as he glanced over at the wall of professional photos and awards garnered by his father.

'I'll get what else I need from reception, if that's alright? I need one of your employee's details.'

'Sure.'

Ward traipsed back to reception, letting himself out of the main office. As he passed, he caught a glimpse of Jennifer's screen—the *Cosmopolitan* website. Something about eating only green foods to "look fine in the sunshine this summer!". Ward suppressed a shudder. He was a pro at beige food, thanks very much. "No carbs before Scarbs", as they said—though he couldn't remember the last time he'd taken a trip to the seaside resort of Scarborough. Or cut down on carbs.

'James has sent me to see you—I need a few details.' Ward employed an easy smile—the same one that had won over Katherine all those years ago, and the one he rarely got to use these days—and leaned on the elbow-high counter. 'I need your employee records for one Claire Parker, please.'

Jennifer frowned. 'I can't just give you that.'

'Of course you can. I'm the police. Besides, James has okayed it—I mean, you can check if you like, but I don't think he'll be mighty impressed at being disturbed today, don't you think?'

Jennifer swallowed and glanced away. 'No, no, you're right.'

'I need that information, please.'

'First off, Claire Parker is no longer an employee of the company. She was fired on Sunday morning. Robert told me to prepare her termination paperwork, get her things ready for her to collect, and to start the recruitment process for a replacement. Stormed off shouting all sorts of profanities. It was awful! We just don't behave like that here, but then I always did say she was a bad egg.' Jennifer scowled.

Ward cut her off before she could continue. 'Do you know why she was fired?'

'Well, no, that's between her and Robert, but...' She leaned closer, over her desk, looking up at Ward, and whispered, 'it's not the first time we've had a spurned woman storm out, if you catch my drift.' She sat back and nodded knowingly.

'You're insinuating they had a relationship outside work?'

'And inside work.' Jennifer shuddered.

Yikes. He wasn't subtle, then. He wanted to ask more, but it would be pure speculation from the receptionist as to the nature of Robert and Claire's relationship. The best gossip was only lightly sprinkled with the truth after all.

'Charming. If I can have her contact details, that would be very helpful, thanks. If Robert was in work on Sunday morning, I don't suppose you know what time he left, and what his plans for the day were?'

Jennifer shook her head. 'Oh no. That was Claire's job—his schedule, I mean. She knew everything. He worked every Sunday from nine 'til twelve. I don't know where he would have gone or what he'd do afterwards. I work til four, you see. Ten-four.' Jennifer sighed. 'Not how I'd fancy it, but we can't complain for Sunday pay—we get time and a half.'

She trailed off, and her face paled. 'I didn't even think, when he walked out...I didn't even think that would be it.' Her face crumpled, and a sob escaped. She clapped a hand to her mouth and turned away, her shoulders trembling.

'Just can't believe it,' she said, her voice muffled and thick with tears. 'Do you think Claire had something to do with it?' She looked up at Ward again, tears glistening behind her glasses.

Ward bit back an impatient huff. *Just give me the bloody files already, woman.* 'I can't comment on an ongoing investigation. As Robert's assistant, who knows his schedule, she might be able to help us. I can't say any more than that.'

'Yes, of course,' sniffed Jennifer. 'She was terminated, so I removed her work systems access myself on Sunday afternoon—security reasons, you know—but I don't have access to Robert's diary. Perhaps Claire will know what he was doing.'

'Thank you. I have to be off now,' prompted Ward.

At last, she printed off an A4 sheet of paper with a grainy, greyscale photo of a woman on it, Claire Parker, and her details.

CHAPTER SIXTEEN

Detective Sergeant Emma Nowak had already learned there were few things she wouldn't encounter on the job. From oddities to aberrations, and the unusual to the downright bonkers, DS Nowak had discovered many colourful sides of humanity already in her time on the force. But this one was a new one.

'Hello Mrs Hodgson, please can you explain why you made and burned an effigy of Robert Craven?' she murmured to herself as she drove to Skipton to meet the very woman. Nope, no matter how she phrased it, she couldn't find a way to say it that didn't sound, frankly, crazy. She sighed. 'Never a dull day.'

It had instantly piqued her interest, seeing the picture of a very self-righteous looking woman standing before a burning pyre, her arms crossed, glaring into the camera, on one of Eliza Pullman's articles. Such a length to go to—but why?

She was genuinely curious on this one. Making and

burning an effigy of someone took anger, and a lot of it. At least she didn't have a nutter with a shotgun to deal with, like DC Patterson. Just possibly a pyromaniac. Ordinarily, she might have been unnerved, but with that comparison, frankly, she felt like she'd got the better deal of the two of them. It had been a good call to leg it out of the office before Ward could land her with the shit job. He'd seen straight through her. His text had called her out—and told her she'd dumped the DC in it. Nowak chuckled darkly. No regrets.

Nowak pulled into the new build estate—now three years old—jolting uncomfortably as she left the tarmac of the main road onto the rough surface. She drove around the raised grates, and eyed the lack of streetlights. It was in a poor state, alright—a stark contrast to the seemly houses and landscaped gardens of the estate, which stood in proud relief.

'Fair play,' Nowak muttered. If she'd lived there, she'd be pissed off buying a house without a tarmacked road and streetlights three years down the line too.

She pulled up by the house listed as Frances Hodgson's. Immediately, she noticed that all the curtains and blinds were drawn. A single car sat on the double driveway, backed right up to a garage door. Nowak eased out and went to the porch—locked. She rang the bell and knocked, her fist rapping sharply on the glass, the sound carrying across the street.

Inside the porch, as she peered in, she could see post littering the tiled floor. Nowak chewed the inside of her cheek. *Are they away?*

She glanced up and down the road. There were a few cars dotted about—she supposed, it was the middle of the working week too, which wouldn't help. People wouldn't be sat at home waiting for her to call.

Across the street, a door slammed.

Nowak turned. A woman with a baby in her arms and loaded down with bags, chivvied a toddler towards the car on the driveway, looking drawn and harassed.

'No, Archie, we're going to the shop. Come on.'

'I. WANT. PEPPA!' screeched the toddler, and plonked himself on the sodden grass.

The woman raised her eyes skyward and murmured something Nowak couldn't hear.

Well, it wasn't ideal, but it was better than a closed-up house. 'Hello?' Nowak said, and crossed the street. 'Sorry to bother you.'

Just as the toddler full-on threw himself into a flowerbed for the mother of all tantrums.

The woman turned a baleful glance upon her. One of the "I-don't-have-the-capacity-to-deal-with-anything-else-on-my-plate-today" looks.

Oh, balls. Nowak fished out her car keys, complete with the ridiculous pink pompom her mum had gotten her for the previous Christmas, complete with googly eyes.

Nowak smiled, trying to disarm the mother, who looked on the brink of tears. The woman turned away to wrestle the baby into a car seat in the back of the car, ignoring the toddler for a second as she at least got one child strapped in.

Nowak unclipped the googly-eyed pompom. 'Look!' she said brightly, crouching next to the child. 'What's this?' She shook the pompom at the bairn, sending its eyes all agog. It was hard to be heard over the toddlers insistent screeching. She dangled it closer.

The toddler paused, mid-tantrum.

Eyes locked upon that offering.

A hand darted out to snatch the pompom.

'There we go. Isn't that cool?' murmured Nowak.

The mother turned back, having got the baby strapped in without fuss.

'Sorry,' Nowak said quickly. 'I didn't mean to interrupt. I have a niece the same age—they can be feisty!'

'That isn't the half of it,' the woman said tiredly. 'Thanks. It's been one of *those* mornings, but if I don't get to the shops now, we have nothing for tea, and I won't have another chance to get out.'

'I'll be quick then, sorry. I need to speak to Frances Hodgson across the street. I don't suppose you know where she is, or have any contact details for her?'

'They're on holiday.' As she spoke, the woman opened the boot, dumping bags inside atop a folded pram.

Nowak's stomach fell. 'When did they go away?'

'About a week ago. They're not back for another week.'

Nowak mentally calculated the days. *Damn.* That put Frances Hodgson too far away to ask any questions—and out of contention as a suspect due to the timing of her vacation. Nowak had been hedging her bets on this one, she realised. If someone were willing to burn an effigy...well, murder wasn't implausible. 'Do you know where to?'

'Spain, somewhere. Sorry, I don't know anymore. I really have to go.'

Nowak flipped out her warrant card, and stood, leaving the toddler sat happily on the wet grass, playing with the pink fluffy abomination. 'Just a minute, if you don't mind. No one's in trouble. I just have some questions. I don't suppose you know anything about an incident with burning an effigy last year, do you?'

The woman's eyes widened. 'No one's in trouble?'

'Absolutely not. Just looking for some background information.'

'Yes, I know about that.'

'Am I correct in understanding Frances Hodgson made that?'

The woman looked at her quizzically, and scooped the diffused bomb/toddler off the grass, patting down his soggy bottom. 'Oh, she wanted to take all the credit—you're *sure* no one's in trouble?'

'Not a bit.'

The woman rolled her eyes, bouncing the toddler on her hip. 'Alright then. It's so *Frances*. The world revolves around her, you know. She took centre stage for that, but it was a community affair. We all helped out—and enjoyed the bonfire. I made one of the arms for her. Quite proud I was too—it had five fingers and everything.'

She gestured to the street. 'In case you haven't noticed, it's a mess. We bought our forever homes, and

Robert Craven shafted us all. It was a PR stunt meant to get some attention on the matter, but even then, nothing happened. The company gave some nice-sounding rubbish, some builders came and looked busy for a couple days, but nothing's changed since.'

Right. So everyone here probably hates Robert Craven then. Just what we need—more people to add to the queue.

Frances organised it, roped us all in, and she was happy to get the limelight too. She said we were "making a stand" and we were going to show him he couldn't walk all over us. Most of us didn't care, to be honest, as long as it helped. She did a good job, I'll give her that. We even had BBC Look North here. We just wish it had worked. Now, we're just back to waiting and hoping. We just want what we've already paid for.'

The woman gave an exasperated huff, and turned back to the car to strap the toddler in—the young boy still waving the pompom monster happily.

'Come on now, Archie, we have to give that back.'

'NO!' snapped the toddler, glaring at her and yanking his hand away.

'Give me strength,' muttered his mother. She whipped out her phone, and a few seconds later, the theme tune for Peppa Pig cheerfully blared out.

The toddler's attention immediately swivelled to the phone. His mother deftly swapped it with the pompom and shut the car door.

'Thanks,' she said, handing it back to Nowak.

'Anytime. It's the small things, isn't it?' Nowak grinned.

The woman just smiled faintly and stepped back. 'Do you need anything else? I have to go.'

'That's all, thanks. Appreciate your time. Good luck.' Nowak chuckled.

She headed back to her car, sparing one more thoughtful glance at the deserted Hodgson property. She'd find no answers there, it seemed—not to the questions she still had about what and why Frances Hodgson had done what she had done. But that was more personal curiosity than professional. At least she had the answer she truly needed.

Frances Hodgson hadn't even been in the country when Robert Craven had been murdered.

One down, and one to go.

Next on Nowak's list to investigate was one Eliza Pullman, mistress of the bitter pen.

CHAPTER SEVENTEEN

TUESDAY AFTERNOON

C laire Parker wasn't too far down the valley from Skipton, in the village of Steeton, across the valley from Silsden. Ward pulled off the street into the converted mill development, where Claire Parker lived, apparently in one of the new-build townhouses beside the mill, according to the address.

Ward wasted no time, even though his stomach was growling. It was almost lunchtime, but somehow, his meagre breakfast seemed an age ago, and he was dying for a good brew. Ward wasn't sure what kind of welcome he'd be getting here, given that he was off to speak to a spurned and fired woman. He doubted he'd be offered anything. *Better make this quick and off I go.*

At a sharp rap, she answered. The match of the photo, though paler, drawn, and with red-rimmed eyes, Claire Parker stood in the doorway.

'Detective Inspector Ward. May I come inside? I

have a few questions about an incident we're investigating.'

'Is this about Robert?' she said, folding her arms around herself and squeezing to the side to let him pass, before she closed and locked the door behind him. 'I heard from work. Is it true? He's...?' She gaped, her mouth opening and closing, but no sound emerging. She couldn't bear to say it. *Dead*.

'It is.' He glanced pointedly around. She invited him further in, taking him to a sitting room upstairs, and perched on the arm of a sofa, gesturing for him to sit down. It was a minimal space, decorated with soft, light colours, family photos decorating the walls. Happy, smiling faces—Claire, a man, and two children in various stages of aging up to about ten—decorated the walls.

Ward lowered himself into a chair, his back turned to the closed Juliet balcony doors that overlooked moody autumn hills crisscrossed by dry stone walls outside. 'As you possibly know, Mr Robert Craven was found dead on Monday morning. At this time, we are treating his death as unexplained, and are conducting further enquiries. As his PA—'

'Executive PA,' she shot at him, before clamping her lips shut—as though it were a reflexive correction that slipped out unbidden. She straightened a little with it, before slumping again.

'*Executive* PA,' Ward corrected—not like it bloody mattered—and continued, 'we're hoping that you might have some information that's helpful.'

Claire nodded, and folded her arms, fiddling with the

hem of her creamy jumper. Ward examined her surreptitiously. With bleach-blonde shoulder-length hair, a solid line of roots showing, and wearing grief as her makeup, she looked older and more tired than her years. The jumper did nothing to accentuate her short, full figure, nor the slightly too small skinny jeans that seemed to be in vogue everywhere these days. Still—he saw a normal woman, a grieving one, not a hot-headed nuisance causing havoc as she had charged out of the office the previous Sunday.

'I appreciate this might be very difficult for you, and I appreciate your help. Do you happen to know what time Mr Craven left the office on Sunday?'

'I don't, sorry. I left just before. He normally goes about twelve.'

'Do you know any particular plans of his, this Sunday afternoon just gone?'

Claire shook her head and swallowed. She produced a tissue from up her sleeve and blew her nose noisily. 'No, sorry.'

'You mentioned that you'd left before Robert, is that normal?'

'No. Normally we finish around the same time, or I work later.'

'But on Sunday you finished earlier, why is that?'

'I just left early.' Her tone grew shorter, more hostile.

'See, I heard that you were fired that day and asked not to return, with immediate effect.'

'What?' She glanced up at him, wide-eyed, the picture of innocence. 'That's not true. Who said that?'

'Were or were you not terminated on Sunday, after which you immediately left the premises?'

Claire coloured. 'No. I mean, I did leave, and we fell out, but no, not that.'

'Can you explain, then?'

Claire cleared her throat. Twisting the tissue in her hands, it was already beginning to disintegrate. 'He was in a foul mood. There was an event on Saturday night—a celebration for the company, for him, at Harewood House. It was going perfectly, but then that horrid girl from the paper showed up, started pestering Robert. Eliza whatever she's called. Saying the most awful things! On Sunday, her article was one of the first things he saw...'

'You were with him, at Harewood?' Ward interrupted.

'Oh, yes.' Claire looked away and cleared her throat. Ward saw the avoidance—what she didn't want to admit. That her relationship with Robert Craven was more than professional. 'I go everywhere with him. He was in a *foul* mood after seeing that. We came straight back to the office—'

'Together?'

Claire frowned at him, as though annoyed by his interruption. 'Yes. And then, it was damage control, trying to get the editor to pull the article, making sure competitors had favourable content out there, reducing the traffic and footprint of the awful thing—that sort of thing.'

'You did that, or him?'

'Both of us. I help in the practical sense, he pulls the

strings—he's very well connected, you know.' She sounded almost proud of that, he noted.

'But by all accounts, things became heated—other staff report that you stormed out, that you were very angry, shouting, and the like.'

Claire's face tightened, and she folded her arms again.

Her sleeve rode up and Ward saw a purple bruise around her wrist, beginning to yellow around the edge, as though already a couple of days old.

'It didn't go well. He gets so angry. I tried to calm him down, but...' Her voice caught, and she trailed off.

'But?' Ward prompted quietly.

'He was awful,' she whispered. She rubbed her wrist unconsciously, but Ward saw the movement. 'I tried to calm him, but he wasn't having any of it. Shouting all sorts at me, slagging me off, a real slanging match. He threw me out—I mean, verbally, not actually. I left. I was so angry and so hurt too, I knew that he wasn't going to calm down then, and certainly not with my help.'

'How did that make you feel?'

'How do you think?' Claire glanced up at Ward, her eyes brimming with tears. 'I was mortified! The whole office heard. I was so embarrassed, I just wanted to get out of there.'

'You haven't been back since?'

'No. I was hurt, embarrassed, honestly, a little angry too. I didn't deserve to be treated like that. I thought I'd stay off yesterday, see how he liked it, having no one to run around for him all day, then this morning, I heard.'

Tears spilled over, and she wiped them hurriedly away with the back of a hand.

'Are you alright? Do you need a moment?'

'I'm fine,' she said between sobs.

'Alright. So you're certain he hadn't fired you, then?'

'No,' she said after a moment of hesitation. 'He occasionally loses his rag so far he says awful things like that, but he's never meant it. He always begged for me back—can't cope without me there.' She gave a weak smile through a haze of tears.

'I see that you have a bruise on your wrist. Did Robert do that?'

'W-what?' Claire glanced down, and covered it with her hand self-consciously. 'No. I...fell.'

'Sure about that? I know it can be hard, but you don't need to suffer if you're a victim of an assault.'

'No,' Claire said sharply. 'It's not like that. No.'

'Alright.' Ward eased back, giving her a few moments of respite as he scrawled in his pocket book. 'I have to ask about the nature of your relationship with Mr Craven, Claire.'

'I'm his Executive Personal Assistant,' she said automatically.

'Of course—but I mean the relationship you had outside the office?'

'We didn't.'

'Your relationship was strictly professional?'

'Yes,' she said at once. 'I'm married. I have two kids.'

That means nothing, these days.

Ward rattled off a phone number. 'Is this your phone number?'

Her brow furrowed, not following the sudden change of tack. 'Yes, why?'

Ward's lips thinned. 'I understand it's not pleasant to have your life aired out to strangers, and it's not my intention to pry, but I hope you understand we have to build a picture of Robert's life to investigate how he died. We know about the messages between the two of you, Claire. We know that you were having an affair.'

Claire paled, silent, as she looked at him, stunned. And then she stuttered into life, blooming red. 'Fine. Fine! Yes, ok, we are, we did, we have...*that*. It's not what you think! Robert was divorcing, and my marriage...' She shook her head. 'It's a mess.'

'Does your husband know about Robert—the affair, and his death, the difficulties you had at work this Sunday?' Ward asked carefully, his mind alight.

Claire had given such a different version of events to the receptionist—and only her and Robert truly knew the truth, he supposed, but still. The receptionist had clearly stated she was terminated personally by Robert, and he'd ordered Jennifer herself to gather Claire's things and begin the recruiting process for a replacement.

Claire would have been upset, but she had admitted to being angry too—angry enough to kill? Especially if it were true, that Claire had been fired, and possibly personally spurned too by Robert.

Hell hath no fury like a woman scorned, and all that.

If the husband knows, he'd be pretty pissed off, to say the least too. Angry enough to seek revenge, perhaps.

'Yes,' she eventually admitted.

Ward stilled. 'Tell me about that.'

Claire coloured, and she dropped her gaze to the floor, clearly ashamed. 'He saw the messages on my phone. About six months ago. I tried to end it with Robert, but...I was too weak, and he's not the kind of man you can say no to.'

'And how did your husband feel about that?'

'Furious, obviously. We've not been in a great place for a few years. Since Benjamin came along, really. We just coexist, I guess. Robert made me feel special again, like I hadn't done in years. I supposed, if Niel didn't care, then what did it matter?'

'What happened when Niel found out.'

'We argued. A lot. But he wasn't willing to forgive or forget and I don't make enough to support the boys by myself. I stayed because I didn't know what else I could do.'

'It sounds like that would be quite difficult.'

'I hate it,' she spat out, and her eyes glistened with fresh tears. 'I just wish there was a way out. We've been talking about divorce, but it's so expensive, and we can't agree on who owns what, we're both so angry and bitter about it all, we're just not getting anywhere. Then the boys are in school, all settled.' Her voice cracked with the strain of it and Ward wondered if that was how she'd felt too—cracking, under the strain of living two different lives. One of drudgery and indifference and bitterness... the other of a fantasy escape.

'Was Niel angry with Robert?'

Claire nodded and swallowed. 'He confronted Robert. It didn't go down well. Nothing happened. It didn't come to blows or anything. I begged them to leave it.'

'And did they?'

'Ha. Robert didn't care. Niel was nobody to him. He could have whatever, whoever he liked, he thought.'

'And Niel?'

'He was furious. Said Robert was just using me, that he was happy to wreck our marriage and that he didn't really care...Neil was furious that I'd broken our vows, and with Robert of all people. I think Niel felt small, second-best next to him. Even though he didn't want me anymore...and he hadn't for a long time...he didn't want anyone else to have me either.'

It was a damning comment. He'd never met the man, but already, Ward had in his mind's eye a picture of a jealous and bitter man who might stretch to extraordinary lengths to get Robert Craven to back off his wife.

'Did Niel know where you were on Saturday night?'

'A work event, of course.'

'Did he know that you spent the night *with* Robert Craven after the event?' It was a guess, not a fact, but by the way she coloured, now beetroot, it was the truth.

'Not for certain, but I'm sure he guessed.' He could hear the burning shame in her voice at it all.

The door downstairs opened and slammed shut.

'Shit,' Claire cursed quietly, jumping to her feet. She mopped at her ruined face in a fruitless attempt to disguise her tears, but her eyes were red-raw.

A man strode in, hard-faced, and halted dead in his tracks when he saw Ward.

'Who the hell are you?' He turned on Claire with a snarl, his assumption clear—another mark of Claire's infidelity.

Ward held up his warrant card and stood, towering over the thin man by half a foot—the man thought again. 'Detective Inspector Daniel Ward. Mr Parker, I presume?'

Caught off guard, the man's mouth flapped for a second. 'Uh, yeah. What's going on?' he glanced between Ward and his wife.

'I'm led to believe you know about your wife's boss's death already?' Ward said gravely.

'Yeah, I know about that. Knobhead probably had it coming to him.' A smug, dark smile passed across Niel Parker's face. Victory and loss all in one. Ward could imagine exactly why Niel felt like that—the feeling that he had triumphed against a rival...and the great and bitter personal cost that it had come at.

'Niel!' Claire said, but her husband cut her off with a glare.

'I have to ask,' Ward said quietly. 'Where were you both on Sunday afternoon between twelve and eight?'

Niel glared at Claire. 'We were here, arguing,' Niel said, 'about Robert himself, as it happens, and the fact that for some stupid fucking reason, you throw yourself at him like a common slut, make me look like a complete mug, treat the kids like you can pick them up and put them down when it suits you and *him*.' Every word he fired at her was filled with scathing venom.

Claire bloomed red and retreated onto the sofa arm.

'We were here arguing about the shit state of our marriage thanks to you,' he directed at Claire, 'and frigging Robert Craven, which isn't how I'd planned to spend my Sunday afternoon whilst the kids were at your mum's!'

'I'm sorry, alright!' Claire burst out, angry tears streaming down her cheeks. 'I don't know how many times I have to say it!'

Niel's voice rose as he responded, 'Yeah, well, what you say and what you do are two different fucking things, so maybe that's why I'm not buying it!'

'Alright, alright, calm down,' Ward said, stepping between them and holding up his hands. 'I understand this isn't easy for you, and the last thing you want is some stranger coming and stirring up trouble for you. If there's anything else either of you could tell me that might help with our investigation, then here's my number.' He held out a card. 'Call me anytime, night or day.'

Robert's death was a crime of passion, alright, and in the past half an hour, it seemed Ward had two more likely suspects to add to the list.

CHAPTER EIGHTEEN

T he fog was just lifting on that side of the hills as Nowak drove up the A65 to Settle, a small town under the brooding peak of Pen-y-Ghent, one of York-shire's famous Three Peaks. It was dark and foreboding that day, with hardly any light seeping into the valley—this far out in the sticks, without the ambient orange glow of the city lights, it seemed like where dawn ended, dusk began in the autumn and winter. Perhaps, Nowak wondered, it was where the saying "It's grim up North" came from.

Even so, Settle was a pretty place, she thought, as she pulled off the main street. One she did not often get to visit. Eliza Pullman had brought the DS there. As the author of so many inflammatory articles against Robert Craven and his business practices writing for the Dales Gazette, they had to talk to her—just in case it had spilled over into anything more sinister in nature.

Nowak had already Googled Miss Pullman. She'd

read some of Eliza's heated articles too. Scathing vitriol from an educated and fairly eloquent young woman. She could hardly imagine the slight young thing taking out Robert Craven...but good police work was never based on assumption.

The woman had priors, after all—a personal assault and multiple trespassing on her criminal record. Robert Craven himself had even attempted to take out a restraining order on Miss Pullman, although it had been unsuccessful.

Nowak had to wonder what had caused that. For Mr Craven to have been so bothered by Eliza Pullman, she had to have done something terrible. Just what on Earth was it? Nowak couldn't imagine how a young woman like Eliza Pullman could have ruffled the powerful Robert Craven—but she planned to find out.

If nothing else, Nowak got a nice jaunt out for the morning—an easy job of sorts. Much better than poor Constable Patterson and the madman with the shotgun. She'd drawn the long straw on that one, thank goodness. Nowak chuckled to herself as she pulled up. The lane was exceedingly narrow but there was just enough room for her Mini to squidge against the unforgiving grey stone covered in sharp, scratchy briars, and still leave some passing room.

Nowak eased out of the car, shut the door, and folded in the wing mirror. She glanced around. Up here, at the top of the village, the buildings ended and the hills simply began. Craggy stone towered over the settlement. Beautiful hiking country that Nowak longed to visit more often—except she always seemed to be working or wedding planning these days.

Nowak sighed and crossed the lane. A small stone yard had a Nissan Micra parked there—the only car that would fit on such a small plot at the corner of the two narrow lanes.

In all honesty, it was such a minuscule house, Nowak didn't quite know who would have been able to live inside the tiny bungalow. *And I thought that Saltaire houses were tiny...*

Flowers—geraniums and clematis—climbed up the exterior, dying off for autumn now, but brightly painted on a small plaque bearing the house name, *The Old Brewhouse*. Nowak approached the dove-grey painted door, and lifted her hand to the brass knocker.

The door flew open before she could reach it.

'Ah!' Nowak said, recognising the flame-haired young woman. 'Eliza Pullman? Police—' Before Nowak could say another word, time seemed to stall. Abject fear flashed over Eliza Pullman's face. And she bolted.

Eliza shoved past Nowak. Instinctively, Nowak latched onto the woman's jacket, tugging her back, both their weights braced against each other as Eliza struggled to escape and Nowak inexorably pulled her closer. Eliza wriggled, throwing Nowak off balance, and shrugged off her jacket. With her fist wound into the puffy fabric, it was all Nowak was left holding. Tugging with all her might—against nothing.

Nowak exclaimed as she reeled, falling onto the Micra and bouncing off onto the hard stone flags.

Winded, she scrambled to her feet with a strangled curse and gave chase. But Eliza was gone. Far ahead, Nowak saw that fiery hair vanish over a dry-stone wall into dark woodland that extinguished the brightness of Eliza's hair as though it was a flame snuffed out.

'Bollocks!' Nowak spat, one of her Irish mammy's favourite curses that she seemed to have unconsciously inherited as a reflexive response. She sprinted up the lane and vaulted up onto the wall, her hip smarting from the impact with the ground—and her pride smarting, too.

Gone.

Distant crashing through the woodland told her Eliza was already far ahead. Nowak would be hard-pushed to find her at all.

So much for getting the easy one.

Smarting, Nowak stomped back to her car to make the humiliating calls. She'd have to ask Ward to authorise an alert on the PNC, and ANPR in case she returned to take the car, plus a mobile trace though...Nowak looked around.

There were more trees than cell towers out here in the sticks of the Dales. More sheep than CCTV cameras. It was practically hopeless, she had to admit. There was not the abundance of surveillance techniques out in the Dales as there were in the cities.

They were blessed really, as far as policing went in Bradford. One couldn't move for being caught on a camera of some kind. Cell towers were so plentiful triangulation was a relative doddle. Number plate recognition was easy peasy. And the fact that the city was crawling with coppers. Out there in the hills, she was probably the only DS in a twenty-mile radius.

Nowak considered whether she ought to wait—but what would be the point? They'd done no surveillance on Eliza. They didn't know the first thing about her life— and therefore, her movements and haunts. If she was smart, she'd run, and keep running, or hide until Nowak had gone. She wouldn't be stupid enough to emerge and walk straight into Nowak's waiting hands, Nowak reasoned. Sometimes, DS Nowak wished it were so easy, though she knew she'd be bored if that were the case.

Why did she run? Nowak wondered next, leaning back in the seat. Running meant one thing usually— something to hide. Nowak had checked Eliza's record. Flawless except for those few misdemeanours a few years back. Without incidents in the past few years, perhaps Miss Pullman was a changed woman? Or, Nowak considered, perhaps tigers didn't change their stripes.

She'd been done for vandalism, graffiti, and antisocial behaviour. Nowak had been surprised by it all, not expecting it from someone who had what appeared to be a longstanding job at the newspaper, or someone who came from the Dales where folk were still raised with decent values.

Nowak waited in her car, just on the off-chance Pullman was daft enough to come running right back. She flicked through the material on Pullman she'd pulled but not had a chance to dig into, having not expected Pullman to be quite so colourful.

Much of it was connected to Robert Craven, though

that had been less surprising given the articles Pullman wrote directed at him and his company. She'd chained herself to their gates to halt building work, camped on a building site to protest against ecological destruction, and even managed to get local TV coverage for the latter, where she'd stayed for thirty-one days before being forcibly evicted.

Nowak's eyebrows rose with every fresh word she read. So, Eliza Pullman was some kind of environmental activist. Definitely not someone who would see eye to eye with Craven, a developer and profiteer through and through.

The thread running through all of Eliza Pullman's work at the paper and her criminal record was one of protectiveness towards the Dales. Nowak wondered if she, like so few of her age, saw herself as the next generation of the Dales, of its rich landscape and history. Fleeing implied Eliza Pullman had done something wrong. Would the young woman protect her home...at any cost? Would she stretch to murder?

The DS chewed her lip as she contemplated it. Eliza had been wiry, strong for her build, but...not enough to take on the likes of Robert Craven, surely? Still, Nowak had seen plenty of bar fights gone wrong already in the CID field. One hit in slightly the wrong place could kill, regardless of strength. One fall and bump to the head. She shivered. Life was too precarious when she thought about it.

On a whim, she glanced over to the cottage. The dove-grey door seemed closed, but Nowak could see it gently swaying in the breeze, bumping shut. Nowak's curiosity piqued. If the door was open...it would be dodgy, she knew, without a warrant, but it wasn't as though she was breaking and entering...*maybe* she would tell herself she was securing the property and potential evidence. Nowak wasn't sure it would fly with DI Ward.

Before she could chicken out, she stepped out of the car, crossed the narrow lane, and slipped inside.

It was cool and dim inside the small cottage. An aged emerald sofa jammed up against a small wooden table with two chairs rammed right under it for lack of room. They squidged up against a tiny kitchen counter that looked as if it dated from the seventies by the finish on the cupboard doors that was now so old, it was probably in vogue again.

It was clean but messy, with handmade ornaments on shelves and woven textiles hanging from the walls, making the small space feel dark and homely—with a touch of claustrophobia too, for Nowak. The pitched ceiling gave some volume, but the low-set narrow windows in the walls made her slightly breathless. She'd never been good in small spaces, especially cluttered dark ones.

Letters, opened and unopened, with paperwork and handwritten sheets littered the lumpy velvet sofa. Nowak shifted the papers to glance through a few. Some of them seemed to be article drafts, red pen angrily dashed across them where Eliza had edited her words. Nowak read a sample.

It was violent stuff, hateful vitriol—the black pen

scribbled out by red. Edits written beside. Calmer, more palatable. Printable, perhaps, given what she'd seen already in the paper. How they were getting away with it without being done for libel was beyond Nowak. Some of the articles she'd seen were nasty.

An open notebook caught DS Nowak's eye. One of the *Paperblanks* brand that she herself loved—she'd bought one from Salts Mill just down the road from her in Saltaire last year to keep a gratitude journal in. Not that she remembered, nine days out of ten.

Nowak flicked through it. Not intending to read it— realising quickly that it was Eliza's diary. Respect warred with professional curiosity as she saw Robert Craven's name in there more than once, written in the same rounded hand as everything else.

She really despises Robert Craven. What's she got against him? Surely building houses on some fields was bad, but didn't warrant this level of hatred.

Nowak stilled as she turned another page and read the worst entry yet. She took a photo of the page for evidence. And called it in. Warrant or not, she needed to arrest Eliza Pullman—immediately.

CHAPTER NINETEEN

Nowak had put out a call for Eliza Pullman's immediate arrest on the basis of what she'd seen in the young woman's diary. The rest of the small cottage —a tiny bedroom and an even smaller shower room and toilet—had made for quick searching. Nothing that stood out amongst a young woman's typical possessions.

Then, she had left, closing the door behind her until the latch clicked into place. Eliza Pullman had still not returned. Nowak glanced up the lane but nowhere could she see that flame-coloured hair signalling a watcher from the woods.

Settle's police station was her next port of call. It was a tiny converted stable block attached to the former police station, that wasn't even open all the time.

Irked, she'd had to wait twenty minutes before the station could cobble together a response to meet her, so that Nowak could put them to task bringing Eliza Pullman in with urgency. But Nowak wasn't sure they understood the meaning of the word. It wasn't a city beat, after all.

Together, they trawled Settle, checking shops and public spaces. With the fog's lifting, a steady drizzle had started, dampening Nowak's already sour mood—and yet still, Eliza did not appear.

Her temporary companion, one PC Tony Braeburn, knew Eliza personally, it turned out—though Nowak oughtn't to have been surprised. In such a small place and tight-knit community, it was one of those places where everyone knew everyone. By all accounts, Eliza was a farmer's daughter and experienced hiker who'd grown up half-wild on the moors and who knew those parts like the back of her hand.

Nowak left Braeburn to it, with strict instructions to find and arrest her urgently, whilst she visited the family farm just up the valley to see if Eliza had headed there.

It was to no avail. By the time Nowak arrived, to be greeted by Pullman's mother, much to Nowak's annoyance, Eliza had come and gone, with no word as to where she headed or when she'd be back.

Nowak hated to admit it.

Pullman had gone to ground.

The diary entry she had read and sent back to Ward lingered in her mind. They needed to find Eliza Pullman to explain herself.

But they wouldn't. Not until she wanted to be found.

Nowak had to call it a day—and she begrudged giving up. She groaned to herself. 'Maybe I should have volunteered to take the nutter with the shotgun.'

CHAPTER TWENTY

W ard reached Trafalgar House—Bradford South Police Station—just as the press release went out that morning. It was the top news story on the radio as he pulled into the station car park, but only a basic statement had been given.

'West Yorkshire Police issued a statement to say they are following several active lines of enquiry at this time, and at present, are treating Mr Craven's death as unexplained. Robert Craven was a local property tycoon who built his empire from nothing, to become one of the county's most successful entrepreneurs. Just last year, he funded renovation of Leeds City Council's chamber as a gift of thanks to the people of the city.'

Ward snorted. As a bribe, more like. From what Claire had said, Robert knew how to grease the wheels to ensure the company mission prospered. People in high places, and all that. It wasn't what you knew, after all, but who. He thought of DSU Diane McIntyre's personal connection to the family. A small part of him wondered—and hoped—it was strictly above board.

'A vigil will be held at the company offices in Skipton this Friday at twelve pm for all mourners wishing to pay their respects.'

The radio was silenced as Ward turned off the car. He was on a mid-shift that day, so he'd enjoyed a much-needed lie in. Until Oliver had demanded a walk, anyway. And then Nowak had phoned. Eliza Pullman had slunk back home at last early that morning—right into the police's waiting arms. She was en route to Bradford South Police Station, arrested and ready to interview.

Ward didn't know what to believe—they had three, possibly four, compelling involved parties, all with plausible guilt from their aggrieved connections with Mr Robert Craven. Miranda Craven. Eliza Pullman. Claire Parker. Niel Parker. All running from something—but was it murder?

Ward entered the busy station and headed upstairs for HMET's shared office, stopping by the canteen on the way. Entirely unsurprisingly, Metcalfe was already there, selecting a plate of biscuits from the offerings.

'I see Marie's given up on the diet, then?'

Scott jumped and turned at the unexpected interruption. 'You what? Er, yes, no, maybe.' He looked sheepish.

Ward sniggered.

'Shut it,' grumbled Metcalfe. 'The least you can do is be a willing accomplice. Makes me look less bad.'

'Oh, go on then.' Ward sauntered over and swiped

the lone chocolate bourbon off the top of the pile—
Metcalfe's favourite going by the disappointing look—off
the top, stuffing it whole into his mouth before DS
Metcalfe could stop him.

Metcalfe squawked in outrage.

Ward laughed. 'Should'a been more specific, mate.'
Ward flicked on the kettle and started making them both
a brew. He needed a good one after the morning he'd had
—and the messages he'd just listened to and seen from
Nowak. Christ, what on Earth had they gotten into with
this case? 'Any updates?'

Metcalfe sighed and munched his way through a rich
tea before he replied. 'Aye. I've spoken to the commercial
tenants in Skipton. A right mithering bunch, if y'ask me.
You Yorkshire folk can't half moan.'

'Only 'cause we have to put up with you Lancs arse-
holes for neighbours,' Ward said with a wink.

'Hmmph. Well, nothing there, I reckon. They didn't
have any contact with Robert—none of them had even
met him. All their contracts and issues are negotiated
directly with an appointed rep at the company. Not for
lack of trying, by the sounds of it—they wanted to speak
to him and wanted him to engage, but he wouldn't. The
company handled everything. The only common thing I
found from them all is they all bloody despised the man,
and none of 'em are sorry to see the back end of him.'

'Charming,' Ward muttered. 'Nowak spent yesterday
chasing the Residents' Association woman in Skipton
and Eliza Pullman—interesting developments there to fill
the team in on, I think. Heard anything from Patterson?'

Like Nowak, Ward hadn't made it back to the office the previous day after doing the rounds chasing leads.

A dirty, dark chuckle escaped from Metcalfe and he grinned, a mischievous twinkle in his eye. 'Oh, Patterson came back alright, and if he had any balls, I reckon he'd be shoving that job down your throat, mate.'

'It didn't go well?' Ward said lightly as he stirred the teas. He hadn't received any urgent phone calls, so Jake was alive and well. Hadn't had his head blown off by a shotgun or anything daft.

'The way he tells it, he fought the man single-handedly. The way I hear it, the mad old bugger waved around his gun and our little friend shat his pants.'

'Oh, Christ. I've got to hear this one first-hand. Where is he?'

'Recovering in the loo, I think. Got another stress poo to get out.'

'Poor little love.' It must have been bad if Jake was suffering the next morning.

They shared a dark chuckle at Patterson's expense.

'Norris wants you, anyway, Daniel. He was hoping you'd be back—told us to collar you when we saw you.'

He stilled, spoon still mid-air. *Who's at whose beck and call?* Ward wondered, amused. Wasn't he supposed to be the boss?

'Where is he?' Ward dropped the teabags into the under-counter bin and gestured to Metcalfe's brew.

'Ta. Interview Room Three. Buried under it all. Says he has a development, and it can't wait. Something about SPF? Not sure what sun cream has to do with it.'

SPF. Slovak Police Force.

Ward's gut churned. 'Right. On it.' He dashed out.

Scott's holler brought him dashing back.

'Brew!'

Burning hot mug in hand, Ward legged it downstairs. What news did DC Norris and the Slovak Police Force have for their Varga investigation?

———

'Perfect timing, sir, I was just about to call her.' David Norris looked up from the laptop as Ward entered the interview room where the DC had holed up. He evidently had nowhere else to work since Varga's case-load had long ago enveloped his desk, and DS Chakrabarti still headed up the burglary task force in the Incident Room and board room on their floor.

'Call who?'

'Our contact in the Organised Crime Bureau of the SPF, sir. You asked me to set up a meeting—I did email the details half an hour ago but I know you've been on the road. The call's in five minutes, as it happens.'

Ward huffed a laugh. 'Couldn't be this punctual if I tried.'

David, wisely, didn't pass comment. 'I've been liaising with a woman in the OCB. As far as I can tell, her rank is somewhere from Sergeant, to maybe Inspector, by our scale, anyway.

'*Práporčík*, or *Prap.*, Marika Milanova has gained the authorisation of her senior officer to speak with us to discuss data pooling our caseloads on Varga and operating under a joint directive. Strictly speculative and confidential at this stage, with no guarantees, of course.'

'Of course.' Ward settled in beside David, who waited a minute, then hit the call button on his laptop. A video of the two of them sat side by side popped up. Ward tilted his face so that it didn't show quite such a horrendous "double chin and up the nose" angle.

David clicked approve, and the spinning wheel of doom rotated until another video screen popped up beside theirs.

Against a white background, a woman stared at them. Late thirties. Long black hair scraped into a ponytail. Tanned skin. Fine boned. And yet, intimidating with dark, inscrutable eyes was Ward's first impression of Prap. Milanova.

'Hello,' David offered first, with a quick smile. 'It's nice to finally see you in person, Prap. Milanova. This is our Senior Investigating Officer on the Varga caseload, Detective Inspector Daniel Ward.' He gestured to Ward, who inclined his head.

'Good afternoon, Detectives,' Milanova said, her expression entirely impassive, her voice tinged with a slight accent.

'Hi,' said Ward.

DC Norris cleared his throat. 'The purpose of today's call is really to introduce ourselves, and discuss our objectives and the possible ways we could collaborate on a case that's incredibly important to both our respective forces, with regards to the bureaucratic difficulties we face in doing so.'

'This call is to be confidential, yes?' Milanova said, narrowing her eyes.

'Yes, and on your end too?' Ward replied before Norris could. On instinct, he wasn't sure what it was, but she grated upon him. And besides which, he didn't trust her. She hadn't earned even a shred of that yet. 'I'm not trying to be rude, Prap. Milanova, but Varga is known to have eyes in the *kukláči*. How do we know we're not just feeding dear Bogdan all the intel we have on him through you?'

Milanova's lip curled. 'I can promise you I'm not Varga's. I could say the same for you.'

Ward scoffed. 'Hardly. I can assure you he has no foothold in my force.' Ward was certain of that at least. His face hardened, as did his tone. 'I lost a good man to him last year. DC Toby Saunders. He didn't deserve the end that Varga gave him. Not to mention the countless victims who have Varga to thank for so much misery, suffering, and death. I uncovered a lorry full of them last winter. All dead. In the worst way. He treats people worse than animals.

'Everywhere he goes, others pay the price, and I won't have it anymore. He and his toxic blight need exterminating from my city and I will make sure that happens,' Ward growled, glaring into the camera at Milanova.

Her reply was cuttingly quiet, every word razor sharp. 'You don't know the half of it, Inspector. I owe that man for what he's done to my city and my people. I'll see him pay for it, and you can get in line for whatever pieces of him are left.'

They shared a common goal, it seemed. He could see from the glint in her eye, hear from the fire in her tone, that she hated Varga as much as he did. 'Then it seems we have much to gain from working together.' He crossed his arms. 'Where shall we start?'

'Tell me what you're working on.'

Alright. He'd give her that and then see what he could get. 'BLS.'

A small smirk crossed her lips and she tilted her head to one side like a cat who had just sighted a mouse.

'You know what I refer to?'

'Oh yes,' she said smugly. 'We know *all* about that.'

'Then you'll probably know more about who owns and runs BLS than we do?'

'Perhaps,' she said lightly, offering nothing.

'The owner of BLS is related by marriage to Bogdan Varga. It's the brother-in-law of Varga's sister that owns and runs the firm. Correct?'

'Yes.'

'We wondered, is it complicity or coercion?' He watched for any response.

She considered her reply, pursing her lips. 'Both, depending on who you refer to. Varga's sister isn't involved. What Varga does isn't her business, but her husband and his brother, now, they're the connections. Her husband is one of Varga's right-hand men. His brother...' Milanova tipped her head from side to side. 'I'd say he's involved whether he wants to be or not. And these days, I think he is more the latter.'

'He's a weakness?'

'Yes. For us to exploit. For Varga to worry about. Whichever. But Varga's sister and her husband...they would never betray him. They would not be stupid enough to, and besides, they are his greatest allies. They have much to gain from him, after all.'

Ward snorted. Quite. Being at the top of a criminal empire had its financial perks. Whoever said "crime didn't pay" obviously wasn't doing a very good job of it.

'We have a growing list of all his business connections and assets relating to BLS, from vehicles, to cloned plates they run on, to those they employ from BLS to run the shadow-side of the business, and we're working on making international links, for example, to organisations on your side of the Channel.'

Ward raised an eyebrow. Such information was pivotal to understanding how it all hung together. 'How have you sourced all this?' He suspected the answer.

Milanova confirmed it. 'We have informants on the inside, and conduct a considerable amount of covert operations.'

'Yet you haven't been able to take him down?'

Milanova frowned. 'If nothing else, you should know how careful he is to cover his tracks. We usually end up with evidence against his accomplices and subordinates. Your lorry driver, for example. Manslaughter.' She let out a dry, bitter laugh. 'We know who the real guilty party is, but you didn't have enough on him...neither did we.'

'What are you hoping for? How can we get him?'

Milanova considered for a second. 'We need the pieces of the puzzle on your end. Perhaps then, if we have all the information, one of us might have enough to go after him.'

'Perhaps.'

Milanova smiled darkly, reflecting his own doubts back at him. '"Together, we are greater than the sum of our parts." Aristotle.'

'Here's hoping. Would you be able to supply intelligence to us on shipments to the UK?' If Milanova could spot which vehicles they needed to target, well, they could bring Varga's operation to its knees.

'Most definitely.' That vicious grin widened, and her pointed canines flashed in the camera's glare. 'Can you give us details of his assets in the United Kingdom so we can expand our portfolio on his business interests?'

Ward shared a triumphant smile with Norris. 'Of course.'

'Excellent. Together, we can cripple his shipping operation. If we can stop his supply chain, he'll be forced to move.'

'And if we have a complete picture of his assets, well, we can starve him of resources to freely do so.'

Milanova raised her chin. 'I think we shall be able to accomplish great things together, Inspector Ward.'

Ward mirrored her grin. The possibilities they had, working together, were far in excess of what he could do alone, working half-blind to all of Varga's doings. 'How quickly can you get me the vehicle data and shipping schedules?' he asked.

'Within a week. You?'

Ward looked to Norris.

'The same,' supplied Norris. 'I have detailed records of everything we're keeping tabs on with regards to Varga's assets, interests, and movements here.'

'Perfect,' purred Milanova.

Ward nodded. Now they had an accord. He could respect that. The overarching goal loomed overhead. Finally. At long damn last. He had a fighting chance. They all did.

We're taking Varga down.

CHAPTER TWENTY-ONE

D I Daniel Ward reeled after his conversation with Prap. Milanova, but as was the way with life in the HMET department, he was pulled to another case the moment he finished up.

He went straight in to interview Eliza Pullman with DS Nowak, who'd filled him in that morning over the phone on what she'd discovered about the young woman and her hatred of Robert Craven.

Ward was torn so far. Who *didn't* hate Robert Craven? It seemed no one had anything other than hatred for the man, except perhaps, his son James.

'I didn't do it,' Eliza said sullenly the moment they walked into the interview room. She was already waiting, her lean muscled arms folded. Partly slouched in the chair and turned away, as though she could deflect their attention. Her hair was greasy, braided in a long plait, and there was a faint odour of sweat hanging in the air.

Wherever she had gone, Eliza Pullman had run far and fast, it seemed.

Ward stared at her for a second until she turned her defiant glare to the floor. He took his seat opposite her in silence, as Nowak sat beside him. She'd be leading this interview—she had all the cards, after all. Nowak started the recording and reeled off the spiel to start the interview.

'Why are you here, Eliza?' Nowak began, her voice neutral.

'Because you think I killed Robert Craven,' Eliza said, her mouth drawing into a snarl. Under her folded arms, Ward saw a fist ball. She'd been fingerprinted on the way in, of course. Forensics would be trying to match her prints to anything at the scene of Robert's murder as they spoke to her now.

'Did you?'

'No!'

'Then why did you run, Eliza?'

'I didn't, I...panicked.'

'You assaulted a police officer to escape, Miss Pullman. You know that carries a heavy sentence, don't you?'

Eliza's ruddy complexion deepened. 'No! That wasn't what happened, I just, just—'

'How about we cut to the chase,' Nowak said, leaning forward, steepling her fingers as she rested both elbows on the scratched table. 'We cut out all the "I didn't do it" rubbish, because that's not going to get us anywhere. The fact of the matter is, you despised Robert Craven. That's fair to say, isn't it?'

Eliza nodded. 'Doesn't mean I killed him, though,' she shot back, unable to keep silent, her eyes darting between the two of them. Nowak's slight form. Ward's silent bulk. No doubt wondering why Ward was there, and who he was. Ward stared at her impassively and said nothing until she looked away.

'Indeed. But you had a campaign of hatred against the man—we've seen your criminal record, Miss Pullman. We know about the vandalism, the antisocial behaviour, even the restraining order that he tried to take out against you.'

Eliza's scowl deepened.

'We've read your articles—scathing, to say the least. They paint a picture of a young woman who would go out of her way in her vendetta against the man.'

Eliza said nothing, glaring sullenly at Nowak.

If looks could kill, Ward thought.

'Those alone would be enough to raise suspicion, but then we found this at your home address, Miss Pullman.'

Nowak, at her leisure, slowly slid a photo out of a file and across the table, rotating it to face Eliza. Both of them watched her like a hawk. Saw the flaring of her nostrils. The slight widening of her eyes—quickly hidden. The tightening in her mouth. And her entire body.

'Can you explain that to me, Eliza?' Nowak said evenly.

Silence.

'For the purpose of the tape, I am showing Eliza Pullman item reference seventeen-R-C-dash-two, obtained from her home address. Can you describe what this photograph shows, Miss Pullman?'

Eliza did not reply, but her attention was wholly focused on the photograph of the page from her journal. Depicting the dead body of Robert Craven with herself standing atop it, artfully illuminated in bright artist markers.

At her silence, Nowak described it instead, and continued, 'You wanted Robert Craven out of business. You wanted Robert Craven to suffer. Most of all, you wanted Robert Craven dead, didn't you, Miss Pullman?' Nowak leaned forwards, a triumphant glint in her eyes.

'No!' exclaimed Eliza, finally uncurling, her hands raised in an emphatic gesture. 'I didn't do it! That's not how it is!'

'Where were you on Sunday afternoon between twelve and eight?' Nowak fired back.

'I don't know!' Eliza's voice held an edge of panic.

'Then *think*, for goodness' sake!'

'Th-the pub,' Eliza quickly supplied. 'I was at the pub.'

'*Which* pub?'

'The Talbot Arms, in Settle.'

'Why?'

'For a meeting.'

'What meeting?' Nowak ground out, laser-focused as she leaned forward, wanting, needing answers.

'To organise a protest against the planning permission decision—for the Settle development he'd planned.'

Nowak looked to Ward, who nodded. Usually, their

roles were reversed. This time, it was Ward who slipped out to quickly ring upstairs—he'd get them to check the alibi with the pub.

'If you had nothing to do with his death, then why did you run, Eliza, hmm?' Nowak said as Ward silently entered the interview room once more and took his chair. 'It's a big step from not wanting to speak to the police to actively pushing a detective out of your way, risking them serious harm, and fleeing so far and for so long that we couldn't find you.

'You waited so long that you were sure I'd gone, so long you were sure there'd be no one waiting for you when you got home because you didn't want to be seen or caught. That doesn't sound like innocence, does it?' Nowak let the question hang, but Eliza gave her nothing.

'You're a smart, educated young woman, Eliza.' She was slightly older than Nowak's twenty-six years, in fact. 'Frankly, you ought to know better than to waste everyone's time.'

Nowak's voice took on a hard edge that had Eliza glancing at her in surprise, as though she hadn't expected, perhaps, to be admonished by someone her junior. 'If you didn't do it, help us help you—and if you did, rest assured we'll build a watertight case against you from the evidence, and you'll spend the best years of your life in prison far away from Settle. Do you want that?' Nowak demanded.

'No,' said Eliza, and Ward could hear a raw edge in the young woman's voice.

'Then why did you hate him so much? Why did you

have such a crusade against him? Why did you draw this picture?' Nowak stabbed her forefinger at the offending artwork.

'Everything I saw suggested you wanted him to come to harm. The diary entries, the articles, the research...You have one chance, right now, to tell your side of the story. I'm not going to say this all looks really bad against you, because it doesn't. It's a thousand times worse. This is catastrophic, Miss Pullman.'

Ward leaned in. She'd never worm out of this, if she had anything to do with it.

But the three words Eliza Pullman whispered next changed everything.

CHAPTER TWENTY-TWO

'Beg pardon?' Ward asked.

Eliza Pullman jumped at the unexpected sound of his deep voice, and fixed him in a watery look.

Nowak stared at her too, dumbfounded.

'He's my dad,' Eliza repeated in a whisper.

Nowak cleared her throat. Shared a look with Ward. 'Robert Craven is your father?' she asked.

Eliza swallowed and nodded, one sharp jerk of her head. 'He didn't know. That it was me, anyway.'

'Go on,' said Nowak faintly. Ward could tell her reaction was the same as his—*what the flying fuck?* That was *not* anything they had expected. If nothing else, this job was not one for steady, easy wins. More like surprises as explosive as Patterson's arse.

Eliza shifted in her seat with a giant sniff. She wiped her sleeve across her nose. 'He knocked up my mum years ago.' Her eyes were downcast, her voice quiet. 'He was married at the time to Mrs Craven. Their son is a year older than me. The daughter's younger. He'd had it with her, and he was going to start a new life with Mum. I don't know what happened, but it didn't work out. He left my mum unmarried, pregnant...she was the shame of the village.' Anger crackled in her words at that—what Robert had done, the suffering he had caused her mother. Eliza swallowed.

'I didn't know for a long time. Mum met Dad—my real dad. Mark Pullman. They married when I was a baby, and he raised me as his own. I grew up on the farm with my little brothers and sister. I had no idea. Mum told me the truth when I was eighteen. I didn't believe her at first—but she'd kept proof, and there was my birth certificate too. *He* was on it. Robert Craven.'

'Go on,' Nowak prompted quietly when Eliza didn't speak for a long moment.

The young woman chewed on her lip. 'He'd never cared. That was the long and short of it. I was an inconvenient truth. The moment he'd found out Mum was pregnant, he got cold feet. It wasn't so fun if it came with responsibilities.'

Eliza's lip curled. 'I was a mistake to him. We both were. He wanted nothing more to do with either of us. He sent a cheque to my mother in her maiden name every year with a small amount for child support. That was it. The first time I met him, as an intern with the paper, a few years ago...he didn't recognise me. Or my name—Mark's surname. He had no idea who I was. None at all.'

Ward couldn't imagine how that would have felt.

Eliza shook her head, her lips pursed, clamping shut. Her fingers fiddled with the edge of her sleeve. 'It took me a lot of years to come to terms with the truth. I was horrified. Disgusted. *Ashamed*, even though it isn't my fault where I come from. I know that Dad—Mark—is my real dad. He raised me. Loved me. He's always treated me like his own, just like the rest of my siblings.'

'But you still bear ill will towards Robert—towards where you came from?' Nowak dared to interject.

Eliza gave her a dark look. 'Wouldn't you?' she said scathingly. 'Wouldn't you be sickened to know that you came from *him*? I *hate* that his blood runs through my veins. I hate it!' She brought trembling fingers to her lips, pausing for a moment, steadying her breath. When she spoke again, her voice was calmer.

'I felt responsible. I feel responsible. I wanted, and I want, and I will do whatever's in my power to stop him and his destructive legacy. I might share his genes, but I can do better. I can fight his greed and his corruption, and I plan to, with whatever platform I have.'

Eliza Pullman lifted her chin and met their eyes. Ward could see pain and anger there, but strength and resilience too. He couldn't help but respect her for that— she'd had a traumatic journey to adulthood on Robert's account.

'Be that as it may, and I appreciate you sharing what must be an incredibly personal matter with us...The diaries, though,' Nowak said.

'They're old ones,' Eliza said quickly. 'Look. I didn't

mark the date, but I signed the drawing with my name, and the year. It's in Roman numerals.' She pointed.

Sure enough, there it was in tiny lettering, hidden amongst the vibrant art. Nowak quickly worked it out— Ward didn't know how to read Roman numerals, but of course, the Sarge did. Another thing he could be surprised and grateful to her for.

She looked up at him and nodded. Several years earlier. Could have been forged, of course, she still could have drawn it last week, Ward's natural suspicion malingered.

'I got them out for nostalgia's sake, I suppose, hearing that he'd died. I don't know what I thought I'd get from it. My more recent diaries aren't half so grim.' A faint smile quickly faded. 'I still hate him,' she clarified, 'and I always will. I'm glad he's dead, but I didn't do it.'

Nowak raised an eyebrow at that.

Ward stilled. He wondered in time if Eliza Pullman might regret saying that. That she was glad her biological father was dead. Grief and anger made people say things that they regretted.

Eliza wasn't finished. 'I wanted to be active in other ways. Yeah, I've caused a nuisance, but isn't that the point? If we don't disrupt the system, the system's never gonna change.' She had a fire of resistance lit in her on the matter, Ward could tell.

A text pinged on his phone.

Upstairs.

Alibi checked out. Landlord confirmed meeting held

on Sunday, 2-4.30pm, Pullman present. Phone location confirmed Settle. Patterson.

He showed the message to Nowak, who sighed, defeated. It wasn't outside the realms of impossibility, but Eliza's phone had been in Settle all day...suggesting she probably had been too, before and after the Settle meeting.

'Your alibi checks out, it would seem.'

Agitated, Eliza shifted in the chair. 'I know you see a criminal record, but I see it differently,' she said. 'The day I chained myself to the plant yard gates, we saved an eight-hundred-year-old oak from being felled to build that bastard a swimming pool. The graffiti campaign—well, isn't he just graffitiing our landscape with his shitty new builds? Call it a metaphor that went way over his head. The site protest—the one I lasted a month on—ended up finding that a rare species lived in the area, and he *had* to protect it, or he'd be fined in court, convicted, and that development would have been torn down.

'I make a difference, and yeah, it's unconventional, yeah, it's outside the law sometimes, but I don't regret a damn bit of it, because I know I'm doing what's right—protecting my home and my landscape from greedy capitalists like *him*.'

She sounded like a preacher, Ward thought. He'd seen one once, on the streets of York, preaching to all and sundry. She had the same fire in her belly. To her, it was both a duty and a calling. He wondered if, in another life, or perhaps in this one, with less unconventional means, she could really make the difference she hoped to.

He kinda hoped so.
He was fed up with the criminals winning.

CHAPTER TWENTY-THREE

'Pullman's a dead end then, sir,' said Nowak, visibly deflated as they returned to the office upstairs, having released the young woman from custody.

'Aye.' DI Ward would have been disappointed, had they not already had such a strong suspicion of Miranda —they just needed to find the missing statuette and gain access to the CCTV system for the evidence that she really, truly had done it. He had known it ever since he'd met her. She had been so cold and unmoved—uncharacteristically so for a grieving spouse.

'Are you alright, sir?'

'Just frustrated. Come on. Let's go see if there's any progress on Miranda Craven. They should have been able to find the car and phone by now.' Ward rubbed his forehead. A dull headache pounded through him.

It was waiting for them.

DS Metcalfe collared him as he entered the open-plan office.

'Update on the Craven case.'

Ward wrenched his train of thought away from the world of potential open to him now as far as stopping Varga went. 'Go on?'

Metcalfe smiled grimly. 'Got the historic ANPR back. Robert Craven didn't leave Skipton that afternoon, that we can see. However, Miranda Craven's ANPR data. You'll want to hear this.' He paused for dramatic effect. 'Miranda Craven's car wasn't in Harrogate all afternoon on Sunday as she'd claimed. It was in Skipton.'

Ward narrowed his eyes. 'What?'

'Yep,' Metcalfe said smugly. 'Double checked it. Skipton. Five in the afternoon. A few hours later, heading away. Harrogate all day, my left arse cheek.'

Ward was already a step ahead. 'Then what are we waiting for? Christ, that's her alibi shot for starters, and it places her in exactly the right place at the right time. We need to bring her in.'

'Arrest?'

'You're damn right we're arresting her. With all the circumstantial evidence we have, she's suspect numero uno, wouldn't you agree, Scott?'

'Aye. I mean, it's a nice pile of suspects we have on this one, but the almost ex-wife with a massive estate to gain from his death and a fib as big as Blackpool Tower for her alibi just about takes the cake, I reckon.'

'She was the only person with access to the house—no forced entry, remember—who we know for sure was there at the time of Robert's death. At the very least, we'll be questioning her under caution. Kasim?' Ward called over the office.

DC Shahzad looked up from behind his desk. 'Aye, sir?'

'CCTV footage yet?'

Kasim winced.

Ward cursed under his breath.

'Sorry, sir. The company hosts all the footage remotely in the cloud, so there's no hard drives or anything to access at the house, and the app on Robert's phone is password protected. Really struggling on the warrant here. No one's in a rush since Craven's already dead, I think.'

'See if the Super will pull some strings.' Ward wagered if DSU Diane McIntyre was such close friends with the Cravens, she'd be apoplectically incensed to discover that not absolutely everything possible was being done to find who had murdered Robert Craven.

Kasim paled. 'Wh-what? You want *me* to ask the Super?'

Ward chuckled. He wasn't about to throw the DC under a bus like that. 'Not likely. But put it to DCI Kipling, and frame it in his best interests. It's all our arses on the line if this isn't done to Her Majesty's satisfaction.'

Ward snagged his jacket from the back of his chair. 'Right. I'm off.'

'Lucky sod,' grumbled Metcalfe.

'Don't be daft. I get a nice drive out to Rudding Park to arrest Mrs Looking Guiltier Every Second, and you get to do what you do best.'

'Which is?' DS Metcalfe narrowed his eyes, expecting a thinly veiled insult. Or perhaps a blunt one.

'Boss everyone around, Lord Office Manager, and eat all the good biscuits.'

Metcalfe smirked. 'Aye, right enough. I've done my running around, you know, so I'll let that slide. You young whippersnappers can do all the hard work these days.'

'Young? Ha! Wish I felt it. Right. Don't work too hard whilst I'm gone.' And with that, back to extravagant stately Rudding Park DI Ward went.

Wednesday late afternoon

Miranda wasn't answering her phone, but that was alright. DI Ward didn't mind. In fact, he rather fancied being there to see the look of surprise on her face when she realised they'd rumbled her. She probably didn't even realise she'd been clocked—but the backroads of Yorkshire weren't immune to ANPR technology.

He pulled into Rudding Park, parked up, and marched into the grand reception. The receptionist's attention piqued when Ward held up his warrant card.

'I need to speak with Mrs Miranda Craven at once. Police business. Which room is she staying in?'

'I can't give you that information, sorry, sir,' said the receptionist with a pearly white smile. 'We take our clientele's confidentiality extremely seriously.'

'Can you please contact her to let her know I'm here,

then?' Ward forced out a smile that was half a threatening grimace. He didn't want to let the cat out of the bag unless he had no other choice. He didn't want her to bolt.

The receptionist thought for a moment. 'Yes, I suppose I could.'

Ward bit back a scathing retort as the receptionist, painfully slowly, found Miranda's details on the system and rang through to her room.

After a minute, he hung up. 'She's not answering. Sorry I can't help.' With a dismissive smile that instantly got Ward's back up, the receptionist turned back to his computer screen, the conversation done.

Ward's temper erupted. He'd planned to be nice. But that didn't account for when people acted like complete knobs. He took a deep breath—the lifesaving kind. For the receptionist, not him. And then he leaned in close, as a couple wandered past behind him, quietly giggling.

'Listen, Theodore,' he said, glancing at the young man's name badge. 'I need to speak to Miranda Craven *now*, and it'd be a very bad move for you to get in my way. You can either whip that pretentious air of superiority off your face and help, or I'll be happy to take it up with your manager and tell him what an utterly overpaid waste of space you've been today.'

'Hang on,' Theodore said indignantly, looking up at him—and then regretting it, in the full force of Ward's disdain. 'There's no need for that.'

'No. There absolutely isn't. I'm investigating the murder of Miranda Craven's husband. As you might imagine, I have plenty better things to do than stand around yakking with you. I have a warrant for her arrest and I'm here to enforce it.'

'Of course,' stammered Theodore, paling. 'I'll take you to her room myself.'

Now, the young, skinny man couldn't move fast enough, his suit jacket flapping as he skirted out from the desk. 'Follow me.' He wielded what Ward assumed was a master key card in his right hand.

Ward followed him in silence along a hallway and up a sweepingly grand staircase.

'I can't let you in,' Theodore murmured as they approached a suite door.

Ward shrugged. That would be pushing it too far—he'd need a search warrant for that and he wasn't about to push his luck by shooting first and asking questions later, so to speak.

Theodore knocked. 'Mrs Craven?' he called, ear to the door. He knocked again, called again. And a third time.

Nothing.

'Excuse me,' Theodore said to Ward with a waspish stare. 'I'm coming in, Mrs Craven, if you can hear me.'

He slipped inside, leaving the door ajar, and Ward waited—and waited. *How big are these suites?* It would have taken him precisely three seconds to ascertain any of his previous hotel rooms were empty, anyway. But then, he'd never stayed in a suite. It was probably bigger than his entire bloody apartment in a place like Rudding Park.

The receptionist finally appeared. 'She's not here, I'm afraid.'

'Are you sure?' Because Ward wasn't—of Theodore's competency to search.

'Yes.' Theodore scowled as if he knew exactly what Ward was thinking.

'Could she be anywhere on the premises?'

'I can check our systems to see if she has a booking with any of the facilities, yes, and do a general search on the site CCTV.'

'Do it.'

Theodore dodged around a cleaner hefting a hoover upstairs as they returned to the desk. Ward narrowed his eyes. He could see from the woman's gait that she had something wrong—he'd walked funny like that for three months with sciatica a couple of years back. Miranda Craven could wait ten more seconds. 'Hold up.'

Theodore paused and turned, as Ward held out his hand. 'Allow me,' he said to the older woman with a warm smile.

She gaped at him, horrified. 'Oh goodness, sir, no, I couldn't. I'm fine, honestly.'

Ward leaned in and winked. 'I'm not a guest, don't worry.' He took it from her and hefted it up the steps, depositing it at the top.

'Thanks, love.' the woman flashed him a grateful smile.

'It's no trouble.' Being kind cost nothing, after all. Ward turned back to a blank-faced Theodore. *Not that this pretentious twat would know that, it seems.* 'Come on, then.' He glared back at the receptionist until the young man galvanised.

Ward chivvied the receptionist back to the desk, the growing gnaw of urgency biting at him. This was supposed to be easy. Why wasn't it easy? Go to Rudding Park. Arrest Miranda Craven. Bish, bash, bosh, as they said. Now, the sixth sense that lurked in him, that police sense that *something* was up, niggled.

The man was slow, too bloody slow for impatient Ward's liking as he checked his systems.

'No bookings anywhere,' he eventually murmured. And then, after five minutes more, 'I'm sorry, I can't see her anywhere on the premises in the public areas.'

'Well, when was she last on your radar? Can you check back?'

'Not across thirty-seven cameras, Detective, in the time I have available.' He glared pointedly at the queue now forming behind Ward.

'I have a warrant for her arrest. I'm not going anywhere until we find her,' growled Ward, 'so I'd call for help.'

Theodore duly did so, sporting a monstrous sneer to make absolutely sure Ward understood just how displeased he was. A minute later, another staff member slipped into the chair beside him with a curious glance at Ward before she unleashed a gleaming smile to the next in line and murmured a graceful apology for the wait.

'I'm looking on the system—she was booked in for breakfast this morning as usual...but didn't show. Mrs Craven's room wasn't checked off the attendance list, and she hasn't missed a breakfast in the last three weeks. Hmm.'

'Mrs Craven?' the other receptionist interjected, with an apology to her current customer. 'I saw her today—seemed in a hurry, actually, which I thought wasn't like her.'

'When?' Ward fired at her.

'A couple of hours ago, if that.'

Ward deflated. He'd just missed her. *Shite.* 'Where did she go?'

'I don't know.'

'Did she come back?' Ward asked.

'I didn't see, sir, I'm sorry.'

'Did she take her car?'

'I-I'm sorry. I couldn't see from the desk, but probably —we're not exactly close to Harrogate, and she didn't have me ring for a taxi like she has done before when she's say, been entertaining and can't drive home.'

Ward didn't reply for a second, thinking through his options—and Miranda's. Where could she have gone? Why would she not have returned? Christopher's, perhaps? The Skipton house, now it had been released as a crime scene?

And the young lady had said Craven had gone in an unusual hurry...Ward wondered if she knew they were onto her. Where would she go and what would she do if that were the case?

'Detective?' Theodore prompted.

Ward returned to the present. 'Here's my number.' He passed Theodore a card. 'The moment she returns, I need you to call me. We have to speak with her as a matter of urgency. Please make sure all your front desk staff know, and your security staff.'

'Of course.' Theodore finally seemed to understand the gravity of the situation.

Ward left, already on the phone to HMET as he stepped outside. They had to find Miranda Craven at once—wherever she had run to. If Ward had had any doubts of Miranda's innocence, now that she'd fled, those doubts were fast evaporating.

He drove to Christopher Dawson's address in Harrogate, seeing as he was close by at Rudding Park, but there was no sign of Miranda Craven or her car there. The house seemed empty, the driveway clear of cars.

Ward ordered the office to trace Miranda's phone and car, and request a warrant to track her financial transactions in case she'd fled without phone or car—at least they'd be able to trace her from any card transactions.

As he drove, Ward rang Christopher Dawson's office —if anyone were to know where Miranda was, he'd bet it would be her lover. But, no joy. The receptionist told him that Christopher was out all day in client meetings, no she didn't know precisely where, and her calls to him were going straight to voicemail because he was otherwise engaged.

DI Daniel Ward nursed his growing foul temper all the way back to Bradford.

CHAPTER TWENTY-FOUR

Miranda Craven's heart pattered in her chest. She clamped her trembling hands tighter on the steering wheel of the red Porsche. It ate up the miles as she sped away from Harrogate, and yet, it seemed to drive painstakingly slowly, as though through treacle.

Too slow. Too slow. Too slow. The thought drilled into her.

All at once, it seemed she was too hot, too cold, too in control, too out of control. Nausea roiled through her. The scent of petrol fumes and the vanilla air freshener were unbearable.

Gods, what a mess!

She had to get out. Go somewhere else. Somewhere she wouldn't be found.

You're done for. The thought terrified her.

She couldn't face it.

Absolutely couldn't face it.

Any of it.

What had she been thinking?

A ragged sob tore out of her.

She choked on it as sirens blared past in the opposite direction, and her heart pounded so fast she thought she would pass out. But it wasn't the police. Just a fast-response ambulance car, blazing down the country road to some other emergency.

Miranda pressed down on the gas, urging her car faster.

Knowing she couldn't escape.

CHAPTER TWENTY-FIVE

I t had been the kind of fruitless end to the day that DI Ward despised. The ones where he left with alto-gether too many loose ends for his liking, and not enough answers. Ward paced the office like a caged animal, unable to switch off from the case whilst they had a crit-ical lead outstanding.

Where was Miranda Craven?

It gnawed at him, right into the pit of frustration seething in his belly. He was tired, his eyes gritty and aching after a long day, and yet, his mind refused to settle. He strode over to DC Shahzad's desk.

'Sir,' Kasim said, but his tone was off. 'I was just about to collar you.'

'What is it?' Ward asked.

'Well, since there's a warrant out for her arrest, I put out an alert on the PNC to see if anyone over that way could pick her up. Her phone's switched off, but the last ping was from the towers local to the family home, and her car's in the area according to ANPR.'

'Right?'

'A car went over to check it out...'

'Spit it out, Kasim.'

'They just called it in. They've found her, alright. But she's been attacked. Unresponsive.'

'What?'

'That's all I know. Signs of a physical altercation. She's unconscious and alive, but in a bad way. They have an ambulance there now stabilising her.'

'Shite.' Ward's mind raced. What did that mean for the investigation?

'There's one more thing, sir?'

Ward hovered, waiting, fighting the urgency in him that drove him to *go*.

'Claire Parker. I put a trace on her phone. On Sunday afternoon at one, her phone was located at Robert Craven's house.'

Ward stilled. 'For certain?'

'Yes, sir.'

Ward whistled. 'Right. Put a pin in that, eh? We need to check up with Mrs Parker, because she definitely didn't give me the same tale. Right now, though, we have to find Miranda. Come on, Sarge. Let's get over there now.' He grabbed his keys and coat from his desk and chair and headed out at a sprint, Nowak a step behind him.

It was a tense drive up to Skipton as darkness fell. They arrived just as the ambulance was leaving. Ward hailed the driver. 'DI Ward. SIO. What's her condition?'

'Stable, for now, but she's had seven bells kicked out of her,' said the driver, 'I reckon they'll put her in an induced coma. We need to go, sorry. Taking her to Airedale.'

'What the hell happened?' Ward muttered to himself as he parked the car in the gravel courtyard.

The two of them marched over to the house, where a local officer waited.

'Thanks,' Ward said to the man. 'We'll take it from here. Have CSI been notified?'

'Yes, sir,' Nowak said, at precisely the same time as the PC. She smiled sheepishly.

'Any witnesses?' Ward raised an eyebrow at the PC.

'Just me,' the man replied. 'I responded to the PNC alert. When I got here, this car was present' —he pointed to Mrs Craven's Porsche— 'and the front door was ajar. I proceeded inside, calling out, but there was no answer. I did a quick sweep of the property—downstairs seemed deserted, so I went upstairs. I discovered Mrs Craven in one of the bedrooms. It was chaos, stuff everywhere. I didn't see her at first, not until I stepped inside. I called the paramedics straight away. She was unresponsive, covered in blood...I dunno who did that to her, but they didn't spare anything.'

'Christ,' Ward muttered. 'Right. Thanks.' He rummaged in his inner coat pocket for gloves and shoe covers—he was starting to get into the habit of carrying the blasted things at last—and slipped them on. They had a quick scope of the downstairs first. The back door was locked, the rooms undisturbed.

Ward trod up the stairs, each footstep muffled on the thick carpet, with Nowak behind him. On the mezzanine landing, it was much the same as before—though now print dusting powder lay in patches everywhere from CSIs original visit. The cleaner hadn't been since the day she'd discovered Robert, it seemed, and Miranda hadn't made other arrangements.

The Roman artefacts on their plinths caught Ward's eye once more as they passed, and he gave each a glance-over. That one in the middle, still missing. Mercury. He wondered where it was—if they found Miranda's car key anywhere, they could check out her vehicle too for forensic recovery. Would they find a statuette inside the boot?

Ward frowned at the open door ahead, and the item of clothing spilling across the threshold. He stepped over the navy garment.

Clothes lay strewn across the bed and floor. Several suitcases were open on the bed, in various stages of being stuffed with clothing. It was all hastily chucked in, not folded, but crumpled. Miranda had been packing for a swift getaway, which *someone* had disturbed.

Was she fleeing for her life, or to evade justice? That was the question Ward could not answer—not now that she'd been attacked, for that raised a whole raft of new possibilities.

Blood speckled the cream carpet beside the bed, and from the debris left—booted steps in the carpet, medical detritus like a stray tape roll and cannula packet, and the way the items on the floor had been swept aside into a great pile to make way for a stretcher—Ward deduced this was where they had found Miranda Craven.

Who could have done this? Eliza Pullman couldn't be in the clear—she'd been with them that afternoon, sure, but who knew when this attack had happened. Did her grudge extend to Mrs Craven too?

He suspected the Parkers somewhat—though he couldn't be sure which. Mr Parker had a great motive, for the Cravens had ruined his life, but then, Claire Parker wasn't innocent in any of it either. Would she despise the woman her lover wouldn't leave? Most probably.

She was here on Sunday... he reminded himself. *Could she have returned today, and attacked Mrs Craven?*

It was circles within circles.

DI Ward needed Miranda Craven to wake up and give him the answers he needed.

Until then, she was under arrest.

CHAPTER TWENTY-SIX

WEDNESDAY NIGHT

W ard and Nowak had been to the hospital after handing the house over to CSI once more for further investigation. However, they weren't permitted to visit Mrs Craven—only to stand guard outside her door, as she was in police custody, unconscious or not.

Just as the paramedic had said, she'd been placed in an induced coma, as she had a small bleed on the brain that they were concerned about. No, they couldn't be sure when she'd regain consciousness. Yes, of course, he would be the first to know when she did.

There'd been no sign of the Roman statuette or bloodied clothing in Mrs Craven's tiny and wholly impractical car, nor any other signs of obvious guilt. She'd been there—she'd returned to the scene of what Ward thought was *her* crime...but she couldn't have done that to herself. Not what the PC on the scene had described.

Ward returned home to a chaos that rivalled Mrs Craven's ruined bedroom.

Oh, shit.

Oliver the dog had not taken kindly to Daniel working overtime, it seemed.

The new sofa cushions he'd bought were now spread throughout the apartment in torn tatters, shreds of stuffing strewn all over like candyfloss. And, proudly in the middle of the kitchen floor was a ginormous turd.

Oliver was *definitely* sulking when Daniel returned home. The dog didn't come bounding out to see him the moment he opened the door. Perhaps he knew he'd been naughty—it was the kind of thing Katherine would have severely punished the dog for, by putting him outside. It only made Ward feel even guiltier.

'Olly? Bud?' he called.

At last, the dog emerged, slinking from the lounge, all sad eyes and low tail.

Ward sighed and sat on the floor. He was two hours late, after all. 'Complaints duly noted, pal. Come here. I'm not mad, you daft thing. I'm sorry, bud. This job isn't very dog friendly it seems. Come on. Come here.'

Oliver at last approached.

Ward grappled him in a giant hug, fussing him.

Oliver erupted into his more typical cheerful energy at the reassurance that he wasn't about to get put outside for a cold night.

'I think, little bud, that we need to find you a doggy daycare, eh?' He couldn't get home during his shifts to toilet Olly, and if he worked late...the dog, frankly, deserved better than being shut in his apartment all day.

He deserved to run, play, be socialised, and not have to hold his bladder and bowels.

As Ward ran him out for a walk and toilet—his own stomach growling ravenously at the late hour—he Googled for some suitable places and sent off some email enquiries. When they returned home, Ward set to tidying up the carnage. Then, at last, though it was so late he wondered whether he ought to bother, it was dinner time.

He sat on the sofa afterwards, Olly curled into his side, with the TV on, but Daniel wasn't paying attention to it in the slightest. As usual, his caseload whirred away, taking over all his mental space.

Who the bloody hell had murdered Robert Craven? Eliza Pullman had spun them a convincing yarn, but really, she had hours unaccounted for that *could* still have placed her as a suspect, given the incredible personal vendetta she'd had against Robert Craven.

Her father, Ward reminded himself. He hadn't seen that coming. He wasn't sure if that convinced him in her favour or against—after all, plenty of murder victims knew their killer, and if the way Robert had treated his daughter wasn't enough of a personal connection to warrant a deadly response, he didn't know what was.

Then there was Miranda Craven. Why on earth had she lied? She'd claimed to be at her friend's—her lover, Ward now knew—Christopher Dawson's house and asleep to boot whilst there. It was an alibi they couldn't verify with any level of accuracy.

Her phone had been switched off, which was surely

suspicious in itself, especially now they knew her car had been in Skipton at or near the house at the time of Robert's death. Ward knew that phone had been switched off for a reason, and no doubt Miranda had driven along the many back roads, expecting to evade detection.

He wanted to ask her. He *needed* to. She had presented so coldly at their interaction, as though she hadn't cared at all that her husband of decades, business partner, and the father of her two children was *dead*. That screamed alarm bells for Ward. And yet, she was in a coma. And they had no significant evidence proving beyond doubt that she had committed the murder. Everything was on hold until she woke up.

Who on earth could have attacked her?

Claire sprung to mind immediately. Claire Parker. Possibly current or former—depending on which account he trusted—Executive Personal Assistant to Robert Craven. His mistress. Perhaps his killer, if it was true that he had fired her, and perhaps dumped her too. He couldn't see that Robert would have done so and continued their relationship.

Perhaps, Claire was Miranda's attacker if Miranda had instead killed Robert—or Claire had suspected Miranda had. Perhaps Claire had sought revenge at the first possible opportunity for the death of her lover, of the person she suspected most.

Then there was her husband...

Either way, he needed to speak to Claire Parker first

and foremost tomorrow morning. Did the fact that her phone placed her at the scene of Robert's murder, in the absence of any other evidence yet, give him enough grounds to arrest her too?

Ward couldn't be sure. But he needed to decide.

CHAPTER TWENTY-SEVEN

THURSDAY MORNING

A subdued Claire Parker entered Bradford South Police Station in handcuffs, flanked by two officers. Ward watched them book her in and met them to take her through to the interview room.

She sat in the unforgivingly hard chair in silence, now uncuffed, as Ward and Nowak set up and started the interview. Her hands were hidden in the sleeves of an oversized powder-blue hoodie, and she wore leggings and slip-on shoes. Her bleached hair hadn't been washed or straightened and was tied back in a messy bun instead. She wore no makeup, her skin blotchy and the shadows under her eyes deeper than the other day. She looked an altogether different person to the Claire Parker proudly preened on the company website where Ward had first seen her photograph.

'You're under arrest at this time,' reminded Nowak, 'so anything you do say may be given in evidence against you. Do you understand?'

Claire nodded.

Ward placed his hands, clasped together, on the table in front of him, the movement deliberate and slow. He could see from Claire's stiff posture, the way she leaned as far away as she could, an edge of wildness in her eyes, that she was nervous.

She had good reason to be, if his suspicions were true.

Every second he delayed was a second for the tension inside her to build. He wanted her to slip up.

'Do you know—or rather, do you understand, there's an important distinction there—why you've been arrested, Claire?' Ward asked, his tone even.

She squirmed under his gaze. A whisper escaped. 'No.'

'You've been arrested, as already stated, on suspicion of the murder of Robert Craven, and the attempted murder of Miranda Craven.'

'It isn't true,' Claire moaned, bursting into tears. 'I love him, why would I kill him?'

'Because he'd just fired you, Claire. You didn't tell us that, did you? You denied it, tried to pass it off, but we have verified all the details with the company. You were terminated with immediate effect on Sunday morning. It wasn't a tiff. Robert Craven specifically instructed admin staff to revoke all your system access, collect your things, and start recruiting for your replacement the moment you left.'

'No! He wouldn't. He couldn't.' But tears streamed down Claire Parker's face.

'You didn't want to accept that, did you, Mrs Parker?'

'I loved him,' she insisted, her voice breaking on the words.

'How did it make you feel to know that he'd cast you off without a second thought?'

'He wanted me back, I know it! He didn't mean it.'

'He did, Claire—you just don't want to acknowledge that. I bet it hurts, doesn't it?'

Claire gritted her teeth and glared at him defiantly, tears streaming down her face.

'I'll bet it made you angry too, didn't it?'

No response.

'After all, you'd taken a chance on him—such a leap of faith. You'd given up your marriage for him, and he tossed you aside.'

'I told you, me and Niel have been over for years.' She roughly wiped her tears away with her sleeves.

'Still, though, it's a big thing to go from unhappily coexisting, to deciding it's over.' He knew personally with Katherine, exactly how bloody hard that was. They'd never strayed into affairs, but the finality of that decision, once it was truly over... 'It's a terrifying moment. A leap of faith. And Robert didn't catch you. He let you fall, Claire. Look at the mess he's left you in.'

He could see it. A truly shattered marriage beyond any repair. An unhappy family. The shattering mess of divorce. The emotional, mental, physical, and financial separation the family would have to endure before they could even see the start of the journey of healing on the other side.

She could see it too, for her face screwed up with the bitterness of it.

'Is that why you lied to us?'

She froze like a rabbit in the headlights. 'W-what?' she said—but Ward could read her like a book.

She's a shitty liar.

'I'll give you that. Perhaps you didn't *lie* to us, per se. More *omitted* some very key information. Why were you at Robert Craven's house on the afternoon he was murdered, Claire?'

She couldn't reply, her mouth frozen open in silent anguish. 'I...I wasn't,' she eventually said. Too late. Too lamely.

'Oh, come off it, Claire,' Ward said, annoyance souring his tone. He'd given her enough chances now. 'We know you were there. We've traced your phone to Robert Craven's house at midday on Sunday. So you might as well tell us.'

Claire shrank back in her chair, shaking. 'I swear I didn't...I was there, alright, I'll admit it. But I swear I didn't do anything to him. I swear it!' Fresh tears erupted. 'I couldn't say anything, because I knew I'd be a suspect.'

'It looks a lot worse when we find out from different sources, believe me. Why were you so far from home, Claire, at the home of a man who was murdered so very soon after your visit, if not by you?' He stared at her flatly.

The answer was a whisper, forced out between sobs. 'I was begging him. Begging him to give us another chance—*me* another chance. Niel and I had been arguing as usual. He knew I'd spent the night with Robert. He told me to get out, not to come home, that it was over and I needed to find somewhere else to stay. The kids would stay there with him.'

Ward waited as she cradled her wrist to her chest and quietly sobbed for a moment.

'I didn't have anywhere else to go. And I thought...I thought Robert loved me. Somehow. I thought I could make it right. I'd do whatever he wanted to make it right. But he wouldn't listen. He...He hurt me. You asked me how I came by the bruise...it *was* Robert. He's never hurt me before, ever. He threw me out. Physically threw me out. I have a bruise on my hip too, where I fell down and twisted my ankle.'

Ward shared a glance with a frowning Nowak. Who knew if either of them believed the woman, really.

'I was in shock. I couldn't believe it. I hadn't anything with me, I didn't have anywhere else to go. I went home. I can't afford to stay in a hotel or rent somewhere else. Niel and I argued all afternoon about it. He didn't want me there. All I could think about was Robert. He scared me. I've never seen anger like that from him. Temper, yes, hot fury sometimes, but that...he was so cold.'

'What time did you arrive and leave Robert Craven's home?'

'I...' Claire stalled, and then she swallowed, trying to think. 'It would have been about one, and I left about half-past.'

Ward would get Shahzad to verify that with the phone records. They'd be able to trace her movements and the time more accurately.

'Where were you in the house? In Robert's house,' he clarified at her blank look.

'Downstairs.'

Ward waited.

'In the lounge—and the kitchen. I made us a drink, or, I tried to, so we could talk, but he wouldn't have it.'

'You didn't go upstairs?'

A slight pause. 'No.'

'Sure about that?'

Claire coloured. 'I tried to,' she admitted quietly, a blush grazing her cheeks. 'I thought if I could get him into bed, maybe he'd reconsider. We've always had amazing...chemistry.'

'I see. Did that happen?'

'No.' She swallowed and unconsciously stroked her wrist again. 'When I tried, he...that was when he hurt me and threw me out.'

'Right. And where've you been since? Specifically say, yesterday afternoon and early evening?'

Claire looked blankly at him 'I don't know. Home? I drove around a bit, and then I came back. I was home yesterday, all day. I don't have anywhere else to go right now.' Her lip wobbled again, fresh tears threatening.

Ward sighed. Maybe they'd be able to verify that from her phone records. But anyone could leave a phone somewhere whilst they went to kill someone. 'Do you know Mrs Craven?'

A flicker of dislike crossed Claire's face before it was quickly hidden. 'No. I've met her, if that's what you mean. But I don't know her. I don't like her, but then, who does?' She let out a bitter laugh. 'She made his life miserable. He couldn't wait to divorce her.'

'Have you seen her recently?' Ward watched carefully for any tells.

'Yes.' Claire pulled a face. 'Saturday night at the event. They—Robert and *her*, that is—were arguing out in the hallway after the party.'

'Have you seen her since?'

'No, why?'

'Have you been to the Craven property since Sunday?'

Claire's lip shook. 'No. I...I've been drinking quite a lot. Not necessarily just at night. I'm not...I wouldn't drive. Never. I'm not like that.'

'Were you drinking yesterday afternoon?'

Claire flushed. 'Yes.' She looked away.

'And evening?'

'Yes. Niel's a supermarket manager, so he works all kinds of odd shifts. It's easier to do it when he's not there.'

'So he was at work?'

'Yeah, on a one 'til ten shift.'

'Right.' That ruled the husband out, then, if it was true. They'd be checking.

'The reason I ask is that sometime yesterday, late afternoon or evening, Miranda Craven was injured in a serious aggravated assault.'

Claire stilled. 'What?' she said slowly...and Ward saw the moment the lightbulb switched on in her head.

'I didn't do it.' She looked between the two impassive detectives. 'I didn't do it,' she said more strongly. 'Just ask her—she'll tell you. It wasn't me.'

'I'm afraid we can't do that,' said Ward, his lips thinning as they pressed together. 'Mrs Craven is currently in a medically induced coma as a result of the assault. Believe me, if we could, we'd be asking her.'

Claire burst out, 'It wasn't me. I wasn't there. I don't know anything about it!'

'Well, Mrs Parker. That remains to be seen. As it stands, you're able to be placed at the scene of Mr Craven's murder on or around the time he was attacked. You have no witnesses or evidence to prove to the contrary that you weren't involved with that—and we'll be putting together the evidence to charge you for that, and Miranda's attack, if we can.'

Nowak calmly wrote beside him. Ward knew she'd be recording their next steps too. Check her phone records. Check her car location. Verify her husband's working pattern. Check any other details they could that would help verify if Claire Parker could be placed near the scene of Miranda's attack at the correct time.

Claire simply gaped at them in stunned silence.

'Do you have anything else to say?' Nowak prompted.

After a pause, they stood.

'You'll be returned to the custody cells and charged or released after a maximum of twenty-four hours,' Ward said.

That got her. 'N-no! You can't put me back in there. It's awful! No! Please!'

They left her in hysterics. Her wail followed them down the hallway.

'*I'm not a murderer!*'

CHAPTER TWENTY-EIGHT

'I reckon the wife did it,' Shahzad said.

'I reckon the mistress,' Metcalfe weighed in.

'I still think it was the mad bastard with the shotgun,' muttered Patterson darkly.

Nowak tutted. 'Wuss.'

'Hey! You weren't there,' Patterson snapped.

'Nope, I was up hill and down dale, getting my arse handed to me by a Nissan Micra,' Nowak smirked. At least her pride wasn't stung so far by it she couldn't make a joke at herself. 'I wonder if Eliza Pullman might have done it, you know. She really had it in for her old man.'

'Aye, but there's no evidence to suggest Pullman was there at Craven's on Sunday. Or the farmer. But we know Miranda and Claire *did* visit the Craven house on Sunday afternoon. Any other possibilities? The Queen's mother, maybe?' Ward said as he strolled into the Incident Room where they'd all gathered. 'Not like we don't have enough people to chase—why not add a few more?'

No one answered, which was probably wise. Ward had definitely gotten out of the wrong side of bed that morning.

He raised his hand. In it, a sheaf of freshly printed papers. 'I have here something rather interesting from James Craven. He's just sent through a scan of a draft of Robert Craven's new will. It's *very* illuminating.'

Ward shuffled through the papers. 'Now, this isn't his official Last Will and Testament. It's not signed or witnessed, and it's on draft paper. *But*, that could be argued in a court of law. That's not what concerns me, however. Miranda told me that as part of the divorce, afterwards, they'd be drawing up new wills—financially prudent and all. It turns out, Robert was prudent enough to get a head start on his. This draft dates from a couple of months ago—so who knows if this draft copy was, in fact, finalised and is legally binding.'

He looked around. Everyone stared back at him with their full attention. 'In Robert's new will, he's cut Miranda out completely.'

His team shared looks.

'Precisely. If Miranda didn't know about this, perhaps she'd assumed that their current or former wills would be up to scratch until their divorce finalised. Perhaps she did know about this. Enclosed with the draft is a photocopy of the current will with changed sections highlighted. In the original, Miranda, as his spouse, gets everything. The moment this will becomes adopted, she gets *nothing*.'

'So, she wouldn't want that new will at all, sir, would she?' said DC Patterson, wide-eyed.

Ward wanted to roll his eyes. 'No, son, she wouldn't.'

He turned back to the team. 'James Craven doesn't know where he stands right now—whether this was adopted as Robert's Last Will and Testament. He'll be able to get that from the solicitors soon, when we've finished with Robert.' The man was still somewhere in Mark Baker's mortuary.

'For him, it's a personal question. For us, it's evidence. Evidence that it was *firmly* within Miranda's best interests that she and Robert were still legally married at the time of Robert's death. Miranda Craven is our prime suspect right now in the murder of her husband. She had access to the property and was in the vicinity when he was killed. The weapon used was a statuette that she herself could identify by memory—that she would be capable of wielding.

'She showed no remorse or feeling at the news of his death, suggesting that she wasn't shocked or grieving for him—a callous coldness that lends itself to the theory that she killed him in cold blood to financially secure herself. Her forensics are all over the house, granted, but they are there. She would know that—it gives the potential for her visit on Sunday to camouflage itself amongst the wealth of her DNA already on-scene.'

'You really think she did it, sir?' Nowak said, her brows furrowed.

'Don't you?'

'When you put it like that, yes. But, she's a woman... Women don't tend to kill like that.'

'Aye. I know what you're saying. Poison, deceit,

maybe...brute strength not so much. But we now know that Robert was violent towards Claire. Maybe he was violent towards Miranda too. Maybe it was self-defence on Miranda's part, if they argued and he became violent.' He was spinning theories, but something niggled. He still wasn't on the money. What the bloody hell was it?

'Who attacked Miranda, then?' Nowak posed, crossing her arms. She stared at the Big Board, at the photo of Miranda there in all her glamour from the Saturday night just gone, hanging off her impassive husband's arm, dripping in expensive jewellery.

'It's gotta be the mistress,' Metcalfe said. He stared at Claire Parker's picture on the board. 'It's *gotta* be. If he fired her and ditched her...' He whistled and winced. 'Christ. If I did that to my Marie, she'd have my balls faster than you could run to the shitter after a bad curry.'

'*Scott!*'

'*Sarge!*'

A round of groans drowned him out.

Scott twinkled with glee at their discomfort, and continued, 'All I'm saying is she'd be mad and then some. That kinda fury...maybe she lost control, or maybe she did it on purpose—premeditated—but I reckon she'd have been furious enough to do it. And, as for Miranda—a rival for Robert's time and money, even if not his affection?

'If Claire thought Miranda was trying to swindle Robert out of money that she thought should be his...well, maybe she took it into her own hands too. She seems unstable enough. I was watching the cameras in the interview. She's lost everything. That makes folks dangerous.'

'Aye,' mused Ward. 'She seemed...*passionate*, if that's the right word. But until the forensics team comes back, and frankly, until we find the murder weapon, we're scuppered. Nowak, can you arrange for Claire Parker's car to be searched?'

'Yes, sir. What about the husband?'

'Check his shift patterns at work, phone location history, and any hits for his car. Go from there. If he can be placed at either...it's worth investigating.'

'Are you discounting Eliza entirely?' DS Nowak asked.

Ward chewed his lip. 'My gut's not there, Sarge. Is yours?'

Nowak grimaced.

'Her alibi's slap-bang in the middle of Baker's window for time of death. She could have, of course. It'd be tight, but it's possible. Personally, I think Claire Parker and Miranda Craven are stronger candidates. And Niel Parker, frankly, if we can place him. They all have a lot more to lose personally.'

Nowak nodded in agreement.

'We just need Miranda to wake up,' Ward said with a sigh. 'She holds more answers, I know it. And we need that damn statuette.'

But who would the guilty party be—Craven, one of the Parker's, or even, if she proved to be more duplicitous than he realised, Pullman?

Metcalfe was right, Ward thought. Parker was too unstable. She'd have panicked. Been too messy. If she could even have done it at all. Craven controlled her, mind and body. Ward wasn't sure whether she had it in her to take that power back.

His gut pulled him away from Pullman, angry as the young woman was with her father.

Miranda Craven still ensnared him. So cold. So calculating. So likely. He desperately needed her to wake up.

'Shahzad, get ahold of Christopher Dawson. He can help us piece together Miranda's movements better than anyone else.' If Miranda couldn't tell them herself, then he'd just have to bloody well figure it out.

Would she wake up just in time for them to damn her —or for her to damn herself?

CHAPTER TWENTY-NINE

D I Ward was still in the thick of searching for Robert Craven's killer. Forensics had recovered Claire Parker's car for testing. No statuette hiding in the boot—that, he'd already checked with Victoria Foster, who was none too pleased to be disturbed by him from her work.

A warrant had been requested in order to get more detailed phone location data from Claire Parker's phone —and her husband's. Expedited by the DCI, given the countdown ticking away on whether they charged Claire Parker or released her within the allotted twenty-four hours.

Shahzad still hadn't managed to track down Christopher Dawson and worry niggled at Ward. That sixth sense that not all was right. Ward wondered, was Chris a victim in all this too? A victim of Miranda—or perhaps, whoever had attacked her?

He'd just phoned the hospital again—and he could tell the nurses' patience was wearing thin from his incessant contact. "Miranda Craven is still unresponsive, and could you kindly piss off" was the theme of their response.

'Sir...'DC Shahzad's subdued voice pulled Ward out of his musing.

'What is it, Kasim?' Ward looked up from his desk, straightening his hunched shoulders with a groan from where he pored over transcripts of Robert Craven's messaging history in an attempt to find any clues.

'I'm looking into Dawson as you asked...you need to see this.'

Shahzad hurried back to his desk without another word. Curiosity piqued, Ward followed. 'Go on?'

'Well, sir. I still can't get in contact with him. His phone's switched off, and his office stated his diary's blocked out for the rest of the week, but that there's no detail on there to say what he's doing or where he is. So, I ran some checks. Managed to prise a bit more out of the network, and, along with our ANPR database, well...'

Ward's intuition prickled. *No...*

Shahzad pulled up Google Maps on his web browser. 'I've pinned some key items I think you'll be interested in. 'Namely on Sunday afternoon at five-ish. Miranda Craven's car was picked up in the Skipton area.'

'Aye,' said Ward, waiting for more.

'But her phone wasn't. Switched off, right?'

'Aye.'

'Well, turns out that there was another phone there at the same time, in that area, triangulating on cell towers around the Craven address.'

'Christopher Dawson's.' Ward groaned.

'Yeah.'

'You don't think...?'

'That she—Miranda—took his phone, maybe? At first, yes. But then...look.' Shahzad pointed to four different pins. 'Here, and here. That one is a vague cell tower triangulation on Christopher's phone again. That one is his car. And this one is Miranda's car hitting the same ANPR shortly before. And her phone at that location, again, shortly before Christopher's.'

'When?' Ward breathed.

'Yesterday afternoon, between three and five.'

'When Miranda was attacked.'

'Yes, sir.'

'Shite.' Ward looked over the pins again—the timings. 'He followed her there.'

'And what's more, he's the only person aside from Miranda herself, obviously, that we can now place at the scene of both Robert Craven's murder and Miranda Craven's attack.'

'And she couldn't have done that to herself.'

'No.'

Ward shook his head, speechless for a moment as he tried to come up with answers. 'Were they in it together, I wonder? She had so much to lose, but they both had everything to gain. But then, what?' he mused aloud. 'She got cold feet, or they argued, perhaps she'd never intended it to go so far—maybe Christopher was the one who struck the killing blow on Robert. And then he turned on her when she wanted out?'

'She may well not have been involved at all, sir. Maybe it was all Dawson,' Shahzad said. 'Maybe she did have a migraine, maybe she was out cold on Sunday afternoon at his, like she said—and he took her car, thinking that he was smart. Maybe she had no idea, but then Robert died, and she pieced it together. Maybe she realised, and silencing her was the only way Christopher Dawson could stay under the radar.'

'Only, he didn't do a good enough job if so.' Because Miranda Craven, despite being in a serious condition, was very much alive. Damn it, Ward needed her to wake up.

'Why, sir? That's the only thing I don't understand. Why would Dawson be involved? He has a successful firm, he's wealthy on his own, from what I can see. Why would he want Robert dead?'

'That, I don't know, son,' Ward admitted. 'That's why I still reckon it was Miranda. She must have found out about Robert's new will, and she wasn't happy. Who would be, right? No matter that she gives the impression of being some kind of ice queen, there's gotta be more to it than that. She's spent her whole life with the man. They built the Craven empire together. That severance must have been hard, even if she didn't show it.

'Maybe she pushed Christopher into being an unwilling accomplice and maybe she pushed too far. Maybe she tried to cover up the evidence—and he took a stand. They fought. Maybe she tried to tie up the loose end that could incriminate her. Him. Maybe Dawson's injured, or dead, or in hiding for fear of her. Shite. We need to find him.'

'Already on it, sir. His phone is still switched off. I've put in a request for recent ANPR hits.'

'Great. In the meantime, I'm off to Dawson's myself. Get local units there ASAP. If he's there, I want him detained until we can get a clearer idea of what on earth's happened. Regardless of Robert Craven's murder right now, he's got to be a prime suspect in Miranda Craven's assault. I want a warrant too, expedited, so we can conduct a full search of his property.'

'There's one more thing, sir.' DC Patterson popped up seemingly from nowhere.

'Yes?' Ward turned to him, Shahzad too.

'We do have some interesting material from Craven's phone,' Patterson said.

'Craven's?' Ward frowned.

'Yes, sir. Miranda's. We seized it to examine. There's some rather interesting conversations between her and Christopher.'

'Like?' Patterson had Ward's full attention.

'Like where he eggs her on to get more in the divorce, and she refuses, because she says she doesn't need any more money, and she doesn't want it from Robert, thank you very much.'

'So she didn't mind if he cut her out of his will?' Ward frowned. Not like most acrimonious divorces he'd heard of.

'Apparently not. There are some very lengthy phone calls going by the call logs, but obviously we don't have any recordings. However, on Wednesday... Miranda tries to call Christopher repeatedly. Leaves voicemails. And a lot of messages. Accusing him of drugging her with sleeping tablets on Sunday afternoon, and taking her car, and then murdering Robert, and that she's done with the two of them and she's going to the police.'

Ward gaped. 'Shite. If that's the case...'

'Then she was fleeing,' Shahzad concluded gravely.

Patterson scowled, put out that Shahzad had nicked his big reveal. He cleared his throat and continued. 'She probably thought the house was safe—he knew where she was staying at Rudding Park, and going by the phone and vehicle locations, he did try to find her there first, before he went to the house. Maybe she'd planned to get her things and stay at the Craven house, or go somewhere else.'

'But he caught her first.'

The room was silent as they let that all sink in. Nowak slipped outside to take a call.

'This all hinges on Miranda's account being true, of course,' Ward murmured thoughtfully. 'And that's the crux of it. These messages, the voicemails, they might be an elaborate lie.'

'I heard the voicemails, sir,' said Patterson. His gaze dropped to the floor. 'She sounded devastated. Distraught. And angry too. I know so far, she's presented as cool, calm, and collected, but listen for yourself. They sound like the most genuine thing we've seen or heard from her yet.'

'And they may well be, if they're private communications not intended for our ears or eyes,' Ward concluded.

'You can ask her yourself,' said Nowak, slipping back inside. 'Miranda's awake.'

CHAPTER THIRTY

THURSDAY LUNCHTIME

Ward settled at the side of Miranda Craven's hospital bed in Bradford Royal Infirmary, with Nowak sat at the foot of the bed, taking notes. It was overly warm and unpleasantly muggy in the hospital—in the fetid way that made Ward's skin crawl, as though he could see germs festering and breeding in the air.

He relaxed slightly as a nurse bustled in and cracked open the window, allowing a cool finger of air to reach in. She eyed the PC on the door as she left, but said nothing. He was there for everyone's protection.

'How are you feeling?' Ward asked.

Miranda smiled weakly. 'Probably about as good as I look.'

Her face was black and blue on one side, her neck mottled with bruises, and her arms too, lying bare on the cover. A cannula sat on the back of her hand, taped in, though there were no longer any tubes attached.

'Are you able to answer some questions?'

Miranda's voice hardened. 'Yes.'

'Do you remember what happened?'

'Yes.'

Ward waited.

Miranda swallowed, wincing in pain. 'It was Christopher. Dawson. He did this. He followed me to the house and attacked me.'

'Why?'

Miranda closed her eyes, but a tear slipped out nonetheless that surprised Ward. 'He killed Robert,' she said in a cracked whisper.

That, they already suspected from the car and phone tracking. Gods, he needed that CCTV footage from the house more than anything right now to be sure of the truth. 'Go on,' murmured Ward.

She took a long moment to gather herself. To distance herself emotionally, Ward realised, for when she spoke, her words were void of feeling.

'On Sunday, I had the migraine I told you about—and a hangover, to be honest. I went to bed, but I was so tired...I think he drugged me with some of my own Temazepam, perhaps in my decaf beforehand. I was out for the count, and I woke up hours later. Usually if I have a migraine, I can't sleep. When I went downstairs, he was there—I didn't think anything of it, but he had changed, which was odd.'

'What time was this?'

'It was dark...' Miranda frowned. 'Maybe eight or nine? I'd been asleep since...maybe half two?'

'And then?'

'I was annoyed. I'd meant to go back to the house that day to return my dress, collect some things for Trixiebelle. And of course, I wasn't going to go on an evening, not such a long way. Not when I might find Robert and the strumpet there. I went first thing Monday instead when I knew he'd be out—but, Robert had died when I got there. I don't think that sank in, not then.'

Maybe she doesn't have a heart of stone after all. Maybe she was just incredibly shocked. He recalled how standoffish and unaffected she'd been just a couple days before. 'How was Christopher acting?'

'Normally, really, in that he's been distant and distracted for a few months—the business has been losing money. He's been very stressed about it. I saw some letters too, from debt collectors.' She shuddered. 'I had no idea it was that bad.'

'Did he ask you for money?'

'No. Well, not in so many words, but...he had been pushing me to get more out of the divorce. Said it was for my new business venture, but I wondered...perhaps, he wanted some for himself, to get him out of the hole he's in.

'I didn't understand why he was so bothered at first. Surely, he understood? I've been bloody miserable for years, and I just wanted out, for goodness' sake. Robert and I both worked hard, and yes, I was sick of his parade of floozies, but I was just glad he was happy to split everything down the middle and have done with it all too.

'But then I saw the letters, and I took a look in Christopher's study when he was in the shower. There were more. His house is mortgaged up to the hilt, the car is leased, and he's in debt up to his eyeballs. He wasn't the successful businessman he'd led me to believe, anyway. I confronted him, and we argued. It was none of my business, according to him.'

'When was this?'

'Monday. I went to the house in Skipton, we met, of course, then I returned to Harrogate to pick up my things.'

'So, you didn't go to the Skipton house on Sunday then?'

'No.'

'Where was Christopher during the time you were asleep?'

At that, Miranda shuffled restlessly, and her eyes flicked away. 'At home. With me. Or so I thought. But...I noticed the next day, Monday, when I went out to drive to the Skipton house, that my car was parked differently. On the other side of the drive. I always park it close to the paving. It's difficult to walk across the gravel in heels. I thought I was going crazy. When I asked him, he said he hadn't touched it. But I could have sworn. Why would I have parked it there?' She frowned up at them, as if they had answers.

'I didn't think anything of it, of course. When I arrived at the house, I mean, the ambulance was there, the police, and I found out what had happened to Robert. I drove away and that was that, I could hardly think of anything at all. It was only a couple of days later that I began to suspect.

'When I had some privacy, I checked my tablets—the Temazepam, I take them for insomnia—and sure enough I was missing a dose. They were in my handbag, so easy enough for Christopher to access, and he knew they were there. He didn't know anything about the missing tablet though, he said, when I rang him to ask. I must have miscounted, he said. But only he and I have access to those tablets, and I *know* I haven't taken an extra dose. I'm one short before my prescription renews.'

Her hands fiddled with the cover. She sighed. 'I mulled that over all night. Then I realised...I have a dashcam on my car. I can access the footage on an app. I checked back and sure enough, it had been driven on Sunday afternoon, but not by me. I had been fast asleep. I fast forwarded, and the car went to the Skipton house. I didn't watch it all. I couldn't.' Her voice cracked. 'I knew then, that he'd done it.'

'When was this?'

'Wednesday.'

'What did you do then?'

'I panicked,' she admitted. 'I called him. He didn't answer. I messaged. Then we spoke—argued. He told me I was talking rubbish, that I sounded like a lunatic, but the more I pushed, the angrier he got, the more insistent he was that I was making it up. But he wouldn't say he *hadn't* done it. I told him I was going to the police, to tell them what I suspected, that if he'd killed Robert, I'd never ever forgive him, and we were done.'

'How did he react to that?'

'How do men usually react when women tell them

no? He was furious, of course. Started to threaten me—I put the phone down on him. I was so shaken. The way he'd spoken to me, what he'd said...' Miranda fell silent, and shook her head.

'He kept calling, but I didn't pick up. He knew where I was staying at Rudding Park, and I knew I wasn't safe there. Or, I didn't *feel* safe. I grabbed some things and left. I was going back to the Skipton house, but then I realised it would be the next place he looked, if he was coming for me, and Robert had died there...'

Ward waited as she stalled, and breathed through some pain both physical and emotional, by the looks of the grimace on her face.

'I was just booking somewhere to stay. Somewhere random, where he'd never find me. Then I could ring you, to tell you what I'd found. Maybe I wasn't thinking straight. Maybe if I'd just phoned you at once, this wouldn't have happened.' Miranda shook her head. 'And then he came crashing in. I hadn't realised, I thought I'd have more time.' She was shuddering, her hands quivering on the cover.

'Take your time. It's alright,' reassured Ward, with a glance at Nowak, whose face was drawn with concern.

'I had nothing to defend myself with. He stormed right in, and the next thing I know...I couldn't get away. Blinding pain. I was on the floor. He was above me, shouting. It's hazy, I'm sorry, but along the lines of I'd spoiled it all, and he was so mad, and it was my fault, and now I had to pay.' She frowned as she tried to remember.

'Something struck me, and I don't remember anything else. And now I'm here.'

She glanced to the door nervously. Fresh tears slid out from between her closed eyes once more. 'What happens now?' she whispered.

Ward chewed his lip, and shared another look with Nowak. Did they have enough to discount Miranda? They couldn't entirely prove she *hadn't* been partially responsible for Robert's death, but her account was convincing, along with what they knew. It made sense. It filled in enough blanks. Either way, they had enough to place Christopher Dawson at the scene of, and responsible for, the attack upon her, and once the forensics had returned, enough to charge him for the murder of Robert Craven.

'I'm de-arresting you on suspicion of your husband's murder,' Ward said finally. 'But you will remain under our protection for now, and we will need to speak to you again.'

Miranda nodded, swallowing.

Nowak sat forward. 'Do you have anyone you want us to contact? To bring you anything you might need, and stay with you?'

Miranda turned watery eyes upon her. 'My children. Please.'

'Of course. I'll do that straight away,' Nowak promised. It was only right that they be with her, all considered.

Miranda sighed, deflating before them. Devoid of makeup, sharp clothing, and her signature attitude, she was a shadow of the woman Ward had met a few days ago. She looked so tired and worn from the emotional, mental, and physical toll of it all.

At the end of it all, their life as husband and wife had been tangled and messy, fraught with pain and anger at times, but they'd planned to end it with mutual respect and understanding that credited to their own personal growth through such difficult times. Now, whatever was left of it all was in tatters.

Whether that was thanks to Miranda Craven's or Christopher Dawson's greed, Ward would make sure justice was served for it.

CHAPTER THIRTY-ONE

Christopher Dawson's grand Harrogate house was deserted. They'd scoped out the door, peered through the windows, vaulted over the gate and checked the back. No signs of life—or Christopher Dawson.

A big red key put paid to the locked front door, however. An alarm blared as DI Ward and DS Nowak rushed in, backed up with local Uniform from Harrogate.

'Christopher Dawson!' Ward called. 'Police! Show yourself!'

Nothing but the siren wailing.

The house was deserted.

One of the PCs dealt with the alarm—a managed system, that crackled into life within a minute of their entrance, the surveillance centre trying to verify if it was an accidental or deliberate trigger. Not the first time they'd had to deal with such a system, of course. The alarm company was able to verify that the police were attending a live incident there. After a few minutes, the terrible siren ceased, and the humdrum of police activity was all that could be heard as booted feet tramped through the building.

'How the other half live, eh?' Nowak said, following Ward along the grand upstairs hallway, both of them illuminated in bright relief by the huge Georgian sash window at the end.

'Hmm.' Ward wasn't sure. They finished checking the rooms briefly—no signs of life *or* death. No signs of anyone at all, in fact. Ward pulled out his phone and dialled Shahzad. 'Dawson's car's gone. No sign of him here. He must be on the move. Have you pulled up the ANPR data yet?'

'Yes, sir. His car went north right after the attack on Miranda. Brief stop at Harrogate, it appears, probably to pick up his things, then right up the A1. Vanishes just after Scotch Corner in the early hours of this morning.'

'Scotch Corner?' Ward repeated incredulously. That was miles north. Implausibly north. 'He's guilty or he's frightened, or maybe both, but he's running from something.'

'Aye, sir. I've already cleared it with the DCI to put a financial trace on him. If any of his cards are used anywhere, we'll know about it.'

'When?'

'This afternoon, sir.'

Ward chewed his lip. 'Right. Good work, Kasim. Keep me updated.' He hung up. 'Did you hear that?' He raised an eyebrow at Nowak.

'Yeah.' Nowak's brow furrowed too 'What's he playing at?'

'I don't know, but whilst we wait to hear back from Shahzad, let's see what we can turn up here. Maybe there'll be answers.'

'Yes, sir.'

They split up, each one taking the rooms on opposite sides of the huge landing. Most were bedrooms and bathrooms. Nowak called that she had the master suite, by the looks of it, and fell silent as she searched. Ward stumbled on Dawson's study, and stepped inside to look through the place.

It was as grand as the rest of the Georgian house. Built-in bookcases so large that a rail with a ladder on it stretched from floor to ceiling in rich, dark wood. They were stuffed with books on everything from history and philosophy to true crime and Tolkien.

No Fifty Shades of Grey, Ward noted with a grim smirk. He looked across the shelves, but there was nothing that seemed to have been recently moved—a light dust had settled on each of the shelves, all undisturbed. The desk was a different affair. Some old-fashioned wooden thing, an antique, by the looks of it, was barely visible under the mountain of papers. Letters opened and unopened lay strewn across it. Ward circled the desk, glancing over what he could see.

PAYMENT DUE.

FINAL WARNING.

DEBT COLLECTION.

AMOUNTS OVERDUE.

BALANCE OUTSTANDING.

Some bank statements for various accounts—all overdrawn.

Shite. Dawson was in a right financial mess if the contents of his desk were anything to go by. Ward glanced around the room. So opulent, so overstated, so *expensive.* All just a veneer over a cracked reality? The mountain of paperwork suggested Dawson wasn't a flourishing individual, but a debt-riddled man struggling to outrun the hungry jaws that chased him.

Could those threats have overwhelmed Christopher Dawson? Ward stilled, his fingers resting atop a paper stating a County Court Judgement for collection of something or other—the amount of sixteen thousand and ten pounds and eleven pence, plus interest and costs, dated a month prior.

Could they have made him a desperate man?

Desperate enough to kill?

Christopher Dawson was in deep financial shit alright. The kind of financial shit that perhaps would benefit from a rich girlfriend's dead husband's will...

There was just one piece of evidence missing from the theory slowly solidifying in Ward's mind. Where was the murder weapon?

The team swept the house from top to bottom, checking the cellars and the attics, but nothing matching the description Ward had issued could be found—nor any bloodied clothing or anything similarly incriminating for Christopher Dawson—or Miranda Craven, who Ward had not entirely discounted. Ward and Nowak were themselves combing through the cellars—mainly wine, old crap, and dust—when DC Shahzad called. Ward picked up on the second ring.

'The CCTV footage has arrived,' Shahzad said immediately, breathless with excitement.

'What?' replied Ward sharply, stopping dead in his tracks.

His phone vibrated against his ear even as Shahzad said, 'I'm sending it. Watch it right now, and call me straight back.'

Shahzad hung up before Ward could reply. Ward quickly opened the notification, and clicked play on the video loop within. Nowak rushed over to watch.

A slightly distorted view of the Craven house's driveway taken from the house—the door—popped up. The time and date read Sunday afternoon, at half-past three in the afternoon. Just then, a red Porsche moved into shot and parked on the driveway. It was silent, no sound on the footage. Reflection momentarily marred Ward's view of the interior, but he could just make out one person inside. One, not two. After a moment, the car door opened.

Christopher Dawson climbed out.

Nowak gasped. Chills crawled down Ward's spine.

There it was. In colour no less.

They had him.

There was no sign of Miranda. It was—had been—Christopher Dawson all along.

Now it all clicked into place.

They watched as Christopher passed inside the house.

Ward called Shahzad straight back. 'Good work, Kasim.'

'There's more, sir.' Ward could hear the edge of energy in the young DC's voice. 'I've got him, sir. Dawson. He's used his credit card to check into a hotel.'

Ward could have laughed with relish. *Stupid bugger.* 'Where?'

'You'll want to set off now, sir. Middleton Lodge. Just north of Scotch Corner.'

Near Darlington, then. A right trek. Lucky they were in Harrogate already, Ward reckoned—that would shave some time off of the journey rather than having to drive from Bradford. Still, they were an hour away, give or take —depending on how broken the A1 was.

'Nowak,' Ward called. 'It's go time.'

She straightened at once and they headed for the stairs.

'Middleton Lodge, Scotch Corner,' Ward relayed to Nowak. 'Anything else, Kasim?'

'No sir. Seems he's run far and didn't think we'd be able to catch up with him.'

Nowak snorted, and held up her phone to show Ward as they marched back to his car. 'Definitely not, if the idiot's on the run in a luxury bloody hotel.'

Ward rolled his eyes. 'Honestly.'

'I know, right?' said Shahzad. Ward could picture the young man shaking his head. 'Beggars belief. I've alerted

Darlington police, but they're already short-staffed as it is today, so don't count on any backup when you arrive.'

'We'll probably beat them to it, then,' Nowak said, glancing at Ward.

'Aye, well if you want the job done properly, do it yourself, as they say,' replied Ward grimly.

'The hotel are aware,' Shahzad continued. 'He's staying in The Coach House. They'll let us know if he leaves the premises, but he hasn't done so far, and he's taken most of his food in his room.'

'Christ, if this is what he thinks fugitives do...'

'He's been watching too much James Bond, sir.'

'Aye, and he's no Bond villain, that's for sure.'

Ward and Nowak slipped into his white VW Golf R and he skidded on the gravel as he accelerated out of the driveway.

CHAPTER THIRTY-TWO

THURSDAY EVENING

It was evening by the time DI Ward and DS Nowak reached Scotch Corner, with Yorkshire long behind them. He pulled off at the infamous junction, taking the single carriageway north that ran parallel to the duel carriageway before soaring over it. On the other side, the sprawling Middleton Lodge estate awaited—and hopefully, Christopher Dawson.

Ward rang the hotel reception to warn them of their impending arrival. The countryside was dark already, the buildings of the sprawling estate twinkling warm and cosy against the cold autumn night, inviting them in.

Ward followed the long driveway. Trees shrouded it, their arms reaching overhead, blacker than the night, like yawning guardians threatening to engulf them. Light bloomed ahead across a vast lawn, where a party was in full swing. Crawling along the tarmacked drive, Ward could stare.

'Who the bloody hell gets married on a Thursday in

October?' he asked incredulously as he caught the white of a bride's voluptuous gown amidst the throng.

'It's cheaper, for one,' Nowak piped up grimly. 'If you book out of season, because they can't guarantee the weather, you get a discount usually. Not that I think we could *ever* afford to get married in a place like this.' Ward caught the edge of bitterness in her voice at that—the longing. She and Adam were to marry the following summer, but at a much more modest ceremony.

'Bloody grim if you ask me,' Ward said. 'Bet they're all half frozen—and they're lucky it's not pissing it down.'

'Aye, well.'

'Hey,' Ward said, his tone a little less gruff. 'None of this bloody matters, alright?'

She turned to him but didn't answer.

'If you want to get married for the right reasons, you'd do it in Tesco wearing a bin bag, because it isn't about where you do it, or what you're wearing, or how much money it costs. Not at all.'

In the darkness, Ward could only just see the small curve of her lips as she smiled half-heartedly. 'I know. But still. It'd be nice.'

'Alright, well if you want to be fancy, then do it at Waitrose,' he joked.

That widened her smile.

Ward turned off where a small illuminated sign directed him the rest of the way to the Coach House. There wasn't parking out front, but he dumped the car there anyway. Police business perks and all that, after all.

Inside, warmth and light blazed out, though most of

the windows were curtained. A small reception desk stood inside the modernised stable doors.

Before DI Ward and DS Nowak had a chance to do so much as raise their warrant cards, the woman there strode out from behind it to meet them, radiating tension and worry in every stiff move of her limbs. A badge on the breast of her suit jacket stated *General Manager*. 'You're the police?'

'Aye.'

She drew herself up, her face soured with distaste. 'Good. Discreet.' She glanced at the car. No doubt, she was glad that they weren't in a marked vehicle. 'We've been keeping tabs on him. There's a wedding on at the Walled Garden, and he's just slipped over there.'

The woman shook her head, her lips pressed thinly together. 'Obviously, he is not welcome to intrude upon that private celebration, and my staff are already ready to intercept him without a fuss to make sure the party isn't disturbed.'

'I wouldn't do that, ma'am,' Ward warned her. 'We're here to arrest him on suspicion of murder and a very serious assault. He may be armed and he's definitely dangerous. Let us handle him—and with respect, safety is our first priority, fuss or not.'

She paled. 'Well then, we'd better get over there.' She led them, practically jogging despite wearing deadly black heels, and Ward and Nowak kept pace. As she trotted, she spoke on her mobile, warning her staff to stay back, watch from afar.

'He's definitely in there,' she said grimly.

The three of them entered the Walled Garden through an ornate wrought-iron gate that was already spread wide. Strings of lightbulbs softly illuminated the party from overhead, and fairy lights curled amongst ornamental topiary as though they glittered with stars. Over the chatter and laughter, a light music wound, classical and elegant, through the babbling water of the fountains further in. But Ward wasn't there to admire the ambience.

In their smart work attire, they looked entirely out of place, and a few heads turned their way curiously as the two detectives stepped into the party behind the manager. They crossed the lit terrace, weaving through guests.

Ward scanned every face. Those soft mood lights were a curse, really. Not at all practical. Shadows yawned everywhere, shrouding half the guests, but he could watch their body language at least. See the ease with which they all blended together, chatted, laughed. No awkward, skulking strangers lurking.

'There!' hissed Nowak, pointing at the back of a silver haired head that bobbed in a suspiciously straight line through the party.

Ward squinted as they changed tangent to follow the figure. Was it him? Was this man a tad too tall?

The man turned.

Christopher Dawson.

A rush shot through Ward at the sight of him.

He caught sight of them, and Ward saw his eyes widen.

Then Christopher Dawson turned, and ran.

Ward broke into a run too, as did Nowak, dodging through guests who let out exclamations of surprise and displeasure as the two detectives darted through the wedding party. Ward muttered a hasty, 'Sorry!' as he jolted into someone's elbow, and they shrieked. He'd knocked their drink flying, for it to smash all over the floor in a cascade of glass and bubbles. Ward didn't turn or slow.

Into the black of night Ward and Nowak went, leaping off the terrace and now, unobstructed, sprinting into the darkness across a cropped, perfectly flat lawn. The glowing light of the party lay behind them, throwing tall shadows of them over the grass.

Ward could just about make out Christopher Dawson twenty feet ahead in the darkness—there! Dawson darted left, off the lawn and *crunch* onto the gravel paths that led through ornamental flower beds. Ward followed suit, following the sound of that crunching, slowly gaining on Christopher. Ward stepped up onto the raised sleeper surrounding a bed of heathers. Leapt across it. And vaulted from the sleeper on the other side onto Christopher.

They went down in a tumble, the sharp gravel scratching at Ward's hands and peppering his cheek as he latched on tight to Dawson. Dawson bucked and rolled, kicking Ward away and scrambling to his feet. Nowak charged him, but he shoved her aside. Nowak cried out as she went flying into a flowerbed, landing hard in the dirt.

'I'm fine!' she shouted immediately to Ward.

He legged it into the darkness after Dawson.

A security light flickered on ahead, giving away Dawson's position. Walls cornered him on two sides.

'I'll take the right,' Nowak called, and Ward could hear her sprinting away on the gravel.

Ward put on a burst of speed, just as Dawson turned at the very far corner of the garden, hemmed in by the ten feet high brick walls. No gates. No gaps. No way out.

Dawson turned right and ran. Nowak leapt to intercept him. Her fingers grazed his arm but he shook her off and she went careening into the wall with the force of her momentum.

Ward sprinted past her. 'Give it up, Christopher! We know what you've done,' Ward shouted after him.

The ornamental bushes ended, and now, he sprinted through neat vegetable patches. Closer and closer. Dawson tiring faster than Ward.

His lungs burning, his legs screaming with the effort, Ward ducked his head, spent his last energy, and launched himself at Christopher once again.

CHAPTER THIRTY-THREE

D own they both went. Ward clamped his arms around Christopher's torso, hanging on for dear life.

Squelch.

The impact was softened—no longer gravel. A smell arose—and Ward was too busy clinging onto a struggling Christopher to register what it was for a second.

Manure.

Stinking. Fresh. Manure.

Their momentum carried Ward into it as they rolled together. Dawson crushed the groan out of Ward as he crushed the detective into the squidgy mess. Ward bucked under him, and then Nowak was there.

Together, they wrestled Dawson to the ground—well, into the shit. He struggled under them but it only made it worse for him as he coated the full length of his front in manure. Ward pressed Dawson's head down into the crap too for good measure to restrain him as Nowak cuffed him.

'You do the honours, Sarge,' Ward said grimly, between heaving breaths. He was fit alright, but chasing Dawson had taken it out of him, and frankly, between Dawson and the pile of shite, that had knocked the rest of the stuffing out of him. His ribcage throbbed where Dawson had given him a well-placed elbow.

Nowak straightened. 'Christopher Dawson, you're under arrest for the murder of Robert Craven and assaulting Miranda Craven. You do not have to say anything. But it may harm your defence if you do not mention when questioned something which you later rely on in court. Anything you do say may be given in evidence. Do you understand?'

Dawson blinked and shrank away as Nowak illuminated her phone torch over the three of them.

She stared at Dawson. And then Ward.

Her lip twitched.

And DS Emma Nowak let out a most unladylike and unprofessional guffaw.

Ward glanced down at himself.

The stench from Dawson was overwhelming, but then...Ward realised it wasn't *entirely* down to Dawson. He was covered in manure too.

Oh no...

Ward's grip tightened on Dawson, which was just as well, because now Nowak had let their perp go. She was too busy bent double and pissing herself laughing, with tears streaming down her face at the sight of them both. Eventually, she straightened, giggling.

Ward glared at her. 'Are you quite done?'

Nowak bit her lip, a mischievous glint in her eye. She nodded. Her lips still twitching, fighting back laughter.

'Not. A. Word,' Ward breathed. 'Not one bloody word.'

The manager caught up with them at last, using her own phone as a torch too. 'Oh, my!' she exclaimed.

Ward turned to her, mustering what little dignity he had left. 'Do you have anywhere private we could go—I could use a freshen up, please.'

'Er...' the woman hesitated, eyeing him and Dawson up and down with distaste.

'Wouldn't want to make a spectacle at the wedding,' Nowak prompted quickly. Like they hadn't already. But parading two shite-stained men through a wedding reception would *definitely* make things worse. A lot.

The woman swallowed and faintly replied, 'Of course. This way.'

Nowak and Ward hauled Dawson to his feet and frog-marched him between them.

The woman led them to a nearby gate nestled amidst an ivy-covered wall in the heart of the vegetable patches.

As she rang the head gardener to get him to come and unlock the gate—to save them all the indignity, unprofessionalism, and frankly, bloody humiliation of traipsing through the wedding in their present state, Ward shucked his shit-stained coat.

'That might not come out in the wash, sir.' Nowak couldn't resist.

She subsided, giggling, under his withering stare.

'Um, on your face, sir, there's just a little...' she gestured to her own cheek.

Mirroring her movement, Ward scrubbed his arm furiously across his bearded cheek, muttering curses under his breath.

The garden gate clunked open from the outside and they traipsed after the manager, following the light of her torch along another lengthy stretch of driveway back to the Coach House, where, with the full blessing of wretched light, Ward could finally see the state of them both.

Dawson, who had finally, it seemed, given up, glowered at him, like a beast caged. He'd not said a word.

The Manager ushered them into a tiny utility space behind the reception desk. Ward squeezed in with Dawson. It was lined with shelves, and the small window was frosted out. Nowak entered last, wrinkling her nose.

'If you don't mind,' Ward addressed the manager, finally glancing at her name badge, 'Theresa, if we could take a look at Mr Dawson's room, please, and if you could direct us to his car.'

Theresa glared at Dawson as if he were a poisonous viper. Her eyes did not leave him as she replied to Ward. 'Of course.'

Ward glanced at Nowak, raising an eyebrow.

She took the hint immediately, nodded, and followed Theresa out.

Leaving Ward and Dawson—and their "eau de manure" scent—alone.

'So,' said Ward ominously. He folded his arms, facing Dawson squarely.

Dawson glared at him, his clenched jaw set, a vein pulsing in his neck. Even covered in shite, he was an impressive presence, those steel-grey eyes unblinking.

'Why'd you do it?' Ward asked.

Dawson didn't answer.

'Why did you kill Robert Craven?' He had a reasonably good suspicion, but from the horse's mouth was the best source of all.

Nothing.

'C'mon,' Ward cajoled. 'We're going to find out anyway.'

Dawson remained silent. His look was all the answer Ward needed. Pure, arrogant hatred that he'd been caught—but for what? Ward still didn't know, truly, who had killed Robert—Miranda, or Christopher.

'Why did you attack Miranda Craven?' Ward's voice hardened.

Dawson clenched his jaw, gritting his teeth.

'That's ok. I have time to wait. We have plenty of time to spend together now, Mr Dawson.'

Ward would get to the truth of the matter, one way or another—either from Christopher Dawson's own mouth, or an irrefutable pile of evidence.

CHAPTER THIRTY-FOUR

D S Emma Nowak slipped into the silent bedroom. It smelled faintly of furniture polish, some neutral vanilla scent, and male aftershave. She flicked on the light, illuminating a rich, contemporary, luxurious room. Large, brown, leather bed, with a decadent chaise longue at the end—the coverlet rumpled and unmade. A generous bathroom with a claw-footed freestanding bath —a used white towel slung across the lip.

Nowak stepped over two dirty socks and a pair of boxers, paying them barely any heed—her fiancé Adam was far worse for leaving his kegs about, despite the wash basket being *right there*, damn it.

A holdall lay unzipped on the chaise. Nowak had a quick rifle through—clothes, personal hygiene items, nothing to worry about there. She checked the drawers in the bedside tables. A bible, room service menu, TV remote. An Audi car key sat atop one table. She grabbed it with a satisfied smile. Nowak looked through the wardrobe—a few shirts, trousers, and a jacket hung there. The safe hung open, unused, under a folded bathrobe branded with the hotel logo.

Nowak sucked the inside of her cheek, and glanced around the room again. There wasn't much to be seen—a typical hotel room, devoid of anything personal. But the car...she glanced at the car key in her hand. Now *that* was what she'd really hoped to search.

Nowak strode out. Theresa waited outside—locking the door behind her. 'Where's the car park, please?' She held up Dawson's key. 'I need to search his vehicle.'

Nowak's nerves raced as she followed Theresa, who walked painfully slowly, and insisted on checking in on Ward and Dawson on the way past. The two men were locked in a silent staring battle, it seemed—but otherwise, still in one, stinking piece.

'Going to search the vehicle,' Nowak said to Ward—but she was watching for Christopher Dawson's reaction at her words, and as she raised the car key.

Something flashed behind his eyes, and his jaw tightened. 'No! You can't, I don't allow it,' he snarled, moving forwards.

Ward stepped to him immediately, forcing him back. 'Oh yes, we can,' he said quietly. 'We have a warrant, don't worry. We already searched your home today. Found some *very* interesting things.'

Nowak smiled grimly.

Dawson paled.

Nowak slipped out and followed Theresa to the car park, where a simple unlocking of the fob highlighted the correct car with flashing hazard lights. A silver Audi Q5. *Nice*. Nowak opened the driver-side door, searching through the side pocket and centre console—the usual choice hiding place for small things one wished to conceal at short notice.

Nothing but detritus there. Forensics would give it a proper going over, though, once they'd recovered it. A quick sweep of the back seats—a briefcase, locked. A suit jacket. Newspaper from the previous week. A pair of shoes under the back of the driver's seat.

It was hard to see into all the nooks and crannies—too dark, and the phone torch cast sweeping shadows.

Now, Nowak approached the boot. 'Could you hold your torch a bit higher, please?'

Theresa did so.

The sarge swallowed. She'd saved the boot until last with good reason. With a press of the fob, the boot slid open nearly silently, the door rising above her head. Nowak stepped forward. Theresa too, unable to help her nosiness—but the boot was flooded with light.

It was empty.

Empty of what Nowak sought, anyway. A pair of wellies, fallen over, lay inside, a slight amount of mud spattered across the black boot liner.

'It can't be,' she muttered, frowning. And then...*Aha*.

She reached in and rummaged around until her fingers found the tab. She pulled, grunting as it resisted, and then gave. The floor of the boot rose and Nowak shoved both hands under it, bracing the weight, before she heaved again. The phone, in one hand, illuminated the underside.

The spare tyre bay.

Or, at least, where one ought to have been.

But it wasn't a spare tyre that she could see, nestled inside. It was a piece of carved stone, the pale marble of a Roman god, speckled and marred by dark spatters and stains, and a bundle of clothes tangled together underneath. Clothes that Nowak would bet her life on were spattered and soaked with blood too. Blood that she knew belonged to Robert Craven.

'Jackpot,' Nowak whispered.

CHAPTER THIRTY-FIVE

FRIDAY MORNING

I t was the next morning that Ward reunited with Christopher Dawson across the interview room table.

It had been a long and late journey back from Darlington to Yorkshire in Ward's car—not Dawson, though. Ward had let him stew in shit for a bit longer. They'd both, at the reluctant hospitality of the hotel manager, cleaned up, and Dawson had been transported back to Yorkshire in the back of a police van, much to the annoyance of the Darlington team who didn't take kindly to being a taxi for a hundred and fifty miles there and back.

But, Ward had insisted. After all—he wasn't about to sully his own prized Golf R with the arse of a murderer. And the shit that said murderer had rolled in. Ward was just grateful his own coat had taken the brunt of it, and with a quick face wash, he looked vaguely presentable. Nowak had even let him have a couple squirts of the small deodorant she kept in her bag for emergencies on the job. Then, he'd smelled the fruity kind of ripe, not the shitty kind of ripe.

She'd been good enough not to say a word, though he knew she longed for nothing more than to take the piss out of him, and royally. Ward was under absolutely no illusions that she'd keep it to herself.

And, sure enough, the moment he stepped into the office, they were all standing with a round of applause and raucous cheers.

'Always knew you were full of shit, boss!' DC Patterson dared to call—and for once, everyone laughed *with* the lad, not *at* him.

'Yeah, yeah, alright, alright,' Ward growled. 'Go on, get it all out of your systems.'

He withstood the howls and the poo gags for five minutes before they wore themselves out and returned to work, chortling—and pissed off that he wasn't biting.

'Right, onto work, then, shall we?' he said more lightly than he felt, raising an eyebrow as he glanced around the room. 'Where are we? Do we have the car yet, any confirmation of *anything* we can use to nail either Craven, Dawson, or the pair of them?'

Nowak shifted in her chair. 'Forensics have only just started working on the car—it came in in the early hours. Took a while to arrange recovery from so far away.'

Ward nodded. That was to be expected.

'They'll prioritise the statuette and clothing for samples.'

They *all* hoped that would give them the answers they sought. That the statuette would be the murder weapon, and the men's clothing would irrefutably belong to Dawson, to prove who had murdered Robert.

––––––––

'Dawson's been stewing overnight. He's sought legal counsel this morning,' the staff member on the custody desk informed him.

'Grand. Have him sent to interview room two please, ASAP.'

'Yes, sir.'

Ward met Nowak in the interview room, where two steaming brews waited already. 'Cheers, Sarge.'

'Do you think he'll admit it?' Nowak asked, clutching her brew. The interview room had a chill to it, the heating loathe to work that day, it seemed.

'I'm not sure,' Ward said. 'He seems a brazen character, but that doesn't mean he won't be a coward.'

A sullen Christopher Dawson soon joined them, with his lawyer in tow. Ward had expected a blazingly defiant man to face them, but Dawson kept in line. Still, though, he answered a seething "no comment" to every question Ward posed to him, at the encouragement of his solicitor, until Ward had to, at last, admit defeat. Christopher Dawson had, he was certain, killed Robert Craven to benefit from the proceeds of his will, in the aim of digging himself out of a deep financial hole.

'Just wait a minute,' Ward said, holding up a hand before Nowak stopped the recording.

Dawson looked up to meet his gaze. There was

nothing behind those steel grey eyes. No emotion, no personality. Nothing.

Ward glanced at Nowak, who took over. Ward had played hardball throughout, and it wasn't getting them anywhere.

'We have sufficient evidence to charge you, Christopher,' Nowak said, and Dawson started at the unexpected change of voice, 'and we will be doing so. But I just don't understand. We know all the pressure you've been under financially. We know what you did and why. Wouldn't it feel good to just admit it? Get it off your chest? Tell us the whole story—from your side? If you ever cared for Miranda Craven, surely, you'd want to give her what small comfort you can now, of admitting to it, so that she can start to come to terms with her family's loss?'

Dawson glanced at his solicitor, who gave the smallest shake of his head.

He turned back to Ward, ignoring Nowak. 'No comment,' he said bluntly.

Ward clenched his jaw. 'Fine. Have it your way. We'll drag it out of you in court. Interview terminated.'

CHAPTER THIRTY-SIX

SATURDAY MORNING – A WEEK LATER

It was a little over a week later that Daniel Ward finally made it back to *Griffith's Fine Art And Framing*.

The forensic reports had been completed on the statuette, bloodied clothing, and the car. All the evidence pulled together. It was undeniably strong. Dawson could be tied directly to the clothes and statuette by prints and DNA evidence. All were covered in Robert Craven's blood.

The footage and location data from Dawson's phone and the various vehicles proved where he'd been and when—for both Robert's murder and Miranda's attack. Christopher Dawson had cracked under his financial pressures, taken matters into his own hands when coercion hadn't worked, drugged Miranda Craven and stolen her car, and killed Robert Craven at the family home.

As a result, they'd charged him with Robert Craven's murder, the drugging and attack on Miranda Craven, and a string of other offences that, if charged, he'd be serving decades for in total.

Miranda Craven was recovering well, discharged from hospital, and staying at Rudding Park once more. Ward could understand why she still hadn't been back to the Craven house, which she'd stated she'd be putting up for sale immediately. Her daughter visited from York most days. Not James, though—he'd thrown himself into the business to deal with his grief.

Eliza Pullman had been silent on the matter of Robert Craven's death—no columns from her in that week's papers or online articles that Ward had seen yet. Perhaps she wasn't wholly filled with hatred towards her biological father, he wondered. Maybe the young woman grieved in her own way for the father she'd never known, for the man who'd never accepted her, for the individual whose values had been so diametrically opposed to her own.

Claire Parker had been released, also without charge, though Ward suspected she wouldn't be getting any kind of happily ever after with the state of the marriage she walked back into.

As for the mad bloke with the shotgun, well, that was anyone's guess. Bill Turner was probably spending the proceeds of his market run on animal feed for the winter, and none too sorry to see the arse end of Robert Craven, much like everyone else.

Ward was glad to see the back end of the case too. Not least, because dry cleaning hadn't managed to salvage his coat. Nope. That had gone to a premature manure-stained grave, much to his annoyance. Forking out for a new one hadn't been on his priority list. But at least work had stopped taking the piss out of him for the incident. Well, every five minutes, at least. Now, it was just once a day. Bloody DC Patterson was the worst of them. It was lucky the lad had started to knuckle down and had a good head for detail, much as he lacked any common sense, or DI Ward would already be pushing for a transfer for the lad.

He pushed them all from his mind as he approached the small shop once more, and stepped inside to the same scent of paint and furniture polish as before, to the inviting quiet of the place.

Eve propped herself up on the counter, doodling in a sketchbook, with the tip of her tongue poking out between her teeth in concentration, half-hidden behind the long sweep of light brown hair falling across the counter. She started as he pushed open the door and set the bell off.

'Sorry! Hi,' he said, colouring slightly. He wanted to ask what she was drawing, or take a look, but bottled it. It felt too intimate and too bold all at once.

Eve smiled, her warm eyes meeting his. She slipped the sketchbook out of sight under the desk. 'Now then, thanks for coming. They're all ready for you. Hang on.'

One by one she brought them out from the back. Half a dozen in total. She stood them up on the parquet floor, leaned against the counter side by side. The glass on them was polished to precision, gleaming in the light. The wooden frames were warm-hued and inviting. The artwork nestled within had never looked as good.

'Feel free to take a look, let me know if there's anything you're not happy with that needs changing,' Eve said. 'But, I hope you like them.' She stepped back, standing beside him, her arms folded. This close, inches apart, he could almost feel the heat of her body radiating, and he could smell the faint floral sweetness of her perfume.

He didn't know what it was about her that he was drawn to, but he was like a moth to flame. *Ask her*, he goaded himself. *Ask her anything. Go on. Strike a conversation*. But his cowardly mouth remained closed.

'Well?' she prompted after a few minutes, turning to him with one eyebrow raised and a small smile grazing her lips.

'They're perfect,' he said. 'Thank you.'

'Brilliant. Let me grab the card machine, and I'll help you load them into your car, of course. Do you need any aftercare products—polish, glass cleaner, picture hanging kits, that sort of thing?'

'No,' he said, too distracted at the fact he was willingly losing his only chance, even though he absolutely did need all of the above. *Why are you bottling it, you absolute idiot?* He was a man who chased down criminals. A man who willingly put himself in harm's way (or manure's). He tangled with some of the vilest of mankind...but he couldn't even pluck up the courage to ask a woman for her number, even though the divorce would soon be finalised, and he wanted to take any kind of step into whatever life he wanted to build in the great *afterwards*. He still didn't want to take the risk of getting knocked back. Take the risk that he wouldn't get any kind of happy ending—because the more he thought about it, the more impossible it seemed.

Eve hummed to herself, entirely unaware of his inner turmoil, as she processed the card payment and returned his card with a receipt. She was a ray of sunshine, he realised. She didn't belong on the borders of the darkness where he lurked, between the criminal and the normal. Or over that line, so much of the time—for that was how it felt. Mostly, it felt like that darkness consumed him, dragged him into its toxic embrace. Reluctant to let him leave. He didn't want to suck her into that.

And so, once they had carefully loaded his car with the precious paintings, wedged down over the dropped back seats, Daniel Ward thanked Eve Griffiths politely, bade her goodbye, and drove away.

CHAPTER THIRTY-SEVEN

SATURDAY NIGHT

I t was the ringing of his phone that roused him from a nightmare-filled slumber, where spectres of Varga and Eve twisted together with those of Katherine and all the victims he'd tried to seek justice for.

It tore into that nightmare and ripped it away, but still it lurked, surrounding his consciousness. Ward's hand smashed into the lamp on the bedside table, nearly knocking it over. Finally, he found the switch. Warm, dim light flooded the room as he answered the phone.

His *second* phone, not the main one. The burner pay-as-you-go phone that he now used to exclusively contact Prap. Marika Milanova—for both their protection.

It had been a week and a half too since their call, and, as promised, they had swapped all relative intelligence. It snowed-under DC Norris, who collated it every hour of every day, looking for new lines of enquiry, and information to fit into existing ones. Already, it had built up an increasingly complex web of data that only added to their own.

'Yes?' he said tersely, rubbing the grit from his eyes and propping himself up on an elbow.

'Dobrý večer,' she said. *Good evening*, in Slovakian. 'Prepáč.' *Sorry*. 'It could not wait. He's on the move.'

Varga.

Using their pooled intelligence, a further three lorries had also been identified, stopped, and seized in transit in just seven days. Two to the UK. One returning back to Slovakia. And more importantly, an unaccompanied container filled to the brim with Class A narcotics attempting to enter via Liverpool.

With that key supply disrupted, Varga's position would become volatile, and quickly, they hoped. As rival gangs sought a turf war to fill the hole his lack of product created. They had been watching and waiting, not expecting any opportunity to arise for weeks. Not expecting that Varga would be forced to move to consolidate his empire.

Ward sat bolt upright—dislodging a grumbling Oliver the Beagle from his legs. 'Where? When?'

'I'm going to text you an address. You need to get there now. Take firearms.'

Ward leapt out of bed at once, the tatters of his nightmare gone. Adrenaline flooded through him.

They were so close.

Varga was going down.

Game on.

CHAPTER THIRTY-EIGHT

Ward slung his clothes on one-handedly. Prap. Marika Milanova still spoke in his ear.

Shite, shite, shite! screeched his inner monologue. The adrenaline coursed through him more with each word she spoke. He had to get there fast. He'd jumped to the wrong conclusion—they probably weren't taking down Varga that night, but by goodness, they had to stop him, or they'd have a major incident on their hands.

'Got it. Uh-huh. Yeah. Ok, bye.' Ward hung up. His fingers fumbled over the keypad in his haste. He dialled DCI Kipling and glanced at his watch.

Three AM.

The DCI would give him hell for this—but DI Ward couldn't do it without him. This was *way* above a DI's paygrade.

If they could catch Varga in the act...

Ward nearly stumbled over Oliver who was busy

getting underfoot, trying to understand his master's sudden waking.

'What in the blazes do you want, Ward?' snarled the DCI as he picked up, sounding groggy as hell.

Ward bit back a swear, having realised he was putting his trousers on backwards, and rushed to correct his mistake. 'Sorry, sir. Urgent update on the Varga case. I'm heading into the station now, and I need a firearms team immediately.'

'What?' DCI Kipling's voice sharpened—and Ward knew he now had his superior's full attention.

'Our contact in Slovakia has received intelligence of an imminent incident in Bradford, sir.' Ward snagged his car keys from the stand in the hallway, ruffled Oliver on the head, and left, legging it down the stairs as fast as he could.

'Seems our work has already had an effect. The significant shipment of product we intercepted has created an imbalance in supply in the area. Varga's running low, and other gangs are looking to muscle in on his turf whilst he's down. Varga's sending a warning.'

He could hear thumping, rustling, and movement on the other end of the phone—sounded like the DCI was mobilising too. A muffled curse was Kipling's reply.

'There's word of a raid by Varga's forces on a warehouse owned by the Khans down in Manningham. It's happening tonight—maybe even as we speak.'

The Khans. A prominent family in the area with known connections to drugs and organised crime. One of Bradford's major suppliers. Varga's growing business had harmed their enterprises significantly. It was war between the two—each would be more than happy to kick whilst the other one was down. Or, more to the point, shoot.

'Please tell me you're joking, Ward.'

'Afraid not, sir. Varga's moving to show territory dominance, and it seems, to obtain some of the Khans' product to fill the gap in his own supply.'

A huff of air came down the line as static, and the line went so silent Ward thought he'd lost the DCI. Then the reply came. 'Text me the address. Meet me at the station—I'll be there as quick as I can. I'll get AFOs authorised and on their way, and speak to the Duty Sergeant to route all units into the area on high alert. Rouse the team. We're going to need everyone for this.'

Chills crawled down Ward's spine as he eased the car out onto the main road and floored it through Thornton village. 'Yes, sir.'

Whatever *this* was. Could they prevent it—and detain any responsible parties without loss of life? That would be ideal. Ward was under no false illusions, however. This would be a bloodbath. The gangs took no quarter and showed no mercy when it came to protecting their turf.

If they got there too late...well, that was another matter entirely. There would, no doubt, be loss of life to deal with. Members of the public could be in danger. Police officers would be caught in the line of fire too in their job to keep the peace.

Echoes of the past caressed Ward from the darkest

parts of his mind. The Bradford riots of 2001 were a legacy that still haunted the city, which remained deeply segregated. That July, the city had, quite literally, burned. A horrific time for all those who remembered it, seared into the memories of hundreds of thousands of Bradfordians.

It had been before Ward's time on the force, but as a Bradford lad, born and bred, he had lived through those dark days. He had no wish to ignite a new war that broke the tenuous peace which had been established since. It was precisely incidents like the one they now faced, which threatened to do so. Disturbances between significant factions of different groups within the city, fanned and stoked by opportunistic thugs.

Ward braked harshly for the speed cameras in the thirty mile an hour zone on Thornton Road. He dialled Nowak, who answered after three rings, and filled her in as quickly as he could. Between them, they rang the rest of the team, until all were accounted for and making their way in.

His hands were clammy on the steering wheel as Ward considered what on earth this meant.

Would they catch Varga in the act of defending his patch?

Would they catch any of the Khans, some of whom they'd also been trying to pin for years?

Would they manage to head off a major incident?

Or, would they already be too late, and left with a pile of bodies to clean up?

CHAPTER THIRTY-NINE

SATURDAY NIGHT – SUNDAY MORNING

Ward was the first of his team into the station. Expectedly so, given that he had been first awake and not too far away. Already, it was a hive of activity, with police officers coming and going.

On a Saturday night, they'd be clogged with the usual deluge of drunk and disorderlies to deal with in the town centre. This was an incident the force didn't need, one that would stretch them too thin. And yet, they would answer the call, as they always did, in the line of duty.

Ward made his way down to firearms. Trepidation of another sort curled in his gut, festering with an unease he did not welcome. It had been a long time since he had trained as an Authorised Firearms Officer. It had been years since he had been called upon to use that training. He was rustier than he was comfortable with.

Authorised Firearms Officers already lined the hall-way, in various stages of booking out their weapons, kitting up, and assembling. They would have been on-call, ready to mobilise at short notice to respond to any incident. Ward also recognised some familiar faces pulled from the police ranks on the front line, who had no doubt stood up to serve too.

By the looks of it, they had a few dozen AFOs in total, and doubtless, many more would be pulled from their beds too to answer the call, should they be needed. It should have been enough—but would it be? One never knew. When it came to the gangs, who possessed a myriad of unregistered firearms and weapons—and plentiful more bodies—one could never truly anticipate.

He dodged through them all to the counter, and filled in the form there to request his own weapon and body armour—a Glock 17 and a bullet-proof vest. Every second seemed to last a damn eternity. His whole body was taut as a bow, ready to release. Urging him to go now. He resisted the urge to tap on the counter, flexing his fingers into a fist at his side instead.

When it arrived, Ward hauled the vest up with a grunt—he'd forgotten how heavy they were—but his fingers hesitated for a fraction before they curled around the cold, smooth weapon beside it. Then he took the gun. And the ammunition.

The Glock held seventeen bullets. Ward hoped he wouldn't have to use a single one. The adrenaline that had just begun to fade surged once more as he retreated through the ranks of heavily armoured AFOs, most of them touting semi-automatic Sig rifles.

Whilst Ward was SIO on the Varga caseload, he would be kept at arm's reach from the firearms operation that night. He spotted the familiar—and grim—face of Jonathan Sinclair through the melee. The very man who had trained him, and now commanded their district's AFOs. 'Sinclair.'

They shared a nod.

'I'm Silver. Pearson is Bronze. Your Kipling's Gold,' Sinclair said, sparing no extra words than was necessary. They didn't have the bloody time. The man didn't even wait for Ward's response before he shouldered past him to the Incident Room, where the flow of bodies ran to. No matter the urgency, they had to be briefed.

Ward followed. That was good. The firearms operation had three commanders: Gold for strategy, Silver for tactics, Bronze for operations. Each making sure that officers were in the right place, at the right time, acting as one, with the proportional response demanded by whatever unique situation they were presented with.

They all crammed in the Incident Room, with Ward at the back. DCI Kipling already stood front and centre and speaking—kitted up too, for he was also AFO trained.

'...the threat identified presents clear risk to life and breaching the peace. Given the urgency on this one, your designated commanders will see your briefs completed en route. All units, move out.'

'Sir!' came the resounding response.

The floor juddered with the stampede of booted officers departing for the car park outside. A fleet of marked vehicles and vans awaited to transport them the short distance up the hill and out of the city centre to the

Manningham area, in the streets surrounding the iconic Lister Mills.

Ward piled into a van with the rest of his team in fraught silence. Only two of them had firearms training aside from the DCI—DS Priya Chakrabarti and himself. DCI Kipling drove.

Not one of them looked half asleep despite the stupid hour, but they all wore the same, grim, gaunt look of trepidation at the task ahead of them. Above all, they had to protect life—protect the public. But they needed this to go well. They needed to find evidence to aid their case against Varga and his empire.

Ahead, the clouded sky illuminated in the garish orange glow of light pollution, a blaze flared. Fire. Unmistakable. And a huge one. Up on the hill, with Lister Mill proudly silhouetted against the glare.

The heart of Manningham.

They couldn't prevent anything.

It was happening now.

DCI Kipling's hands strained as they clenched yet tighter over the steering wheel as the convoy thundered up the hill, blue lights and sirens a cacophony of light and sound through the city outside. Through red lights they charged. The streets were deserted. Their radios erupted as the local station in Manningham itself responded to the incident. The convoy slowed as three fire engines overtook them to tackle the blaze looming ahead.

They arrived to chaos.

Ahead lay the turning off Heaton Road, but they could go no further. Fire engines and police personnel already clogged the street. DCI Kipling barked commands back, for units to surround the area with a cordon on Toller Lane, Lilycroft Road, and other key roads—so if anyone fled, they had a cat in hell's hope of catching them.

The AFO teams were faster than HMET, already disembarked and passing in a line. Their weapons were out and pointed down as they charged towards the heart of the incident. Kipling led the HMET unit behind them, with Ward at the front and Chakrabarti at the rear —if nothing else, they had some small protection aside from bulletproof vests. Police officers joined them, swelling their ranks to double.

On the street outside the warehouse, figures lay on the ground.

'Check for signs of life, weapons!' roared the DCI.

Ward followed him into the heart of the fray as individuals peeled off the team behind them. Victims, suspects—they didn't have a bloody clue who was who at that point. In the dark, it was impossible to tell.

Ambulances wailed up the hill towards them.

Ahead, fire engines deployed as close as possible. Hoses snaked across the street. Water jets battered at the flames which spilled ferociously out of shattered warehouse windows, billowing dark smoke into the night. The cold autumn air was unnaturally warm, and Ward sweated buckets under the protective vest. The heat of the blaze dried out his eyes, and the smell of smoke heavy on the air, adding a sting to every blink and every breath.

AFO teams systematically cleared the streets, but

they couldn't enter the warehouse—couldn't even get close. It was clear that the fire had taken solid hold inside that building, and neither the AFOs nor HMET would get anything of use from it whilst the fire still raged. The fire crews would already be inside in their specialist suits, searching for casualties or fatalities.

It was deafeningly loud—the roaring of the fire, cracking, spitting, licking, and snapping its way through the warehouse. It drowned out the shouting, screeching, sirens, hoses, and everything else. Ward could barely hear himself think.

He charged down a side street alongside DCI Kipling, flanked by HMET and police officers. Ahead, shadows scattered as people fled—curious onlookers or parties with more nefarious intent, they would never know, for they were lost in a blink to the shadowy alleys.

'Sir!' Norris called from behind Ward, and Ward followed his pointing finger, down a narrow side street that was little better than an alley.

Red tail lights.

A sleek, black Range Rover skidded as it accelerated off the mark. It clanged past a street light—a wing mirror went flying.

'I know that registration plate!' Norris said. He veered off to give chase, and Ward legged it after him.

'One of Varga's!' Norris hollered. Norris stopped after a few strides. The car was almost at the end of the alley.

'How certain are you?' Ward said.

'Hundred percent. One of his cloned plates.'

Ward ducked his head and sprinted past Norris, who shouted at him to stop. Ward skidded to a halt.

He pulled the Glock. Planted his feet. Lined up the gun. And fired.

The sound deafened him.

A fraction of a second later, the back windscreen shattered—just as the vehicle's brake lights flared red at the end of the alley.

Ward fired again.

Ding!

The shot ricocheted off the back of the boot.

Shite! Ward cursed.

The Range Rover turned.

He fired again.

Bang!

Impact.

One of the rear tyres—but it wasn't enough.

The Range Rover screeched away and was gone.

By the time Ward reached the end of the alley, the car was nowhere to be seen.

'What the hell was that?' Kipling yelled at him—ruddy and blowing out of his arse when he caught up with Ward.

Ward crumpled. Pain assaulted him. The impact of the running on his knees shot pain up and down. His ankle throbbed where he'd turned it on a pothole. His chest tightened, wanting to simultaneously explode and implode from the exertion.

'Varga, sir,' he gasped out, bending double, gun still in hand.

'Sir, that was Varga's vehicle, I'm certain of it,' Norris said, only just catching up. 'I recognised it immediately—it's from the pool of clones he's currently using.'

And, Ward knew, there would be no low-level thug driving a car of that calibre. It would be Varga or one of his trusted associates.

Kipling glared at Ward—and Ward knew he'd be getting a right bollocking at the very least for discharging a weapon in a residential street. He turned back to survey the scene behind them in grim-faced silence, to the hungry wolf of that fire devouring the warehouse, and slowly being brought under control by the fire crews.

They'd have a right fucking mess to sort through when the new day dawned. Not just in the clean-up, but the red tape. An investigation of all aspects of their response. An investigation into what the hell had even happened at the warehouse.

Kipling handed his radio to David. 'The eye in the sky is on hand, DC Norris. I suggest you give them, and local units, a description to follow on and best be hoping we find that car. DI Ward, you'd better find your spent bullet casings. They'll need to be evidenced.'

Even more so, since they hadn't even resulted in capturing Varga or whoever drove that vehicle—about the only things that could have saved Ward's bacon.

Ward gritted his teeth. What the hell had he been thinking? This wasn't a damn movie. He was out of practice, shooting a moving target, and in a built-up area. He was never going to make a critical shot. He'd fucked up. Big time.

DCI Kipling strode away without waiting for a reply.

Oh, yes.

DI Ward was in a shitload of trouble alright.

———

They found the Range Rover abandoned an hour later. It'd been unsuccessfully set alight. The rain driving sideways through the wide-open doors had dampened the piss-poor fire before it could take hold. The same rain that, a mile away, was helping douse the warehouse fire.

'All clear,' Ward said as he finished scoping out the vehicle. He holstered the Glock and approached the car, DS Nowak and DC Norris closing in with him. They peered in, but made no further move.

The contamination wasn't worth it. Preserving this crime scene was, in that moment, probably more valuable than Ward's hide.

CSI would be let loose on this gold mine.

A hiss of excitement escaped DS Nowak as she too spied the crimson upon the seats.

Blood.

Along with the other detritus in the vehicle, alongside what Ward hoped would be a wealth of DNA evidence, forensics would be able to write a book off the forensic findings inside. Forensic findings that, if they could tie to the warehouse fire and Prap. Milanova's intelligence, could well pave the way for them to finally arrest and convict Bogdan Varga.

If they could finally, evidentially, tie Varga into this whole fucking mess...

If they could conclusively prove that he was connected to even a fraction of the crime empire they knew he ran...

It filled Ward with fresh energy. He could practically taste the potential.

Or, maybe that was just the acrid tang of smoke on the air.

Despite the smouldering wreckage of the warehouse a mile away, and the absolutely bloody nightmare it was going to be to deal with it all, DI Daniel Ward felt the thrill of the chase anew.

For the first time in a long time, he finally felt as though he were just one, single step behind the monster.

I'm coming for you, Varga.

You'd better be ready.

THE END

A NOTE FROM THE AUTHOR

Thank you for sticking with DI Ward and myself (plus Olly the dog, Patterson, Nowak, and the gang!) for another book. I sincerely hope you enjoyed this case and the merry little dance it led us all through some of the most beautiful places Yorkshire has to offer.

I hope you haven't been scared off by "the nutter with the shotgun" – Yorkshire is home to the most kind and welcoming folk, and I have *definitely* never had a shotgun waved at me on a trip to lovely Grassington! He is entirely fictional, as is the new build estate – though the issues Eliza Pullman raises are very real ones faced by the youth of the Dales today.

I highly recommend a trip to Grassington if you're passing, in any case. The pubs have great food and drink, the village a lovely atmosphere, and there are some cracking walks to enjoy locally. I can recommend the riverbank walk to Burnsall, or up into the hills via

Trollers Gill just a little further down the valley at Appletreewick.

Settle is another place dear to my heart. On many a weekend as a kid with my parents, we'd pass through there to hike up Pen-y-Ghent. It is still my favourite of Yorkshire's famous Three Peaks, not least because, like any good walk, it ends with a *pub* (note: all the locations mentioned above have fantastic pubs...these are as important as good hiking boots, in my humble opinion!). My reward for publishing this book, in fact, will be a hike up there in August 2021. I'll wave to you from the top!

As usual, it's been really lovely to take you through some of Yorkshire's finest places. If DI Ward isn't *too* annoyed at me for taking such creative licence as to rub his face in horse manure...perhaps he'll let me write another tale (I write this full well knowing he has no choice, of course, luckily for us all!).

Hmm...where to next, dear readers? See you soon, in the next instalment! Please do sign up for my newsletter at www.megjolly.com to be the first to hear of new books in the series, and I would also be most grateful if you could leave a positive review of this or any book in the series. These very much help new readers discover the series. Thank you.

Warmly yours,
Meg Jolly

ABOUT THE AUTHOR

Meg is a USA Today Bestselling Author and illustrator living amongst the wild and windswept moors of Yorkshire, England with her husband and two cats. Now, she spends most of her days writing with a view of the moors, being serenaded by snoring cats.

Want to stay in touch?

If you want to reach out, Meg loves hearing from readers. You can follow her on Amazon, Bookbub, or sign up to her newsletter. You can also say hi via Facebook or Instagram.

You can find links to all the above on Meg's website at:
www.megjolly.com

Printed in Great Britain
by Amazon